FRANCES M

The PULPIT IS Vacant

To Ruth, Jim
love
Fran

Frances McGrath

Copyright © 2010 Frances Macarthur
All rights reserved.

ISBN: 145637673X
ISBN-13: 9781456376734

CHAPTER I

Stuck in rush-hour traffic on the Kingston Bridge on their way home to Shawlands, from Killearn, having been across the city to pick up the last of their belongings, Mary Gentle was trying, without any success at all, to calm down her husband Robert. He had just demanded for the umpteenth time, "What is holding this traffic up?" Tempted to say that she hadn't got her crystal ball with her but knowing that she would never have the courage to make a retort like this to her irascible and at times humourless husband, she contented herself with the same reply that she had been giving for the last twenty minutes:

"I don't know dear."

They had been living in Killearn for the last four years and Mary hoped that she would find happiness in this their seventh move, to Shawlands, on the south side of Glasgow. She certainly had not found it anywhere else but then the cause of her

Frances Macarthur

unhappiness was the man sitting beside her and there was no escaping him.

Travelling some miles behind them, helping them to carry some things and not yet stuck in the traffic jam, their daughter Ruth was saying to her boyfriend Kevin Grant on her mobile phone, "Why couldn't my father have taken a job somewhere further away then I'd have an excuse to leave home?" to which Kevin replied, "You wouldn't want to leave your Mum Ruth, you know you wouldn't."

This was true as Ruth foolishly thought she acted as a buffer between her mother and father. She would have been horrified to learn the true state of affairs.

In between these two cars was Colin Tait, making his way to work. For the first time in a number of years he felt really happy. He loved his job and his love life was the best it had ever been. He sang to himself and thought what a lovely day it was. It was May at its best with all the blossom on the trees and the rhododendron and azalea bushes in their full beauty. He was not seeing these right now but had spent lunchtime yesterday in a park near his work and the memory was with him this morning.

Bill McFarlane was on the pathway of his house on his way to work in the bank. He too felt like singing. His wife was expecting their first child after seven years of marriage. She was nearly at full term and he could hardly wait. He stopped to look at one of his almond trees. It too was in bud like

2

The Pulpit is Vacant

his wife and soon the buds would burst open, each bud giving birth to a beautiful flower.

Mary Bell and her twin brother Andrew were on the circle line going into Glasgow. Both were at university there. Andrew was looking forward to taking part in a debate that evening while Mary, much the quieter of the two, was just looking forward to the long, summer holidays which would mean that all her exams would be over. She was not as clever as her twin who seemed to float through exams.

Claire Davidson was on her way into town to meet her mother who was coming from Edinburgh for a visit. With four young children, Claire was hoping for some free time if her Mum would babysit for her. Her husband Bob was on the oil rigs now. He had only got the job two months previously and would not get leave for some months. She was finding it hard to cope alone. Even her Guide work which she usually loved was becoming a chore and she was snapping at the children so often.

Jim and Elizabeth French were setting off in their individual cars heading for secondary and primary schools respectively. Jim had their daughter Jill with him as she went to the same school in which he taught. He would drop her off a little way from the premises as it would not do her street cred much good to be seen arriving with a teacher. Elizabeth was looking forward to her day, although her present class was quite a challenging one. Coping

3

Frances Macarthur

with these youngsters would take her mind off the shaky relationship she had with Jim, she hoped. It usually did.

Philip Gentle had the furthest to go to reach Glasgow. He was setting off from Australia in a few days' time, hoping that he could heal his relationship with his father, Robert. He was scared of the man but hoped to be able to stand up to him now, with the help of his feisty sister. He had a new career move in mind and hoped for his father's blessing.

Charles Davenport, driving to work in Ayr, was soon to be heading to Glasgow and the start of a new career as DCI in the new station on the Southside of Glasgow. He was wondering if this career move would be a good one. He would be uprooting his young daughter Pippa and taking her from her school and friends and he just hoped she would settle down quickly and happily. He and his wife had recently divorced and the youngster had gone through enough upheaval. He was also a bit nervous though when he arrived at the new place no one would be able to tell this, not his second in command DS Fiona Macdonald and certainly not his young constables.

PCs Penny Price and Frank Selby had met on the street leading to the police station. It was unlike Frank to be on time. Penny on the other hand was usually early. Both were wondering about the new chief who would be arriving shortly. Their last boss had been easy-going and they were apprehensive as they began this new week.

DS Fiona Macdonald, quite new herself, was also wondering about the new DCI. She had been unhappy at her last station and had come here to get away from the colleague who had stolen her heart then broken it. She knew her colleagues here found her abrasive.

Salma Din was making her way to a police station in the East End. She was moving across to the Southside the following week. It was promotion for her and she was happy about that but she was also worried about the racism she was sure to meet unless the Southside was very different from other sides of the city. She was learning how to cope but wished she didn't have to.

The paths of all these people were converging though they were not to know this at the time.

CHAPTER 2

Mary Gentle was looking at her husband's hands as they moved the steering wheel. Unlike the rest of him which was remarkably firm for a man of his age, his hands were plump, plump and white. They reminded her of two pieces of fish, two fat pieces of lemon sole to be precise and she found her eyes glued to them, remembering their treatment of her. She had read once in an English exam passage of a spoof horror scene in which fat, white hands had tried to knock on a castle door and had made no sound. She shuddered. Why was she thinking now of fat maggots?

The car stopped.

"Well? What are you waiting for? Get the gates open woman."

Mary Gentle got out of the car wearily to open the gates of the manse. She had only been the passenger on the road from Killearn but how wearing it was to sit beside Robert complaining all the time. She was small and in her late forties but looked older, her faced lined with wrinkles.

All she had to look forward to now was endless unpacking. The furniture had all been put in place by the removers, using her carefully prepared plan, but she had to make at least one room habitable as Robert was planning on having some church meetings at the manse quite soon. As usual he had not consulted her, just barked out an order to get a lounge ready for the coming week.

No doubt he would go immediately to his dark room. They had gone on a trip to the Holy Land with a party from their last church and Robert had hundreds of photographs he wanted to sort out. Not for him the new digital camera and instant snaps. He liked to develop his own photographs. He always had to be in control of everything even photographs.

After that he would retire to his study which had been the first room to be seen to. In the middle of all her rearranging of the kitchen cupboards, she would of course be expected to produce a three course meal that night. Robert was adamant that there should be no prepared meals from the likes of Marks and Spencers though she did use these occasionally when he was not at home.

Ruth would be home soon. She had left at the same time as them but was stopping off on the way to see a friend. She might be lucky and miss the worst of the traffic.

The Pulpit is Vacant

Dear Ruth. What a pleasure it was to have such a wonderful daughter! At 21, Ruth would love to be independent, leave home and start up her own home, probably with Kevin her boyfriend but she stayed at home, Mary knew, for her Mum's sake. She knew that she would be banned from visiting if she ever took the step of flat sharing with Kevin of whom Robert did not approve.

Robert had already alienated their son Philip who, aged 23, now lived in Australia, in Melbourne. He was coming home very soon and she hoped that some sort of reconciliation would be possible. Philip, unlike his father, was a quiet, peace-loving young man but he had found the courage to thwart his father a few years ago when instead of going to university, he had left for Australia.

Mary often caught herself wondering why she had married Robert.

She had been at university and they had met in the students' union. He had been tall and slim - he still was in good trim she admitted to herself - and she had been flattered when he had chosen her to dance with that night. She was a regular churchgoer and had thought that having a husband who was a minister would be wonderful.

Certainly he had hidden his aggressive, sadistic side on their first dates and when he had lost his temper it was never with her. Things had started to change after both their children had been born. She knew she had allowed herself to be dominated.

Frances Macarthur

After all he was the breadwinner and he felt that this gave him the right to control her.

Sometimes she wondered what life would have been like had she finished her course and gone on to teach. She could have gone back to teaching after the children were at school. She would have been a person in her own right and not the subservient creature she had become.

Mary sighed. All this wondering would not get the kitchen sorted or the meal made.

Ruth Gentle, almost at the manse, rang Kevin again. She felt that whenever she closed the manse gates behind her they clanged like prison gates. She tried to stand up to her father but knew that rows only hurt her mother. She wanted so much to be with Kevin but hoped that her presence took some of the pressure off her mother as when she was the brunt of her father's anger it possibly saved Mary from being the whipping boy. Little did she know that her mother bore the brunt of every disagreement she had with her father.

Kevin Grant, on the other end of the phone, tried to cheer Ruth up with the fact that he would meet her outside the manse that night and also the fact that they now lived nearer to each other as he lived with his mother on the Southside. He hated Robert Gentle but knew that to get into a confrontation with him would only make things worse so he tried to calm Ruth and make her believe that one day they would be together. Kevin

The Pulpit is Vacant

was a handsome young man but unlike Robert he had a kind, gentle nature.

Philip Gentle, sitting in economy on the Emirates flight from Dubai, felt apprehensive about the coming meeting with the father who had not spoken to him for a couple of years. He knew that the interview would not be a pleasant one as he was coming home merely to tell his family that he had chosen to make his future in Australia and he knew that his father would only mellow if he promised to remain here and go to university. He hated arguments and often wondered why his so-often angry father had never resorted to violence, not even when he and Ruth were young

The Gentle family knew nothing of the future events which would change their lives.

CHAPTER 3

It would be easy to say that I had a premonition of doom as I drove home from school. I had taken my car that day because I had decided to do the weekly shopping. Other days I walked. Today as I drove home from Morrison's, I could not shake off a feeling of mild depression. No, that was too strong a word. I felt down. I turned into our avenue and parked on the street, leaving the garage for my husband Jim. My blue Vauxhall Astra was old. His white Ford Mondeo was comparatively new.

As I got out of the car the rain, which had been threatening all day, decided to arrive in full force. I went to the boot and grabbed two of the bags of groceries. Running up the path, I hoped that Jill had heard the car pulling up and would have the door open for me, but no, it was shut. I fumbled for my keys, opened the door and placed the two bags inside before returning to the boot for two more.

As I placed these two inside I shouted, "Jill. Come and help me please!" There was no reply.

She was probably in her attic room playing the latest single from 'Take That'.

Dashing back to the boot, I tried to lift the last four bags at once and of course, half way up the path I dropped one. Out spilled half a dozen small bags, tomatoes from one splattering on the path, spraying red in all directions. Some tins rolled back down, clattering down the few steps to the road. An egg box fell to the ground and the lid opened. I watched as, in what seemed like slow motion, an egg slid from its cardboard nest. I stared, mesmorised, as one brown, speckled shell cracked open and a glutinous yellow eye oozed from it. Unable to tear my eyes away even though I could feel the rain dripping down my neck, I saw red, jagged lines slice through the yellow as needles of pain started to slice my temples. The iris of the egg eye distorted and, holding my head in both hands, I went slowly to the front door.

Soaked, furious with everyone - Jill, God, myself for being stupid - and now in the grip of a migraine, I took all the bags into the kitchen.

Our 'baa' clock which made sheep noises on the hour, chose to 'baa' at me. The noise sounded more like a lion's roar. Why, I wondered, had I ever found the clock funny? Nothing was funny these days.

The primary class of eleven year olds which I taught, was the worst class I had ever had in my ten years of teaching in Glasgow : my daughter was going through a giggly, teenage stage : my relationship with Jim, my husband of nineteen years was shaky.

Had I locked the car? In spite of the rain and the headache, I knew that I had to check. Opening the front door I tried to run back down the path, nearly slipping in the mess of spoiled tomatoes and gooey egg.

"Can I help you clean that up, Miss?"

It was William Paterson from my school class.

William was one of the few quiet boys in the class. He had become my little shadow these days.

"No - it's OK William thanks." I said as I went to the car. "You should be getting home. Your Mum will be worried about you if you're not home in time for your tea."

"No she won't Miss. She'll be glad to have one less to think about, especially with the baby being ill just now."

As I checked the boot which was locked, I thought that this was probably true. Poor Mrs Paterson had eight of a family, their ages ranging from six months to about sixteen years. She usually kept them very well, always turning them out neatly dressed and clean but recently I had noticed William appearing at school a bit less clean and tidy. She probably wouldn't tear her hair out with anxiety if he was an hour late home from school. As he'd been following me about like a puppy for the last few weeks, no doubt she

Frances Macarthur

had got used to his late arrival. I looked at him standing there in his school uniform, wet through, one foot hooked behind the other, and the tip of his tongue exploring his upper lip and wondered for the umpteenth time why he seemed to like me so much.

I was always telling him off, for being late, for forgetting his homework and yet he still seemed to like me. I suppose a psychologist would say that I was a substitute mother and that he liked my annoyance because it showed that I noticed him.

I only knew that right then I had no time for him. I was wet, Jill wasn't there when I needed her, my tomatoes and an egg were lying ruined, and I had piles of exercises to correct. A migraine was beginning to play through its orchestral symphony in my head. I had no patience for a small boy. Pushing tendrils of wet, dark brown hair away from my forehead, I barked at him,

"For goodness sake, William, haven't you any friends to play with? Can't you see I'm busy?"

As soon as the words left my mouth, I regretted them. The other boys had no time for him. To them he was a sissy who preferred to sit for hours bird-watching rather than play football down at the old 'muddy', the piece of spare ground behind the school. He was an enthusiastic twitcher and had made himself a hide among the bushes which fringed the path in the grounds of the rambling manse which had lain vacant since the retiral of

The Pulpit is Vacant

the Rev Alex Tasker a few months ago. The old man and his wife had pretended not to notice him as they passed by. They had grandchildren and liked small boys.

William had a large, yellow notebook which he filled with information about the various birds which came into the manse garden and he had waxed eloquently on them when his turn came to give his talk about his hobby in school a few weeks ago.

Even the boys who usually made fun of him had been impressed with his knowledge.

"Oh come on. I'll give you a glass of milk before you go home."

He picked up one undamaged tomato and the egg box and scampered into the house. I could hear his school shoes squelching so I told him to take them off. I took his blazer and hung it up to dry off a bit and gave him the kitchen towel to dry his face. It wasn't till he was sitting across from me at the kitchen table that I remembered that Jill was having her evening meal with her friend Helen. Helen was the daughter of my own close friend, Paula. We had met at a primary school parents' night years ago and been close friends ever since.

Our daughters went everywhere and did everything together and Paula and I shared moans about them.

I went to one of the kitchen cupboards and, taking down a packet of migraine tablets, swallowed one with some water from the tap.

Frances Macarthur

Jim was also going to be late. He often was these days. As a teacher of English at one of the local comprehensive schools, Bradford High, he had many commitments - parents' evenings, parent-teacher events and school board meetings as he had been elected as teacher representative on the board. His school had been threatened with closure so the school board was writing up a response to this proposed shutting of the school and met at least once a week.

Sometimes I wondered if he would do anything rather than spend evenings with me. Other people in my situation might have suspected that their husband was having an affair but not me. Jim was extremely moral and had come from a Free Church background. Although he seldom went to church nowadays, the code of his formative years was still firmly fixed in his mind. It was this extremely moral nature that made him avoid being with me too often yet stay with me.

You see it was I who had made a mistake and I was still paying for it.

CHAPTER 4

It began a few years ago, on Jill's tenth birthday to be precise and we'd gone as a family to the afternoon showing of some film - I forget now what it was. We came out laughing about 6pm and Jim went over to look at some brightly-coloured posters advertising the next films to be shown there. Jill and I were happily discussing the film.

Then I heard,

"Liz. Liz."

I paid no attention at first as no one called me Liz any more, Jim preferring my full name of Elizabeth and other friends sometimes calling me Beth.

"Liz. Liz Boothroyd."

My maiden name brought me turning round without thinking. I saw coming towards me across the foyer a woman I'd thought, and hoped, I would never see again. I tried to look blankly at her but she persisted.

"Liz. It *is* you. Surely you remember me. I was Joan Haldane. It must be about twenty years, no, more than that since I last saw you. Is this your daughter? Is Peter with you? We all envied you you know. He was so handsome."

She took another look at Jill.

"This *is* your daughter? She doesn't look a bit like Peter, nor you come to that."

"Mum, who's Peter?"

"Yes this is my daughter Jill. I'm sorry for not recognising you Joan and I'm sorry too that we have to dash off but..."

Of course I had reckoned without Jill.

"Mum. We can't dash off without Dad."

"Oh is Peter here with you Liz? I really must see him."

At this point Jim appeared and Jill ran to meet him.

I was trapped, like a tiny fly in a spider's lacy web.

Joan looked from me to Jim and Jim smiled, waiting for an introduction.

"Joan, this is Jim my husband."

As I spoke, I half turned away from Jim and sent Joan a pleading look. Surely she would not be so gauche as to mention Peter now.

Unfortunately Joan had not changed. She had always, as a girl, been famous for blurting things out either at the wrong time or to the wrong person.

The Pulpit is Vacant

"Oh...but. Liz...I'm so sorry. You must think I'm insensitive mentioning Peter. Did he die? What happened?"

"Peter? Who is Peter?" Jim sounded as puzzled as Jill had been.

"Have I put my foot in it?" queried Joan anxiously.

"Yes Peter died and now if you'll excuse us we really do have to dash."

"Oh but Liz, we must arrange to meet up for a chat while I'm here. I can't believe I'm seeing you again after all these years. Do you live in Glasgow? I moved from Hastings too and I live just outside London. I'm here for a week visiting my cousin."

I really don't remember how we got away. I think I made some vague promise to call her as I later discovered a slip of paper with her name and a 'phone number beside it in the pocket of my jacket. I tried to talk to Jim on the way home but he said curtly, "Pas devant l'infant" which was our code word for 'not in front of Jill'.

Somehow I got through the drive home, the supper we ate and watching TV till it was time for Jill to go to bed. It must have been only a few hours since we arrived home but it seemed much longer. I felt sick and my tummy knotted painfully as I came downstairs from saying goodnight to Jill.

"Well, do you want to tell me the whole story?"

I knew it was hopeless to lie. How I wished that I had told him all about my past life when we had

Frances Macarthur

first met. If he had decided then that he did not want to continue our friendship it would have been hurtful but less traumatic than this was going to be if his granite expression was anything to go by.

"Jim I was only sixteen. I......"

"Never mind that. Just get on with it."

I had never seen Jim like this. He seemed like a stranger, some alien on my home planet. I felt fear then a sudden anger overrode the fear. The sick fear was gone and in its place was a cold determination to get this over quickly. What did he think he was? A high court judge?

"You don't need the details. The bald fact is that he was a soldier. I met him at a dance. We went out a few times. He went over to Ireland about six months after we first met. I never heard from him again."

"Is that all?"

"What more do you want - his shoe size?" I darted back.

"Well did you sleep with him? No, don't answer that. You must have done as I remember you felt no pain on our wedding night. What was the *story* again? Oh yes. You had had a D&C some months before we met. Was that right?"

His scathing words brought a flush to my face but I held my ground.

"That was true. I admit it made it easy to explain my lack of discomfort that night but it was true."

"So that's all I'm to be told about my predecessor then is it?

The Pulpit is Vacant

"Yes. It was a teenage romance. What more do you want to hear?"

Jim sent me another cold look and went up to bed.

I waited till I thought he would be asleep then went upstairs myself and by the time I got up the next day, he was already up and dressed. Jill was at the breakfast table so no more was said.

In fact no more was said ever again about Peter but my easy-going, warm relationship with Jim had gone and as I said he seemed to do everything possible not to be alone with me. If I went to bed early, he came up late and if I waited up he would suddenly want an early night. We shared the same bed it is true but never again a passionate embrace or even a cosy cuddle. We shared only things which concerned Jill and I made excuses to friends so often for not being able to visit them that Jim got the reputation of having become an ambitious workaholic and I made noises about him wanting promotion soon.

It seems silly in this day and age, in our permissive society, that Jim should take such a moral high ground but coming from Skye as he did and having been brought up in the Free Kirk, he was very upright and expected everyone else to be the same. He had moved on from his Skye roots and seldom went to church but he had no patience with today's looser morals.

Frances Macarthur

Things had improved slightly in the last few weeks and I was willing to go along with any small improvement as long as we were together.

However, enough of my reminiscing. I had a lot of school work to do and my dinner to get and thinking of the past was not going to get a meal cooked and thirty essays marked.

I opted for something easy and unhealthy, two fried eggs with sausage, my favourite meal-for-one.

The meal over and the dishes washed - I still preferred to wash them by hand though we had a spanking new dishwasher in the kitchen - I settled down at the kitchen table with my pile of jotters and the short essays they contained. I loved my job although this year's class of ten year olds could be very trying at times.

I had longed for another child, a brother or sister for Jill but adoption had proved very difficult the second time around and then, more recently, Jim had said that he didn't want another child to have to keep up a pretence for, the pretence being of course that we had a happy marriage. Maybe he had thoughts of a divorce when Jill was old enough to understand. All I knew was that I loved and needed him.

I sighed and turned to the first jotter. It was torn at one corner and had a smudge of blood or maybe tomato ketchup on the front. Fred's jotter. Fred was one of quite a large family and his father was out of work at the moment and the only time I

The Pulpit is Vacant

ever saw his mother at parents' night she was there to complain about something, not to listen to me talking about Fred's work or lack of it.

I picked up my red pen which would be used quite often if Fred's other pieces of work were anything to go by.

He had chosen to write about An Exciting Evening and as I read on, I could feel the bile rising in my throat. He had described how he had gone to the top of a multi-storey building in Pollokshaws and watched as an older boy had thrown a cat out of a window. I couldn't finish the part where he started to describe the poor, mangled body on the street.

What was I to write at the bottom of the page, always remembering that we had to write something positive as well as highlighting the mistakes?

"Don't do this again. It's not nice but you did make it sound exciting."

"Your spelling is poor but you remembered a full stop at the end."

"What about paragraphs?"

I was delighted when at that moment the 'phone rang.

"Hello Elizabeth. It's Bill here. Look, Alison's been rushed into hospital. I'm 'phoning from there now. They think the baby will come sometime in the next few hours. The thing is I promised to go to the manse tonight to meet the new minister. Remember I told you that he wants to meet all the

Frances Macarthur

leaders of any organisations- you know, the Guild the Men's Club, Dramatic Society, Youth groups. Would you be a pal and go instead of me? You help me out with the BB and probably know most of what we do with the boys."

"Oh Bill, I'm so glad about Alison. She must have been getting worried. A nine month wait is long enough without the baby being three days late into the bargain. Of course you can't leave her but are you sure that there's no one else who could go? I'm up to the ears in work at the moment."

"I know. I'm sorry but there isn't anyone else who knows as much as you and anyway I think you'll be interested because...

He spent the next few minutes explaining why he thought that the evening might prove to be more interesting than I thought.

I agreed to go. Fred and his appalling essay could wait.

CHAPTER 5

The new minister had only just taken up residence in the manse a few days ago and the whole neighbourhood was agog with curiosity about him and his family. I didn't often attend the church, Holmwood Parish, and hadn't even heard his name till my conversation with Bill. I had however noticed a new face among the shoppers at the local convenience store and had guessed that this might be the minister's wife. She was a small, anxious-looking woman and Mrs Brodie, the loud but kind-hearted woman who owned the store had informed me, "She's a very nervous lady, Elizabeth. Perhaps she won't want to chair the Women's Guild. I asked Bill McFarlane. He was on the vacancy committee that chose the new minister but he's that wrapped up with the thought of the baby coming that he couldn't remember much at all. Isn't that just like a man? If it had been Alison on the committee, she'd have got all the details. Men are so hopeless aren't they when it comes to important things?"

I just nodded. That's all anyone has to do with Nan Brodie. She would talk on and on for hours to a statue with a nodding head.

If the minister was not the father of a large family, he was going to find his new home rather spacious. The manse was a rambling old building, ideal for children, with a long, sloping front lawn and a lot of trees at front, sides and back. There was also a small pond at the back, a source of pleasure for young William. I hoped that, large family or not, the new minister would not object to the little bird watcher keeping his hide in the trees. Old Mr Tasker and his wife Ivy who were now living near the home of one of their daughters in Perth, had neglected the manse garden in the last few years. I believe from stories I had heard that when their daughters were young, the manse had echoed to the sound of children's laughter. The old man had loved to hear the sound of children's voices and had encouraged the youngsters of the area when they weren't busy playing football elsewhere, to play in his garden. William hated it when other children played there but his hide was skilfully camouflaged and none of them had ever found it. He had been careful in his school talk not to mention where he had seen the various birds he had talked about.

The Pulpit is Vacant

".....but for a man of God, I don't think he's very charitable." Nan Brodie's long diatribe was ending and she was looking at me expectantly.

"Oh Nan, I'm sorry. I'm afraid I was woolgathering. What did you say?"

"Really, Elizabeth, you are the limit. I was saying that Mr Gentle the new minister has a son In Australia and a daughter still living at home but he's not all that nice to her."

"Oh come on Nan. You hardly know them. How can you say that?"

"Well the poor girl wants to marry a fellow she met at university but her father won't hear of it. He says the lad's a layabout - a long-haired lout he calls him."

"Nan Brodie! How did you get all this information?"

"Well to tell the truth I overheard him talking to her the other day. Ruth her name is. They were in the manse garden, at the foot of that front sloping lawn and I was passing on my way from the library. My shoelace came undone and I...."

"Nan that's eavesdropping!"

"I couldn't help having to stop and you know how bad my fingers are with the arthritis. It took me some time to tie the knot."

Really the woman was impossible but I was as bad I suppose as I continued to listen to her.

"The girl has some spunk though. She said if he wouldn't agree to the marriage, she'd just leave one night and not come back."

"What did he say to that?"

"I'm coming to that, Elizabeth, just hold your horses. Honestly, I shivered at the tone of his voice. He said, "Oh no Ruth. You'll never leave while your mother's alive. You're too fond of her, aren't you? You know that without you to protect her from me she'd have quite a miserable life.""

"I'll get Mum to come and live with Kevin and me," she said.

He replied, "She would never leave me and you know that."

"Oh Nan, you must have heard wrongly," I protested. "Only a monster would say such things, certainly not a minister."

"Well I heard what I heard," came the reply. "You wait till you see his wife properly. She certainly looks a shelpit creature to me."

"Probably terrified of all you guild committee people," I joked and left her looking indignantly after me.

Later that evening, having waited hopefully for a 'phone call from Jim, which never came, I took out some old photographs of myself and Peter. There were only three, black and white and wrinkled at the edges. I don't know why I had kept any. Typical womanly dislike of throwing things out I suppose. I think my thoughts that afternoon had made me nostalgic. I looked again at Peter, laughing out of one of the photographs,

The Pulpit is Vacant

so handsome in his uniform. He almost seemed to be mocking me from the picture:

"Well girl, thought you could sweep me under the carpet did you?"

Angrily I ripped the photographs apart and put them into the fire which I had lit as soon as I had come in, after William left.

About twenty minutes later, I was hurrying up the path towards the manse door when the thunderstorm which had been imminent all afternoon broke and by the time I reached the porch I was soaked for the second time that day. I must have looked a pretty sight with my hair clamped to my cheeks and water dripping from the bottom of my grey, poplin coat on to the porch floor.

The thin, middle-aged woman who opened the door looked preoccupied but kindly. She obviously did not have an eye for fashion but was dressed in an unbecoming mustard jumper and brown tweed skirt. Her mousy fair hair was permed and old-fashioned.

"Oh my dear, you're drenched," she said.

"If you wouldn't mind telling Mr or Mrs Gentle that Mrs French is here for the meeting. Maybe they would let me use a bathroom and borrow a towel." I smiled at her.

"I *am* Mrs Gentle," she said with a rather sad smile, "and of course you can use a bathroom. Look this one's nearest. It's the one my daughter

Ruth calls her own but she won't mind you using it. I'll get a towel."

She opened the door of one of the downstairs' rooms and then said, quite nervously, I thought, "I do hope you won't mind if I leave you but my husband does so like me to answer the door and I think I hear someone else arriving."

She vanished.

As I tidied myself up as best I could without the aid of the towel which she had obviously forgotten, I thought back to what Nan Brodie had said. I was beginning to believe her because the little woman I had just met certainly seemed frightened and not at all as I'd expected a minister's wife to look and act.

I was just about to open the door when she returned and knocked on the door. I opened it.

"I really am sorry I had to run off like that Mrs French. Did you manage without the towel?"

I hastened to reassure her.

"Really Mrs Gentle, don't apologise and please call me Elizabeth or Beth if you prefer."

"I couldn't do that my dear. Robert doesn't like abbreviated names but I will call you Elizabeth if I may."

"Certainly you may. I teach at the local primary school and actually I'm here under false pretences. Bill McFarlane who takes the BB has just heard that his wife has gone into labour and..." I became

The Pulpit is Vacant

aware that she was only giving me half of her attention and I stopped.

"Oh I'm sorry Elizabeth. What did you say? I thought I heard footsteps again. It might be my daughter."

She turned abruptly and went out. I was about to follow her when I heard her talking to someone and not wishing to appear nosy, I kept back in the doorway.

"Oh Ruth dear, you're so wet. Go and change your clothes quickly before you catch cold."

"OK Mum."

I heard footsteps coming towards me and then:

"Ruth have you been out with Kevin again?"

"Yes Mum."

"Oh Ruth, you know your father has forbidden you to see him." Mrs Gentle sounded tearful and I felt sorry for her.

"Really Mum," came the fierce whisper. "This isn't the eighteenth century. I'm twenty and *I'll choose* my own friends."

"I beg your pardon!"

Safely hidden in the bathroom, I shivered at the icy tone which accompanied these words. Here was a man who would not tolerate being disobeyed, who would never tolerate human frailty. In fact if Nan Brodie was correct I thought, he actually might enjoy being in a position of power over his family. Mrs Gentle would be the ideal fodder for such a man. Charity and loving kindness might be preached by him but not practised. I stopped myself. How could I glean all this from one sentence?

"Did I hear you correctly?"

"Father - you can't stop me seeing Kevin. I love him."

"Love! That good-for nothing, long-haired layabout. Love! I'm warning you Ruth, if you ever see him again I'll have him drummed out of university. A boy like him from the East End with a father in Barlinnie should never have been accepted in the first place. Added to a disobedient daughter, I've got a namby pamby son, doing odd jobs round Australia. He's probably a poofter knowing my luck."

"Philip is not gay and on what charge would you have Kevin put out of university?"

"Drug taking."

"That's a lie. Kevin only experimented with hash and that's not much worse than smoking cigarettes."

"Do you think anyone would believe his word against mine, a man of God?"

"Man of God? More like man of the devil," Ruth choked out.

There was the sound of a stinging slap then silence.

"Ruth dear," Mrs Gentle's voice was a mere shadow of sound.

The Pulpit is Vacant

I jumped back as a figure burst into the bathroom. She saw me and her hand fled to her face too late to cover the tell-tale red hand print on her left cheek then she turned abruptly and ran off.

At this point Mrs Gentle, trying to catch up with her, arrived at the door.

"Ruth I ... oh sorry Mrs French, I mean Elizabeth. I had forgotten all about you. I'll show you to the lounge. I think the others are all here now"

She took me across the hall and down a passageway towards the back of the house and pointed to the nearest door. I had never been in the manse when Mr Tasker was the minister and I hadn't realised that it was so big. Poor Mr and Mrs Tasker must have rattled about in here when their daughters left home. I knew that manses were supposed to have at least one extra bedroom for needy people but there must be about six bedrooms in this place if the size of downstairs was anything to go by.

I knocked on the door and went in. Gathered round the room were a number of people, some whom I recognised, some I had seen at church on the occasional time I went and one complete stranger, a tall, greying, middle-aged man dressed in the uniform of the minister-at-home, grey woollen cardigan, white shirt and clerical collar atop black trousers. The only one standing, he dominated the room.

"Good evening, good evening." His voice, warm and rich, was the total contrast to the one I had just heard. The man was obviously a chameleon though only in the ability to change his personality as the little creature changed its colour. A chameleon changed colour to protect itself but this man changed to create an impression.

"Hello Mr Gentle. I'm Mrs French." I didn't invite him to use my Christian name. I don't know why. Was it solidarity with his daughter and his wife or reluctance to be even a little friendly with this man? I wasn't sure.

"I'm representing the Boys' Brigade. Bill McFarlane who runs it couldn't manage along himself. His wife's about to go into labour. I often help him so I'll probably be able to answer any questions you might have."

"She'll be glad, poor soul," said Claire Davidson, leader of the Girl Guides. "She's not had it easy for the last two months."

I said hello to the others and received smiles in return.

"Sit down, please," said Mr Gentle. "Now everyone I'm sure knows everybody else. I'll soon get to know you all. Never been one to forget a face." He smiled round genially.

Later I was to remember his words but the face that no doubt paled went unnoticed as the talk turned to particulars of the various clubs represented there.

The Pulpit is Vacant

Well, what's he like, the new minister?" asked Jim as he sprawled in the chair in front of the fire. The nights were still not warm even though we were into May and I was glad that we had decided to keep a real fire instead of having it replaced by electricity or gas. I was also glad or rather grateful when Jim instigated a conversation so I was happy to tell him details about my evening at the manse. I told him about my meeting with Mrs Gentle and the incident with the daughter, Ruth and I told him that Mr Gentle was a Jekyll and Hyde character, one face for the family and another for parishioners. I told Jim that we had to go back, in smaller groups over the next few weeks and that he wanted me to go with Bill and Claire and the Bell twins who help with the Brownies and Anchor Boys to discuss the uniformed organisations.

"Do you think he'll be more interesting to listen to than the old man?" said Jim who only went once a year, on Christmas Eve because Jill wanted him there. Although she didn't belong to the Guides, she did quite often attend a youth club on Friday nights and she loved the candlelit Watchnight service.

I could not say in all honesty that I thought that Mr Gentle would be an inspiring preacher. He'd been a bit prosy tonight, although he did have a lovely voice to listen to, when he wasn't berating his daughter or speaking down to his wife.

"We had a lovely supper, homemade scones and cake. I thought we might just have tea and biscuits as so many ministers' wives these days work and haven't time for these things. I guess Mrs Gentle doesn't work."

"Trust a woman. I ask what the minister's like and she describes the supper."

We laughed.

There was a brief silence then he said, "Elizabeth. Let's start again. I wish you had been honest with me from the start but it all happened before I came on the scene. It's taken me a while to work through the whole thing and I know I've been difficult to live with. Forgive me?"

I went into his arms.

CHAPTER 6

Timid and frightened of what she knew was to come, Mary Gentle sat on the double bed in the bedroom she shared with Robert. She looked round at the decor. It was a very masculine room, shades of black, white and grey, the wallpaper and paintwork chosen by her husband. She had bought the bed linen but had been told what its colour had to be. She had only been allowed to choose the colour scheme of their first bedroom together, in the early years before Robert had changed. Oh, he had always been the strong one, the decision-maker but he had never been cruel. What had changed him had been his time as army chaplain. He had had the utmost respect and admiration for the leaders of the squads, those sergeant majors who ruled their troops with rods of iron and had copied them in his home life by ruling his wife and family. His son, Phillip had been a happy little boy in his first years but as his father changed, he too became different, becoming shy and introverted.

Ruth on the other hand had always stood up to her father and had protected her older brother as often as she could, often taking the blame for something they had both done which was wrong or seen to be wrong in their father's eyes.

Robert had hit her only once and Mary would never forget the scene. Her daughter stood facing her father, her face red where he had hit her.

"I expect I'll have a bruise on my cheek tomorrow Dad," she had said. "Now I'll tell my teacher at school that I walked into a door but I'll only do that this time. If you ever hit me again, I'll tell the truth."

At twelve Ruth was small and it looked to her mother as if a female David was facing Goliath but like David, Ruth was the winner and from then on Robert never physically punished either her or Phillip. What Ruth did not know was that each time Ruth disobeyed or was insolent, her father meted out the punishment to her mother, Mary.

Tonight he had slapped Ruth for the second time. Maybe he realised that she had no teacher or adult to run to now; maybe it had just been an instinctive action, now regretted. Mary did not know but what she did know was that once again she was going to suffer the consequences of Ruth's rebellious nature.

She had caught her husband looking at her throughout the part of the evening left to them after the youth leaders had gone home, a look that

The Pulpit is Vacant

said he was looking forward to something. If he'd have been a cat he would have licked his lips, she thought and shuddered.

She had sat there for about half an hour. This was part of his cruel treatment of her. He made her sit and think about what was to come. There was no point in getting undressed and putting on her nightgown - the nightgown Ruth would be amazed to see and which she had to wash by hand and dry over the radiator in their bedroom if Ruth was living with them as she was now. It was a whispy, black affair, very short and completely see - through, certainly not her own choice. Neither was her underwear. It amused Robert to know that underneath the sensible tweed skirts and serviceable blouses that he insisted on, she was wearing sexy black or red bras and skimpy panties with suspender belt and stockings.

If she undressed now, Robert would only insist on her dressing again. She picked up the book by the side of the bed, one of the books which were her pathway to escape and which he laughed at.

"Mills and Boon," he would say derisively. "Happy ever after and soppy romance! Life's not like that."

Her life certainly was not like that though recently with both Ruth and Phillip out of the house she had been comparatively happy. She loved her children dearly but dreaded their arrival too as Ruth especially brought upon her times of sadistic punishment.

41

She heard footsteps on the stairs and hastily returned the book to the bedside table.

Robert entered the room looking every inch the minister with his dog collar round his neck. He carried another collar and a red dog's lead. Something inside her seemed to shrivel. So the scenario was to be disobedient dog and master routine. She did not move even though she knew what to do, as Robert enjoyed issuing orders. He did this now.

"Pull up your skirt, take down your panties and go down on all fours darling and remember to be quiet."

She obeyed, in a hurry to get this over.

"Who's been naughty then?" he spoke very quietly.

"I have."

He bent down, fastened the collar round her neck and attached the lead. Tugging the lead, he began to walk round the room. She crawled round behind him, remembering to stop as he liked to tug the lead and if she forgot he would make this last much longer. As she crawled, her panties were left behind. At last he stopped and unfastened the lead. Lifting it he began to bring it down on her buttocks, saying, "Bad dog, very bad dog."

It was quite a thin lead so the strokes did not hurt much but she felt as always the total shame of her subservient position and she knew that worse was to come.

The Pulpit is Vacant

He had finished now. He moved away from her but faced her as he began to undress, slowly. When he was naked, he came to stand in front of her showing off his erection.

"Would the little doggie like a bone?"

He pulled her up to kneel in front of him and pushed himself into her mouth. He was so excited that he climaxed almost immediately. This was bad news as now he would want another orgasm.

"Stand up my dear. Bend over and hold onto the bed. Look, I want you again already."

She looked and saw that he was rising again. She went over to the bed and braced herself with her hands on the bedspread.

"Look to the right dear and you can watch in the mirror."

She did as she was told. He had never asked her to watch before. He came up to her, parted her buttocks and with one swift movement entered her. It no longer hurt as it had done at first but the humiliation was almost unbearable. Seeing them in the mirror made it worse as she now knew how it would look to someone else.

When it was over, he simply climbed into bed and told her to put out the light when she was ready. She wanted to shower but this she had discovered annoyed him.

Lying beside him in the dark, she heard his soft voice. "Try to keep our daughter from making me angry again, my dear."

CHAPTER 7

I went into school the next day, still on cloud number nine. My room was two along from Colin Tait's. He was my best friend at the school, the other teachers being younger than us. He stopped me in the corridor for our usual chat. Fair and slim with gentle features, he had the infants' class every year and he loved his little ones who must be so different from the youth club teenagers he catered for on Friday evenings. I often wondered why he hadn't taken a better paid job teaching secondary age children. He had a degree in Biology and Botany and sometime William would ask him for information about his birds - the feathered variety. I also wondered if he had ever been married as he would have been an excellent father. I knew he wasn't married now. As it was I knew he lived at the other side of the city and made a long journey every day to the South side.

"Hi Beth! Ready to face the foe?"

"Just about, Colin."

I went on to tell him about my meeting the night before.

"There were too many people there really. Must have been about twelve of us so he only managed to get across the fact that he was, as minister, in charge of all organisations, even the Guild he said. He ruffled a few feathers I can tell you."

"How did you like him?"

I felt it would be wrong to either spread Nan Brodie's story or repeat what I had heard last night. It would be fair to give the man a chance so I kept quiet.

"He seems OK - a bit of a control freak I would say but we'll soon find out. He seems to want to keep a special eye on the youth leaders. We've to go back next week. In fact you should come along the next time Colin as you're a youth worker too."

"It's probably this child protection thing that's in his mind. You know, forms to fill in for every worker with youth even if they've been doing the job for years."

"Yes. Remember that one we got some years ago where we were asked to write down if we had any convictions with regard to child abuse. As if anyone's going to admit it," I laughed.

The bell rang and we went our separate ways.

"Good morning." I smiled at my class.

"Good morning Miss," they chorused.

We spent the morning involved in our World War Two project. They seemed to enjoy it and especially liked working on the ration cards we were currently engaged in making. They couldn't imagine what it was like to have hardly any biscuits or sweets and to have very few clothes to wear and they seemed to think it would have been fun to queue for even basic items. Fred and William probably knew better than most of them what it was like to have few new clothes and not many luxuries although I suspected that Fred managed to steal a few things every now and then! I had put the class into little 'family' groups for role play, each group having a Mum at home, a Dad in the army and either two or three children. We had drawn a wall frieze with all their houses and a few extra ones and only last week we had pretended that one house had been bombed and the inhabitants killed. This meant that we discussed the nasty reality of war as well as doing the more fun things like the ration cards.

I looked at William, busy colouring in the ration book front cover, the tip of his tongue sticking out in concentration. I felt a rush of affection for him.

The class filed out for its midmorning break and I was about to follow when I noticed that William was still sitting in his seat.

"William. It's playtime dear."

"Please Miss, can I speak to you?"

When you are happy, you are quite amenable to listening to others' problems so I smiled.

"Of course you can. Fire away."

"Miss. Oh please Miss. Will you speak to the new minister for me?"

"Why, William?"

"Miss, he met me the other day in his garden and he's told me not to come into his garden again and Miss my den is there."

He stopped speaking and started to cry, the sobs wracking his thin little body.

"Did you explain to him, William, about how you like to watch birds and that you never caused Mr Tasker any trouble?"

"Oh yes Miss," he hiccupped, "but he just laughed and said it was a cissy thing to do, watching birds."

My blood boiled. Surely the man had some Christian feelings. Yes I certainly would speak to him!

"I'll speak to him William. Don't cry any more. Go out and play and leave it with me."

I hoped that I would be able to convince Mr Gentle of the harm it would do to tear William away from his hideaway. The boy trusted me so fully. I would hate to let him down.

The bell rang and the class came back in. I told them that we were going to try to live like the people did in the war and that I wanted them to only put two inches of water in their next bath and to try not to eat any sweets for a week. I took out a banana from my desk and told them that a lot of young folk during the war didn't see a banana

The Pulpit is Vacant

till they were about their age, that fathers had queued for hours when they heard that there were to be some bananas in the shops one afternoon. The children could not understand a world where things like bananas were luxuries.

At home I discussed William's predicament with Jim.

"Do you think I should go up to the manse and see Mr Gentle?"

"Sure love. You've promised the boy so you owe it to him to try but I've warned you often about getting too involved with that wee boy. Don't be too disappointed if you let him down, if Mr Gentle refuses to change his mind."

"Surely he will?"

"As long as you've tried that's the main thing. However, I doubt you'll fail. I'm certain that once you explain that it's only for one wee lad, he'll make an exception for him."

He smiled at me.

CHAPTER 8

As I walked up the path to the manse later that evening, a dark shadow slipped into the bushes in front of me.

"William?" I called quietly.

There was no answer.

At the house a door closed. Was it Ruth having a secret meeting with her boyfriend? If so I wished them luck.

Again it was Mrs Gentle who answered the door.

"Oh Elizabeth," she said. "Can I help you my dear?"

"I wanted a brief word with the minister," I replied.

"Oh dear. Did he ask to see you? He's busy just now in his dark room, sorting out and unpacking some equipment I think. Is it important?"

She looked nervous at the thought of disturbing him, one hand twisting the other in its grip, so I was just about to say that it was not important and turn away when a door opened and Ruth came into the hall. Her pretty face was becomingly flushed - so she *had* been out seeing her young man.

"Hello. Sorry I didn't get a chance to speak to you the other night, Mrs ...

"French. Elizabeth French."

"Do come in. Mum, why haven't you invited Mrs French in? Come in and have a chat with Mum. She could do with a rest and a friendly face. She's been busy all day with unpacking. I'll get us all a cup of tea."

She propelled us towards the lounge door and almost pushed us in then went off down the hallway, to the kitchen I presumed.

"Mrs Gentle, I'm so sorry. I seem to have been foisted on you somehow but I don't need to see your husband right now if it's a bad time. If you have time, let's just do what your daughter - Ruth isn't it? - suggested and have a wee chat together if you're not too busy. Can I call you by your first name? You know mine already."

"Oh yes. It's Mary. Please do. It's always nice to have new friends." She added wistfully, "We've had so many moves since we started off in Sussex. Robert keeps feeling the call to move on. I do hope we stay here for some time."

"Where else have you been, Mary?"

"Oh we went from Sussex to a place in Yorkshire then to a country charge, on the outskirts of Aberdeen, then to a smaller village in Fife, then to Killearn, now here."

What a lot of coincidences there were. I had also lived in Sussex, as had Colin Tait and Bill McFarlane, prior to his marriage, lived in Aberdeen. I wondered if anyone else around me had lived anywhere in Yorkshire or Fife. But I was getting whimsical and a bit silly now. I smiled.

"Ruth tells me that I should try here to get about and make a life for myself but it's so difficult being the minister's wife. People expect me to run the guild and be full of confidence and I'm afraid that I'm a bit shy. I've never worked you see as I met Robert during my second year at university and he persuaded me to give up my studies and become a full time wife and mother."

She came to a halt suddenly and I felt sure that she had not confided in anyone for some time.

"What were you studying Mary?"

"I had done two years studying English mainly. I would have liked to teach."

It was hard to imagine this timid little woman in front of a class of teenagers.

"I'm sure that no one in the church will expect too much of you. I'm not a regular member of the guild but when I have attended they had a president and it wasn't Mrs Tasker the last minister's wife, though she was there I believe."

"Do you go to church Elizabeth? I hope you don't mind me asking."

"Well occasionally. I go at Easter and Christmas. I've never joined the church I'm afraid."

"Maybe we could be friends then. It would be easier if you're not a member. I remember at our last church there were always people wanting me to talk to Robert for them for some reason or other. It was very difficult in Sussex when he was an army chaplain - all those army wives, jolly hockeysticks sort of people."

She laughed and I realised that she could be a pretty woman when she was happy and smiling.

At that moment the door opened. Expecting it to be Ruth with our tea, I turned round smiling only to discover that it was the minister himself.

"Hello Mrs...French isn't it? Was it my wife you came to see or myself?"

"Well I did come to see you but your wife said you were busy so your daughter offered to make me a cup of tea and...

"Now Mary, you know I'm never too busy to see anyone from the parish."

His smile seemed a bit forced but I was probably imagining things now. Jim would say that it was unlike me to take an instant dislike to someone but I disliked this man.

Mary Gentle, it seemed, never argued with her husband.

"Sorry dear, I was going to come along once we'd had our tea. Look here's Ruth with it now."

"Well you girls enjoy your tea and chat. I'll be in my study when you're finished Mrs French."

He brushed past Ruth. The look she sent after him was not a loving one.

I did not really enjoy the rest of my time with them as we were all aware of the fact that he was waiting for me in the study, probably keen to get back to his darkroom. However, we sat for a while talking about Sussex and Hastings my home town which Mary at least knew quite well, Ruth having been just a baby then. Colin Tait, like Peter, had once been a soldier in Aldershot. We had often swapped stories of that part of the world, he telling me of his days exiled from his home country of Scotland, leaving the army and training as a teacher after four years at Stirling University, and me telling of my teenage years in Hastings then coming to teacher training college in Glasgow. It's funny how English teenagers tended to travel to far away towns for university and college whereas the Scottish young folk tended to go to their nearest place of learning.

"Well Mary, Ruth, thanks for the tea. I'd better be getting along to the study if you'd point me in the right direction."

Ruth did that, leaving me to knock on the door and go in by myself.

Why did I feel so nervous around this man? Was it because of Nan Brodie's' story or because of Mary Gentle's fear of him. Fear? Was I being melodramatic? Lots of wives, especially non-working ones, still treated their husbands as if they were the boss even in these emancipated times but it didn't necessarily mean that they feared the men they lived with.

"Well Mrs French. I won't ask you to call me Robert as I like a bit of distance between myself and my parishioners but if you like I will call you Elizabeth, if it makes you feel more comfortable."

"Thank you but no, just call me Mrs French."

I felt as if I had made some sort of stand in a small way, childish really.

"I've come to see you about a young boy called William Paterson. He's in my class at school and he's a timid little boy, hasn't got any friends so he wouldn't be bringing a horde of other boys.

Robert Gentle gave a small smile.

"So you're a school teacher Elizabeth. You must have a real love of children." He paused, "I'm afraid little ones tend to annoy me when they're unsupervised but I suppose I could make an exception for one quiet wee boy."

"Thank you."

Why when I'd got what I wanted did I still feel wary of this man?

"Now if that's all, I'll show you to the door. I believe we're meeting again next Tuesday when the uniformed organisation leaders are coming back for another meeting. Why don't you come a bit early and we can have a chat about your youngsters. I believe very few of that particular age group come to Sunday school. I'll be school chaplain too so I'd better get clued up about them."

He laughed.

I promised I would do my best to be a bit early next week and left.

On Saturday afternoon, Paula and I took our daughters into town. They had been promised some holiday clothes' shopping and a MacDonald's' meal. Paula, a widow and Helen, were going off for the first time abroad, to Minorca so were looking for warm weather clothes whereas Jill, Jim and I were going to Cornwall and wanted a mixture of things as the weather could be changeable.

We traipsed round the shops for nearly four hours, as usual going back to the shops we'd visited first and buying there. Jill had to be talked out of a bikini when Helen was allowed to buy one. It would be so impractical in the cold water off the Cornish coast. She had to content herself with new denims and some colourful tops. Thank goodness she was not yet at the age where fashion was everything. I dreaded being asked about belly-button piercing!

At last we sat down in Macdonald's and ate hearty meals of hamburgers and chips before getting on the bus to come home. Neither Paula nor I liked driving into town especially at the weekend when parking was difficult.

When we arrived home, Helen came in with us. It was her turn to stopover with Jill and I had asked my neighbour to come in to baby-sit, a term which

Jill hated. To appease two offended teenagers I had said that they could stay up until Jim and I got back.

I was in a happy frame of mind that Saturday evening as Jim and I drove round to the burgh hall to attend the retiral function for the Reverent Tasker. It was a wet and windy evening for May, quite warm but not very summery and I thought back fleetingly to the balmy, May nights of my childhood in Sussex.

For such a small island, what a difference there was between the South of England and Central Scotland where my home was now, in Glasgow, on the south side of the Clyde.

How did that song go? "The summers were longer, the winters were warmer." Winters were certainly warmer but much wetter and here we were in summer having yet another wet spell.

My memories of Sussex were of warm, scented evenings, walking over the twin hills which were a feature of Hastings, my birthplace. The East Hill especially, with its more rugged scenery was my favourite and I loved taking my neighbour's dog for walks there.

I had traded these conditions for a house in the suburbs of a noisy city yet I had been very happy until Joan had turned up a few years ago.

I shuddered and a voice in my head said, "Stop harking back. Things are better now". At the same

The Pulpit is Vacant

time, Jim said, "We're there" and stopped the car outside the gates of the hall.

"Would the car not be safer inside the grounds, dear?"

"No doubt but someone would probably block me in and I don't intend to stay till the bitter end."

Not wanting an argument, I kept quiet. I knew that Jim had only come along tonight for my sake and I did not want to jeopardise our fragile relationship by arguing over something trivial.

Again that song ran through my head "...the way we were." What was it called? 'Memories'. How beautiful were my memories of our life before that evening when we met Joan and why did I have to keep remembering it?

I mentally shook myself and got out of the car.

"Thanks for coming Jim," I said.

"Ok but remember I don't want to be here till the end. We can skip the tea and cakes afterwards. I like the old fellow but I can't stand some of the church worthies and their idle chat."

The hall was brightly lit and rang with voices. We made our way to where there were two empty seats at the back of the hall. There were plenty at the very front but no one ever seemed to want to go there, like school kids in a classroom.

A young woman in front turned round, brown curls dancing. It was Penny Price one of the local policewomen.

"Hello Mrs French. Who's the handsome man then?"

I looked quickly at Jim. He was smiling. Penny had that effect on most people.

Her charm was so natural and unselfconscious. It worked on stray dogs, lost children and no doubt on hardened criminals.

"This is my husband Jim. Jim, this is Constable Price. She's up at the school quite often returning our truants. We're not at school now Penny, please call me Elizabeth."

Jim smiled again.

"Pleased to meet you Penny. I'm not a churchgoer so that's probably why we haven't met before. One of your colleagues was at my school at the start of last term telling the staff about various kinds of drugs. I'm at Bradford High."

"I don't go to church that often either Jim as I work on a lot of Sundays. That would be Frank Selby who came to your school. He's been on a few drug courses recently so knows the score, if you'll excuse the pun. She introduced the woman sitting beside her. "This is my Mum."

Her Mother was so like her. They could have been sisters. We all shook hands.

Just then the platform party started filing onto the stage so Penny turned round and Jim and I settled into our seats. Made of red plastic, they would not be comfortable for very long.

The Pulpit is Vacant

As speech followed speech, I sat in a happy haze. Jim had been so much warmer lately. It was ages since he had been so relaxed in my company and how lovely to feel once again that glow of pride at introducing him to someone and seeing admiration in their eyes. Jim was a handsome man and I had always been the envy of my friends when we were younger till I had spoiled it all with my deceit.

"No that's not true," I chided myself. I had not meant to deceive Jim. At the time I had thought that I was simply keeping from him facts that were better hidden. I had not lied, I had simply stayed silent.

A round of applause woke me out of my reverie and I realised that the first part of the evening was ending. We filed out of the church into the hall, Penny behind us.

"Can we give you a lift Penny or are you both staying for the tea?"

"Thanks Jim. That would be great. No I want to get away now and we walked over tonight."

When we got to our street, I asked them if they would like to come in for a coffee but Penny declined for both of them, saying that she would have to be up early the next day as, although it was Sunday, she was on duty. Her mother thanked us too.

"We have a new DCI starting on Monday and I want to make sure everything's in order. I heard that he ran a tight ship at his last place and I don't want to start off on the wrong foot," Penny added.

We dropped them off at their house and drove home.

CHAPTER 9

After having been at the retiring minister's farewell do, we decided to go as a family to the first service taken by the Rev Robert Gentle BD MA. I was surprised that Jill was willing to go but I suppose she was as curious as everyone else.

The church was quite near us, as was the manse. It sat back from the road and had only a small garden at the side. It had no steeple and was not popular for weddings, being situated in the midst of multi-story flats. It was always being broken into which was surprising as it was right next door to the small local police station.

We had been married in it and had chosen a hotel with lovely gardens for the photograph taking as there was nowhere outside the church suitable. I had felt a loyalty to the church as it was the one my aunt and cousins had taken me to when I first came to go to college in Glasgow. Jill had been baptised there, not as a baby but as a toddler.

We took the car as we had been late in setting out and had some difficulty parking as churches, like hospitals, had been built before cars had become more numerous and had no car parks.

We arrived about five minutes before the service started and took seats upstairs in the gallery which gave us a good vantage point over both congregation and pulpit.

The church had no charm inside or out. It was bare of decoration of any sort and not at all like the church of my youth in Sussex. I looked down and saw Bill McFarlane with Alison minus their new baby boy. I wondered if they would be having him christened and if they did would they ask this new man. Maybe that was why they were here, to see what he was like. I know that I was curious to hear what he preached after hearing Nan Brodie's story and meeting him myself.

Soon the five-person choir filed in, followed by the beadle with the bible and then Mr Gentle. He looked distinguished in his black robes with his blue and gold hood.

The first hymn was Guide Me O Thou Great Jehovah and the singing was loud and enthusiastic though I suspected that about a quarter of the congregation were not regular churchgoers.

The service progressed with prayers and bible readings. I nearly said, "Forgive us our trespasses" out of a habit formed when I was young and went to the Church of England service every Sunday

The Pulpit is Vacant

with my grandmother but remembered just in time to say "debtors".

Then it was time for the sermon which was entitled "Taking the Hard Line". I had read this on the pew leaflet.

One of the readings had been from Exodus, the part about the Ten Commandments and this was the basis of his sermon and although I couldn't agree with the man I had to admire his confidence in taking such a black and white stance over these laws.

He was particularly firm about adultery which in this day and age was almost laughable. I admit that my idea of God was of a wonderful being who would forgive us lesser creatures our human failings but Mr Gentle's God was an awe-inspiring, vengeful one. I am sure many folk were squirming a bit that morning. I suspected that Robert Gentle would be hard on wrongdoers, would not tolerate other religions and certainly would not conduct same sex marriages - I almost laughed out loud at the thought.

It was very warm in the church. One of the blinds had not been closed properly and I saw Bill shift his head about as he sat in what was almost a spotlight. Beside me, Jim was beginning to fidget and I knew that he was thinking that the sermon was a bit long. It was however finishing now as the minister summed up the points he had been making.

The last hymn, like all the rest was a traditional one, "Oh Jesus I have Promised", in spite of the new hymn book, CH 4 which we were using. I imagined that although he was a new minister he was definitely not a 'new man' in any sense of the word. He expected his wife to be the homemaker, the answerer of doors, and the maker of tea. He expected his daughter's unquestioning obedience. He wanted to be called Mr Gentle, not Robert which would suit his older parishioners but I wondered at the vacancy committee who had listened to him preach and spoken to him afterwards. There had been more young folk than old on that committee so Bill had told me. Maybe they felt that in this day of fewer ministers we were lucky to get somebody who wanted to come to an inner city charge. The pulpit had certainly been vacant for almost a year from the time when Mr Tasker had announced his imminent retirement.

I had not gone to the service last week when Robert Gentle had preached to the congregation prior to them voting for or against him but I knew, again from Bill, that this church had followed the rather old fashioned system of asking those in favour of calling Mr Gentle to stand and then those not in favour to stand. The new man was not present at this of course but would be informed of both numbers. I wondered how many had stood like sheep, following the majority and how many had had the courage to stand for the second

The Pulpit is Vacant

vote. Maybe his sermon that day had been more congregation-friendly.

These thoughts had occupied my mind during the last hymn and we stood quietly for the doxology, singing the threefold Amen before filing out to shake hands with the minister at the door. He was most affable, thanking us all for coming and to me saying that he had found our chat most enjoyable a few days ago and that he was looking forward to seeing me again soon. I looked round outside and saw that Colin Tait had also been in the congregation and of course Nan Brodie. I saw too the minister's family, Mary looking faintly embarrassed by the attention she was receiving from church members and Ruth looking protective and trying to edge her mother away to where their car was no doubt parked round the back of the church. I took Jill and Jim up to them and introduced them to each other, at the same time walking away from the throng of people. In this way we reached our respective cars and said our goodbyes.

"Well I don't see him doing anything modern with the nativity at Christmas," Jim laughed as he drove home and Jill echoed this with her, "Dead old fashioned isn't he?"

Old fashioned maybe; intolerant certainly. He was going to ruffle some feathers I was sure.

CHAPTER 10

In her room in the large police station in Govanhill, Fiona Macdonald, a woman in her late thirties, was sitting thinking about her career move. Hers had been a sideways move from a station in Paisley. She had been happy there for some years, extremely happy when romance had blossomed between her and the other detective sergeant, an Irishman called Pat McDade. She had felt that life was perfect. They worked together and socialised together and she had been on the point of asking him to move in with her in her flat in Glasgow when she heard rumours about him and one of the young constables. Thankfully, she had not committed herself to sharing her flat with him because the rumours proved to be true and Pat had told her that he no longer loved her.

Fiona, a shy woman, had only had this one, serious relationship in her life and took the rejection very badly, finding it impossible to work alongside Pat any more. She had asked for a transfer and been given one, to this station on Glasgow's Southside.

She had only been here for a few months when the DCI, a family man with whom she had worked well albeit for a short time, decided that it was time to retire and now she was awaiting the arrival of her new boss Charles Davenport.

She knew that she had acquired the reputation of having a short fuse and promised herself that she must lighten up a bit and not let one disastrous affair ruin her relationships with others.

Penny Price, true to her word, had tidied up the main room at the station, much to the chagrin of her male colleagues who were now not able to find the things they had left lying around. She had made sure that her uniform, navy suit, white shirt and tie, navy shoes that she could have seen her face in if she had tried, was immaculate. Her last DCI had been a man in his early fifties on the edge of retirement, an easy-going man who made life at the station pleasant and informal most of the time but she had heard that the new man, Charles Davenport, was a bit of a perfectionist. It was better to start off on the right foot.

"Hi, Penny! You're here bright and early. Your love life not so hot these days? No late Sunday night?"

Frank Selby, her fellow PC, tall, slim and boyish apart from his thinning fair hair, had arrived, just on time for once.

The Pulpit is Vacant

"Morning, Frank. Still the same old patter? Well for your information, I had a night in last night after Saturday night's soiree for the retiring minister."

"Wow Penny! I wouldn't have been able to stand the excitement! Have to see if we can remedy things. How about coming out with me next weekend?"

"Frank, you know the answer. I keep telling you that as a workmate you're fine but you're the most sexist, racist man I've ever met and I know we'd be at loggerheads before the evening was half over."

"Come on darling! Just because I use the word Paki."

"Well don't. It's insulting to our Asian folk to be called Paki and while we're on the subject, the Chinese don't like to be called Chinkies either and *I* don't like being called darling!"

"Penny my love..."

"I am not your love!"

"I'm sorry to break up this interesting conversation," a dry voice interjected.

Penny and Frank, both startled, spun round and found themselves facing a tall, elegantly-suited man in his late thirties.

"I'm DCI Davenport, Charles Davenport, your new boss. And you are?"

He was looking at Penny as he spoke.

"Penny Price, Sir. PC Price. Nice to meet you, Sir."

"And you are?" He had turned to Frank.

"Frank Selby. PC Selby. Pleased to meet you."

"Sir."

"Sorry...Sir."

Penny suppressed a smile. She had the feeling that the new DCI had noticed the slight hesitation before the "Sir" and that the new DCI was not going to be Frank's type.

The rest of the morning was spent on routine police work.

On her way out to her car, en route to the Catholic primary school where she was due to talk with the head teacher about the worrying rumour that drugs were being handed over to the youngsters outside school at the end of the school day, Penny met DCI Davenport again.

"Hello Constable Price. Where are you off to?"

"The primary school down by the library, Sir. St Theresa's it's called. I'm going for a chat with the head teacher over drugs being sold to some children after school."

"Mind if I tag along? I'd like to attach myself to each member of staff this week, just to get to know how they work."

"Of course I don't mind Sir," Penny replied, wondering how slapdash Frank was going to like this innovation. It was not unusual for him to have to be reprimanded even by an easy-going boss. He got himself into trouble because of the way he addressed the public, especially women and members of the Asian community which was large

The Pulpit is Vacant

on the South side of Glasgow. DCI Turnbull, now off to retirement in Aberfoyle, had tended to meet any complainers himself and give Frank a light warning but Penny doubted if DCI Davenport would take such a lenient view. Frank was also often late though he lived quite near the station. DCI Turnbull never seemed to notice this as he had stayed in his office a lot but she had heard that Davenport was a hands-on sort of man. She must remind Frank to be on time tomorrow.

They were about an hour at the school and the new DCI seemed pleased with the way Penny talked to the head teacher and managed not to ruffle her feathers over the delicate matter of some of her pupils having been found in possession of mild drugs. He told her so as they walked to the car.

"Well done, Constable. You handled that well. Now, what about a quick cup of coffee before I head off to pick up my daughter?"

Penny took him to the nearest tearoom which was attached to the nearby Newlands Bakery, thinking what nice manners he had as he complimented the waitress on the array of cakes. Again she grinned inwardly at the thought of DCI Davenport suggesting a coffee to Frank who preferred a pint. She studied the man across from her while he chatted to the waitress and liked what she saw. He had thick, brown hair with eyebrows to match and surprisingly blue eyes. He came to the end of his conversation and Penny looked down quickly at her coffee then looked up again to ask him what age his daughter was.

"Just over nine. She's started at Southview Primary. I'd have liked her to have stayed on at her old school with her friends but the travelling would have been a nuisance.

"I'm sure she'll settle in quickly Sir. I know one of the staff there, Elizabeth French. She'll not be your daughter's teacher but I'm sure she'll look out for her if I ask her to."

"That's kind of you. Her name's Pippa, short for Philippa."

"Do you have to pick her up every day, Sir?"

"No. My sister will often do it. I just want to pick Pippa up for the first couple of days."

They travelled back to the station where DCI Davenport got into his own car and drove off. Penny went into the station and about an hour later she was called into DS MacDonald's office. In her usual brisk manner she said, "Penny. We're having a new body joining us next week. She's Sergeant Salma Din. I wonder if you'd do me a favour and get Frank to stop saying, "Paki" in less than seven days. He tends to be racist and I don't want any unpleasantness in the station. Have a word with him please. It'll be less official coming from you."

Penny looked at her immediate boss, a bit on the plump side, short fair hair and as she had found out a short temper to match and wondered why she had been given this job. She sighed.

CHAPTER 11

Tuesday was a busy day at school and I forgot for a while about the meeting that night. I managed to talk to William at lunch time. I found him alone as usual, sitting in the doorway of the janitor's shed watching the other boys playing football. He looked forlorn as he often did but he smiled when he saw me.

"William. I managed to talk to Mr Gentle, that's the name of the new minister. Sorry I haven't got round to talking to you till now. He says it's OK for you to keep on using your hide in the manse gardens but he doesn't want you to bring anyone else and I said you wouldn't."

"Oh thanks Miss. No Miss, I wouldn't take anyone anyway. No one else would be interested."

He had a yellow notebook on his lap, not a school one.

"Is that your bird diary William? You used it for your talk didn't you?"

"Yes it's my notes on the birds I've seen. I write down what I see every day then when I get the chance I go to the library and check-up what each new bird is. I copy the best bits into my hobby jotter. At the back I write down things for our war project."

"Can I see it?"

"Oh yes Miss. Would you like to borrow it tonight? I could get it back from you tomorrow."

"Not tonight William. I've got a meeting tonight but some other time perhaps.

I wasn't really interested to be honest but I felt sure that no one at home would have any time to share in his hobby so it wouldn't hurt for me to spend a bit of time on it.

The bell rang for afternoon classes and we went in together.

It was our afternoon for English. Now that the 5-14 programme had been introduced, grammar had become popular again and I was trying to instil in my ten year olds knowledge of nouns, verbs, adjectives and adverbs, not the most riveting of topics I have to admit. The afternoon did not pass quickly!

They seemed to understand that a verb was a doing word and a noun a naming word but adverbs and adjectives confused them even when I told them that adverbs 'added' something to the verb. David Smith, always smart at the wrong time immediately wanted to know; "If adverbs

The Pulpit is Vacant

add to verbs why isn't it adnouns which add to nouns?"

I could see his point. I was just glad that I was old enough to have been taught such things. I felt sorry for the young teachers who had come up through the system in which grammar was not taught and who were almost as baffled as their pupils. I had caught one student teacher writing on the board, "We have did." In Glasgow, the common mistake was, "We done." Obviously this poor girl had realised she was going wrong but went wrong again in trying to correct herself and as for getting the young teachers and pupils to understand that 'yous' was not the plural of 'you'- well, that was almost impossible especially as a lot did not know what plural meant!

The phone was ringing as I opened my front door. It was Paula.

"Elizabeth, Paula here. Look, Helen and Jill want to do their homework together. Is that OK? I'll feed her tonight. In fact she can stay the night if you like. Give you some peace and quiet. She can wear one of Helen's school shirts tomorrow and a pair of her knickers."

"Oh Paula, you're a pet. As a matter of fact I've got another manse meeting tonight and Jim might be late in after the badminton club so it would be a great help not to have to worry about feeding Jill."

"I heard them talking about putting a colour through their hair. Would you object to your Jill having some blonde streaks? Helen's such a mousy colour, poor thing but Jill's so blonde they probably won't show up in her hair."

"Oh I suppose not. As long as it's not permanent. Her hair's almost white blonde."

"Funny her being so fair when you and Jim are dark."

"Be much more worrying if we were fair and she was dark."

We laughed.

"Look Paula I must dash. Have to get something ready for my dinner and something to leave for Jim. I hope this dratted meeting doesn't take long as I've a pile of marking to do, as usual."

We said our goodbyes and I hung up. In spite of having things to do I sat for moment thinking about what Paula had said about Jill's hair.

We hadn't got round to telling Jill yet that she was adopted. No doubt the time had come, especially after comments like Joan Haldane's and now Paula's.

It was quite normal for two dark haired parents to have a fair haired child and I could pass it off by explaining about a fair-haired grandparent but why should we prevaricate any longer? Maybe now that Jim and I were on friendly terms again, we could sit her down soon and tell her between us how important she was to us and how we had chosen her from all the other babies in the home.

The Pulpit is Vacant

She was a level-headed girl and I hoped that she felt secure and loved by both of us.

I sighed, went into the kitchen and started to peel some potatoes.

Once again the phone rang. This time it was Jim. How nice it was to have him phoning again!

"Hi love. Sorry I'll be even later than I said. I'll not be in till about nine. An extraordinary school board meeting about the proposed closure of the school has been called at 7pm and it won't be worthwhile me coming home and turning round and going out again. I'll bring in a fish supper so don't worry about feeding me. I know you have to go out."

As I put down the phone I realised that things were going to be easier than I had thought tonight. Not so many potatoes to peel for a start!

CHAPTER 12

I went early to the meeting. It was a warm evening so I walked over, deciding not to take the car as there was little room for parking in the manse grounds and I would have had to walk up the long, winding drive anyway.

In a childish frame of mind I had decided to wear trousers as I felt sure that Robert Gentle preferred women in feminine clothes, even dowdy ones like I had seen Mary wearing. I felt good as the black, boot cut trousers were new ones bought recently in Marks and Spencers and I had teamed them with a jade top which went well with my dark hair and black boots. No need for a jacket tonight though as it was May it could be cooler later. I had decided to risk it. I arrived slightly breathless at the front porch and this time it was the minister himself who opened the door.

"Good evening Mrs French. Do come in."

He escorted me to the lounge at the back of the house. It was a pleasant room. I took notice this time of the decor: beige with splashes of yellow and orange in the cushions and curtains and I wondered if they had managed to get all their rooms ready as quickly as this one or if this was the colour scheme of the last residents.

We were soon engaged in conversation about the children whom I taught at school. Did I know why so few came to Sunday school? No I did not know but I guessed that their parents did not come to church so did not bring their children. I did know that there had been no recruitment drive as such but I knew that Bill had come along a few years ago to talk to the older boys and girls about the Boys' Brigade and the Guides with disappointing results.

Mr Gentle then asked if I thought he would be welcome in the school if he came to talk to the pupils and I said I was sure that the head teacher would welcome him as she had the Reverent Tasker, especially if he offered to take some services for us as he had done. He mentioned that he had phoned the school that day and had spoken to Mrs Hobson on another related matter and that she had seemed receptive.

We moved on to more general chitchat and I asked him where he had previously been minister, knowing from Bill and Mrs Gentle that he had once been in Sussex. He said he had recognised my accent as coming from the South of England and I said I had lived in Hastings as a child. He

The Pulpit is Vacant

asked why I had come to Glasgow. If I kept back some things it was because I felt instinctively that I could not trust this man with personal details. I just did not like him. I need not have worried about my reticence as he was only too glad to hold the floor, telling me about the other places in which he had been minister.

I was relieved when the doorbell rang and Mrs Gentle showed in Claire and Bill.

They had hardly sat down when the leader of the Brownies, Mary Bell, and the leader of the Anchor Boys, her twin brother Andrew, arrived together. There were no senior boys so Bill was the leader of the Junior Section of the BB.

The minister told us that he was expecting Colin Tait as he ran a youth club in the church halls. We waited for him to arrive but there was no sign of him and after about ten minutes the minister took the floor.

Mr Gentle wanted, apparently, the syllabus for every organisation as he had made clear at the last meeting. This was OK for Bill who was organised and he had brought his along but Claire was a slapdash sort of woman who tended to make things up, as she went along and she had never been asked for this before so she became a bit argumentative. However it was the minister's right to have what he was asking for as the Guides were under the umbrella of the church though not a Christian based organisation like the BB so she

83

had to agree eventually. I admired her for standing up to the man. I guessed that this did not happen often to him.

Pleading a lot of marking to do, I was first to say I was leaving. Just as I got up, Mary Gentle came in with a tray of cups and saucers and a plate of scones and her husband spoke sharply to her:

"Mary. What kept you so late? Mrs French has to leave without supper."

I hastened to reassure her as she stammered an apology. I was horrified that he should speak to her like that in front of visitors.

Bill got up to take the tray for her, saying as he did so that he too was having to leave because Alison was still a bit nervous at being alone with the new baby. Her mother, he said, came over during the day but they could not expect her to stay in the evening too as she had her own home to run.

We went out into the hallway, accompanied by the minister and saw Ruth coming out of what was probably her bedroom.

"Give your mother a hand, Ruth," he barked. "Where have you been anyway? Not out with that good-for-nothing I hope."

Ruth looked a bit embarrassed at being treated like this in front of strangers but she stood her ground.

"I've told you before Father. I'm twenty-one and old enough to see whoever I like."

"Not while you're under my roof you'll not."

The Pulpit is Vacant

"Then I'll....."

Her expression softened and she said, "Sorry Mum. Come on. I'll give you a hand with supper." She walked past me and when she stepped back there was a tray in her hands.

She looked down at it.

"Scones! How on earth did you find time to bake with all the rooms you've been trying to get ready?"

She took the tray and glared at her father who I suspected had demanded the home baking.

I turned round to see Mary Gentle standing behind us. I thought that wringing one's hands was an exaggerated description of a worried person but it wasn't as Mary was definitely wringing hers... She let herself be led back into the lounge by her daughter.

Bill and I left.

"Enjoyed our chat, Mrs French!" the minister called out after us.

As we walked back down the drive, Bill said,

"Gentle by name but not by nature eh Elizabeth?"

I agreed, adding that I would not like to get on his wrong side.

Just as we opened the gate, someone was trying to get in from the other side. It was Colin.

"Oh hello Beth,"

"Hi Colin! Do you know Bill?"

85

"We've met a few times in the church halls," said Bill.

"What kept you Colin?" I asked him.

"Traffic as usual. The Kingston Bridge was jammed again. Probably an accident somewhere. The minister phoned the school today, Beth to ask if he could talk with the infants' teacher. Mrs Hobson didn't know I was to meet him some time in my role of youth leader. Don't know what he will want to see me as tonight."

He sounded a bit nervous and I did not blame him. The Reverent Gentle had that effect on me too.

We all parted company at the gate and I was home in a short time.

Jim came home shortly after me. He too had marking to do and we sat in a companionable silence at the kitchen table. At around 10.30 he sighed gratefully and declared that he had finished his batch of close reading pieces and he was going to have a coffee and then an early night.

I told him that I still quite a lot to do but would have coffee too. Jim was lucky as he would fall asleep almost as soon as his head hit the pillow even having just had coffee.

We finished our drinks and kissed at the foot of the stairs. I told him that Jill was away overnight and went back to my marking. The class on the whole had grasped the concept of nouns, verbs and adjectives but not adverbs, especially the ones

The Pulpit is Vacant

which did not end in -ly. This was going to mean another lesson tomorrow and I might try to make up a cloze passage with adverbs missing. That might make things more fun. I knew that I was not going to get to bed early tonight.

CHAPTER 13

All was quiet.

In the garden, little furry things went about their business in the twilight. A bat flew overhead. After the hot day, the garden drooped but began to slowly revive in the comparative coolness of the evening. The house, becoming a large black shape against the darkening sky, was quiet too. All its inhabitants were probably watching television or reading in the peace after the evening meal.

All was quiet.

Suddenly, there was the creak of a door in the garden wall (He must remember to bring oil for the hinges next time. What a pity he could not use his usual entrance) Never mind he was in now. Hooded and scarfed against what might be a chilly night, he crept past the front windows whose unlit faces stared blankly at him. There was the smell of wood smoke from a nearby garden. It filled his nostrils and he sniffed appreciatively - it was one of

Frances Macarthur

his favourite smells though it made him feel hungry as it was some time since his meagre dinner.

All was quiet.

He was making his way to the bushes at the side of the driveway when he heard voices. They frightened him and he hurried, making a tiny noise as he crossed the path. They had not heard him. They were talking in whispers. He could not make out what they were saying then he caught one word - "dead". He shivered though it was not yet cold. The word sounded harsh. The owners of the voices passed by within feet of him. He shrank back just in case.

A few minutes, then a door of the house opened and there was the sound of one person's footsteps on the path. He hardly breathed as once again a human form passed his way. There was a moment of almost dense silence. He moved a little further into the undergrowth.

All was quiet.

He had been dismayed to find three adults, two of them his teachers, at the main gate to the manse. Usually he used this gate and walked up the grass verge to the bushes and trees at the side of the house. He would hang his old binoculars (his Dad's) on the lowest branch of his favourite tree and then settle down. He came most often in the late afternoon after school but when Mrs French had asked them to imagine what it would be like to live in blackout conditions he had hit on the idea of

The Pulpit is Vacant

coming here when it was dark as it was impossible to get any room in his house dark with his Mum and Dad and all his brothers and sisters there. As it was, he had had to give George, the brother nearest to him in age, fifty pence not to tell his Mum that he climbed out of their bedroom window occasionally to come here at night. He shared the room with another brother as well but Robin was only three and sound asleep by the time he went.

He had walked up the hill to the small side gate which was not much used hence the creak.

There had been another two people round that side of the house - he had heard the faint sound of their voices and that one scary word - dead. What or who was dead? The voice saying that word had been very angry though low.

Mr Tait must have taken longer than himself to come up the manse path and this was him now going up to the front door which he could see from his position in the bushes. Mrs French and the other man must have been leaving as they were not with Mr Tait. The door was opened and a male voice invited Mr Tait in.

In the light of his torch, he drew out his notebook. At the back he was noting down things he felt and things he saw in the blackness as he pretended that it was during the war. His Mum had been amused at him wanting only two inches of water in last night's bath but she was probably glad to save water with another seven children to get clean. He had not enjoyed the bath. Not having sweets was easy as he did not get much pocket money to spend on sweets especially with the fifty pence going to George every time he wanted to sneak out at night.

Every time a plane went over, he pretended that it was an enemy plane and noted the time. He imagined Mr Tait as a secret agent coming to get his instructions from his commander-in-chief.

The manse door opened again and this time he heard a woman's voice saying "Cheerio."

He invented army ranks for them all.

He wrote these comings and goings down in his war diary, as he called the back of his notebook. He could pretend that the manse was army headquarters. He had a good imagination, so Mrs French told him. He liked Mrs French and wished sometimes that she was his mother. His own mother was too busy to spend any time with him now that she had the baby to look after.

After a while he took out his rations, two tea biscuits and a banana. He knew that the banana was wrong but he hadn't been able to get anything else. He ate and was thinking about setting out for home when the manse front door opened again. This time a figure rushed out, slamming the door. The figure ran down the path, passing him where he stood in the bushes. He thought it might be Mr Tait but was not sure. Why would a secret agent be running?

While he was deep in thought, the door opened again and in the hall light he recognised the minister.

He stood at the door and watched the fleeing figure then he stepped back and closed the door.

William wondered how many people were now inside.

He had sat down to write. It was comfortable in his little nest. Some time ago he had brought an old grey blanket and a dark green cushion his Mum was throwing out. He shut his eyes.

Sometime later he woke up. The garden was even darker now, the deep velvety darkness of late evening.

Carefully he stored the banana skin in his plastic bag along with his notebook and stood up getting ready to go down the main path, keeping onto the grass verge.

Then he heard it.

The creak of the side gate.

Quickly he crouched down and going onto his knees, he peered through the bushes. In the pale light of the crescent moon he saw the dark figure pass the front door and make for a side window. It came very near to where he stood and stopped. It moved again towards one of the smaller windows. The window was pushed up and the figure heaved itself up onto the window ledge and went silently inside. The window was pulled down again. No light went on inside the house

William Paterson noted the name of the person in his notebook and the time. It was ten minutes to twelve.

CHAPTER 14

Mary Gentle, waking to birdsong, lay for a moment savouring those comfortable, half asleep, half-awake minutes when the stress and cares of the day ahead had not yet presented themselves. Then reality pushed its way into her cocoon and she remembered the night before. She had known when Ruth argued with him in front of the youth workers that Robert would get his revenge through her and he had. This time he had simply taken a belt to her, making sure that the marks would be hidden by her clothes. As she turned over her nightie stuck to her weals and she winced.

Robert's side of the bed was empty. She had better get showered and dressed quickly. He was probably downstairs impatiently waiting for his breakfast. It would never occur to him to get it for himself.

Frances Macarthur

Her shower was cursory and painful and she was downstairs in about ten minutes only to find the kitchen empty.

There was the clatter of footsteps along the as yet uncarpeted corridor. This would be Ruth whose bedroom was on the ground floor. Robert always insisted that when Ruth was at home she was on a different floor. It would not do for her to hear what went on in her parents' bedroom.

"Morning, Mum. Sleep well?"

"Yes thanks dear. You?"

"Yes like a top." She paused. "I wonder why we say that. Does a top sleep?"

"No and we say, sleeps like a baby yet most babies cry, well you both did anyway."

"Poor Mum and we're still a trouble to you."

"No you're not dear. I love you both. I just wish you would both try to please your father more."

"Mum! We have to live our own lives. Isn't it enough that you let him bully you?"

"OK dear I suppose you're right. Have you seen your father? I thought he'd be in here waiting for his porridge."

"No. Haven't seen him and haven't heard him either."

"Do me a favour love and see if he's in his study. Maybe he fell asleep in there. It's happened once or twice. Or maybe he's in the dark room getting things sorted out."

The Pulpit is Vacant

She knew he had slept beside her to begin with last night but being something of an insomniac he often left her side.

It was just like Robert to get his study and dark room ready before the hall, lounge and dining rooms, she thought. She got down two bowls for porridge and got the milk from the refrigerator. The porridge was steeping in the pan - none of the instant stuff for Robert.

Ruth poured herself a plate of cornflakes before going to the back of the house where the study and darkroom were situated. She would add the milk and some fruit later.

There was no sign of her father in either room.

Deciding to try the temporary lounge at the back of the house, she moved through the downstairs corridors of the house. The large front room not being finished yet, her father had decided to put the furniture from their last lounge into a smaller room meanwhile. Their lounge furniture matched the last residents' colour scheme.

She opened the door. The room was dark, the heavy gold-coloured velvet curtains permitting no sunlight to enter the room. Her father obviously wasn't here either.

Striding across the room to the windows, she stumbled over something on the floor.

Apprehension came with the realisation that the obstacle was not furniture. She stepped sideways and moved on towards the windows.

She pulled the curtains open and turned round, stifling a gasp at the sight of her father's body on the floor.

Thinking that he might have taken a heart attack or a stroke, she bent down.

He was on his back.

She noticed a large wet mark on his chest but it took a few moments before she realised that it was blood on his black vestment. A little of the blood had run down his side and turned the cream carpet a reddish brown.

She got up and left the room hurriedly to find her mother before she came this way herself. She must prevent her seeing this at all costs.

Mary Gentle was stirring the porridge on the stove. She looked up as Ruth rushed in.

"What is it dear? What's the hurry?"

"Mum, it's my father. He's...."

"He's what dear? Not ill...."

Mary's face went white. Ruth put her arm round her and drew her towards a chair.

"Mum, sit down. Now please keep calm. Look there's no easy way to tell you this. It's...someone's killed my father."

"Killed... what...?"

"He's lying on the lounge floor with a big bloodstain on his chest. It looks like he's been stabbed. I'm sure he's dead."

Before she could stop her mother, Mary Gentle was up off her seat and out of the door. Ruth ran

The Pulpit is Vacant

after her and together they stood and stared down at the prone figure.

Feeling shaky, Ruth bent down and put her finger on the side of his neck. There was no pulse.

"Mum, I'll have to phone 999. Will you be OK?"

Mutely Mary nodded.

She heard Ruth in the hall dialling, then her words.

"Please send someone. My father's dead. He's on the lounge floor. I think he's been murdered."

Mary heard Ruth giving her name and the address of the manse. She shuddered.

CHAPTER 15

Early Wednesday morning was quiet at the police station. DS Macdonald and DCI Davenport were together in his office and the constables without a sergeant to supervise them were enjoying some free time. Penny Price, a conscientious girl, was feeling a bit guilty but she really had nothing immediate to be getting along with and she did not want to be accused of being teacher's pet as she would be if she suggested that they should get themselves busy with routine things like getting reports up to date.

"Wonder what the new sergeant will be like," she mused and of course that started

Frank off.

"Salma Din. Well she'll be well suntanned. We'll have the smell of curry round here soon. Just as well I like the stuff."

The two older constables grinned then looked guilty when Penny said,

"Frank. You must try not to show your feelings so obviously. Why must you be so racist and sexist? You're really a nice guy otherwise and..."

The 'phone rang and Frank who was nearest picked it up.

"Shawbank Police Station. PC Selby speaking. How can I help you?"

His laid back demeanour underwent a sudden change. He straightened up and said,

"In the lounge you said? Who found him?"

He listened again then hung up.

"That was the desk, Penny. They've had a call from our local manse. There's been a murder."

He disappeared along the corridor to inform the DCI and DS Macdonald, bursting into the room without knocking.

"Sir, Ma'am. Sorry to interrupt you but there's been a murder at the local manse. A young woman has phoned in. She found the body."

Immediately the station was a buzz of activity. DS Macdonald phoned the police surgeon while DCI Davenport organised his constables, stopping first to say to Frank.

"Please don't burst in without knocking, Selby. PC Price, you come with me. Whoever the woman is will be upset. She seems to have found the body. PC Selby, get two other PCs to help you search the grounds of the manse. The weather's been dry for some days now so our chances of finding footprints are probably nil but we might get lucky with something else. Look out for a weapon."

The Pulpit is Vacant

"Yes Sir." Frank looked mutinous after the reprimand.

"Check the windows first for any sign of a break-in and the ground underneath the windows."

He swept like a whirlwind from the room, leaving Penny to run after him, grabbing her hat as she went.

As they pulled up at the manse gates, the little yellow car belonging to Martin Jamieson the police surgeon was just drawing up. Penny got out and opened the gates and the two cars moved in tandem up the path. There was only room for the car already there, at the front door, so they parked on the driveway one behind the other.

Penny just had time to tell her DCI the name of the police surgeon before they had stopped at the manse front door.

Martin got out of his car. He was immaculate as always, in a pin striped dark grey suit, pale pink shirt and silver grey tie. At odds with this tidiness his fair hair looked windswept.

"Martin Jamieson. You must be the new DCI."

Davenport seemed to tower over this young man.

"Yes. Charles Davenport. Pleased to meet you." He rang the bell.

The door opened almost immediately.

"Oh thank God you're here. It's my father, someone's murdered my father."

"Calm down Mrs...Miss..."

"Gentle. Miss. Ruth. My Mum's here too. I tried to stop her seeing the body but she has seen it. She's in the kitchen."

"Just take me to the body then. PC Price here will get you and your mother a cup of tea while I see what has happened for myself."

"Cup of tea? Is that all I'm good for?" fumed Penny to herself. She would rather have been out in the grounds looking for evidence. She hoped that the DCI was not going to be sexist too, like Frank. Then her common sense took over as she realised that with DS Macdonald having to stay behind to get things organised at that end, she was the only woman available and these women would probably welcome her administrations rather than Frank's.

Miss Gentle came back and took her into the kitchen where she met Mrs Gentle who was white faced but tearless.

"Mrs Gentle, I'm Constable Price. How about I make us all a nice cup of tea while we wait for my boss to see what has happened."

She had just poured out the tea, putting plenty of sugar into two of the cups when DCI Davenport came in.

"The police surgeon is with him now. I'm sorry Mrs Gentle - Miss Gentle - but I have to ask you some questions. My name is Davenport, DCI Davenport."

They nodded mutely.

The Pulpit is Vacant

"Now who found Mr Gentle?"

"I did Mr Davenport," said Ruth Gentle.

"When was that?"

"At about eight thirty this morning. Mum came down for breakfast. She asked if I'd seen my father and when I said I hadn't, she asked me to go to his study to see if he had slept there - he does sometimes fall asleep in the chair there. I went there and to the dark room then I tried the lounge. The curtains were closed so I went across to open them and almost tripped over his...body. There was blood. It had seeped into the carpet and..."

"Robert would be so annoyed Inspector. It must have been an expensive carpet and we were going to leave it down and..."

"Mum please don't. He's dead. Don't you understand? He won't know about the damn carpet."

"Don't swear dear. You know your father doesn't like it."

The girl put both hands to her head and shook it as if trying to shake something away.

DCI Davenport said gently, "I have to go back to the lounge now. PC Price will stay with you. Is there anyone else you want to call?"

"No Inspector," said Mary Gentle. "My son is at this moment on his way here from Australia and we have no other relatives."

"But Mum...."

"What dear?"

"Nothing. Mum. Can I get Kevin here?" Ruth asked

Mrs Gentle looked shocked and the DCI asked, "Who is Kevin?"

"He's my boyfriend. But my father didn't like him and I imagine it wouldn't be a good idea to upset Mum right now. Sorry Mum."

"Who is your doctor?"

"We haven't registered with anyone yet. We've only been here a few days."

Penny offered to contact her doctor as she lived nearby and was told to go ahead.

DCI Davenport went back to the lounge where he found Martin Jamieson taking off his latex gloves.

"Well, a straightforward stabbing. The knife went cleanly into his heart."

"Knife?"

"Well sharp instrument I suppose I should say right now but without further tests I would guess a kitchen knife, the type with a long thin blade."

"How long before you can tell me the time of death?"

"About two hours maximum. I have nothing else on hand at the moment."

"Good man."

They shook hands and Martin Jamieson left.

The DCI stood looking down at the body. The man was slim and, he thought, tall. His features

The Pulpit is Vacant

were sharp, the thin mouth drawn back in a grimace of pain. He must have been facing his assailant at the time of the attack, the entry wound being in his chest. He must find out the man's actions last night.

The bell rang and he went across to open it and let in the SOC team who would dust for fingerprints and mark the position of the body prior to it being taken to the city morgue. Another man had come in with them and he stood hesitantly, waiting for Davenport to finish his consultation with the team leader.

"Dr Forrest, Inspector. Where and why am I needed? Penny Price who rang me just now asked me to come quickly. I don't know the folk who stay here."

"Well Doc, Mr Gentle is past your administrations I'm afraid. He's been murdered. I would be grateful if you would take a look at Mrs and Miss Gentle. Miss Gentle found the body and her mother is almost too calm right now. As a layman, I would say she might be in for delayed shock."

The DCI took Dr Forrest to the kitchen and they found the three women drinking tea.

"Here's the Doctor Miss Gentle. While he sees to your mother could I have a word with you please?"

They stepped into the hall.

"Who was the last person to see your father alive?"

"Well he met with quite a few people last night. He was seeing the church youth leaders. I believe Mum let out a couple quite early in the evening but there were five people involved and I'm sure someone came along later. I don't know when they left."

"Thank you. I'll ask your mother if she knows more about these folk then perhaps if the doctor gives her a sedative you can get her to lie down and I'll ask her some more questions tomorrow."

They went back into the kitchen.

"I've given Mrs Gentle a mild sedative Inspector. Perhaps you would be kind enough to leave questioning her till tomorrow."

"Yes of course. Just one question before you go, Mrs Gentle. Did you see who left last night and when they left?

Mrs Gentle blinked at him and he was reminded of a deer caught in the headlights of a car. She looked frail and he hated having to ask her anything right now.

"Oh dear, I let Mrs French out and there was a man with her. They went quite early. After that my husband must have let the others out. I don't know their names I'm afraid. After giving them supper, I went to bed with my book. He came in later but he could have got back up at any time. He seldom slept well."

Ruth Gentle interrupted.

The Pulpit is Vacant

"Did someone else not come in after the others Mum? I thought I heard the bell ring."

"Oh yes dear there was another young man. I let him in and took him to the lounge."

"Their name s might be in my father's study," Ruth volunteered. "He is...he was...a methodical person and he will no doubt have entered their names in his diary."

She led the way to the study and the Inspector picked up a large leather-bound diary which was lying on the desk.

"Do you mind if I take this away?"

"No please. Take anything you want."

She went back to the kitchen and he hoped that she would take her mother to her bedroom.

He looked in the diary. There were six names written in for last night at 7.30. He looked at them. Elizabeth French. Now where had he heard that name before? Ah yes, she was the primary teacher whom Penny Price had mentioned to him recently.

Bill McFarlane (BB) and Andrew Bell (Anchor Boys) Claire Davidson (Guides) Mary Bell (Brownies).

He knew where he could find Elizabeth French. Penny had mentioned her and she would no doubt be able to direct him to the others. He knew the school, it being the one his daughter went to.

He went back to the kitchen. Ruth and her mother were standing saying goodbye to the doctor who left.

The DCI asked Ruth if she was OK and she said that she was and led her mother out of the room.

"Penny. See if Miss Gentle can get someone to come in to keep her company for the rest of the day. I believe a brother should be arriving soon from Australia but she needs someone now. I'll meet you in the car when you've done that."

"Right Sir. I imagine that she'll want to see her boyfriend and there will be no problem with that with her mother in bed and her father dead. Sorry Sir that sounded a bit callous. I didn't mean it to be."

The DCI smiled and went off to the lounge to check that the SOC team had everything they wanted. He passed a stretcher with a covered body on it being taken out the front door.

It looked as if once again the pulpit was vacant.

CHAPTER 16

Wednesday was not my favourite day and I had not slept much the night before. I quite often had nights like this when my brain refused to shut down. I would get up for a cup of tea and try either a Sudoku or a Codeword from the Glasgow Herald newspaper.

Last night I had done both and read a chapter of my library book and at 5am I had still not slept. What made it worse was that as well as falling asleep quickly, Jim never stirred till daylight.

I didn't like Wednesdays at school because I was on playground duty and that meant no welcome break and cup of coffee at the interval.

I had to come between two boys fighting, Fred and another well-built boy called Liam who both wanted to be in goals for the quick football match. I told them to take ten minutes each and added that if there was any more trouble, they would be sent inside and lose their break. I noticed William sitting reading his notebook. I was always afraid that he might be bullied but luckily so far it had not happened, at least not to my knowledge.

After the interval we continued with our project. No one had liked the two inches of bathwater and quite a few had tried the 'no sweets' rule and had not much liked that either. They were beginning to understand how different the life of children had been during the war years.

"My Dad said his dad had queued for hours when he heard that there were some bananas for sale and that he and his brother were so disappointed in the one he had managed to get but had pretended to like them as their dad was so thrilled to get them," reported one girl.

I told them about liquorice root which could be bought in the chemist.

Today I was beginning with them the children's novel "Goodnight Mr Tom" in which a young boy is sent away during the war to live in the country with a childless widower. After we had finished the book, I was going to show them the film of the book as a treat.

As I read with them I tried to make them understand just how awful it would be to be sent away from their families to the countryside when they were used to town life.

"What things would you miss?"

"Going to the pictures."

"Having a MacDonald's."

Then came the questions:

The Pulpit is Vacant

"Why did the children have to leave Glasgow Miss?"

"Because it was near Clydebank and Clydebank had docks and the Germans might bomb the docks to destroy our ships."

"Did they have computers in those days?"

"No."

"What kind of toys did they play with?"

I talked to them of peever, of exchanging scraps, of skipping ropes and for the boys, days spent playing cowboys and Indians, kick -the -can and of course football. I promised to draw a peever bed in the playground and teach the girls and I said I would bring in my old treasured scrap book.

One of the boys had heard of "Ring, Bang Scoosh" and wanted to describe it to the rest. I just hoped that they would not put into practice the game of ringing peoples' doorbells and running away! Another boy told of his dad telling him and his brother about a game called chickie mellie which involved tapping someone's window from upstairs with a stone on a string. I felt sorry once again for William who had nothing to tell.

After this talk I went back to my reading of the novel and was in the middle of doing this when the head teacher, Mrs Hobson, came into my room to tell me that there was an Inspector of police wishing to see me in her room. She would supervise my class while I went there. I did not much like this idea because the woman pried when left with a class. Oh I know it was her job to know what went on but she did it sneakily and seldom mentioned what she had seen. I had returned from a day's illness once to find many things out of place yet she never talked about what I was doing as if she was pretending she had seen nothing.

I hurried along the corridor and down the middle stairs to her room, knocked and went in.

Standing by the desk was a tall, handsome man in a smart grey suit and Penny Price, smart in her uniform and looking faintly embarrassed.

"Mrs French. I'm pleased to meet you. Penny here was going to ask you to keep an eye on my young daughter, Pippa Davenport, but unfortunately we meet in the most unfortunate of circumstances. You see there has been a murder at the local manse."

I gasped.

"Who has been murdered, Inspector?"

"The minister himself, the Reverent Gentle."

"Who would do that? Was it a burglary gone wrong, an intruder?"

"We don't know yet. The body was discovered by his daughter this morning."

"Oh, poor Ruth."

"Oh you know the family Mrs French?"

"Well not know exactly but I've been to the manse a few times and met the minister, his wife and daughter. I believe they have a son but he lives in Australia."

"I believe that you and a few others were at the manse last night for a meeting."

"Yes I was there with Bill McFarlane, Claire Davidson and Mary and Andrew Bell, oh and Colin Tait but Bill and I met him arriving as we were leaving."

"Why were you all there?"

"The minister wanted to meet all the leaders of the uniformed organisation. I help out with the BB at times so I went although not strictly a leader and I was there earlier than the rest because the minister had found out that I taught the ten year olds here and wanted to talk to me about getting some of them to come to Sunday school. We weren't alone for long before Bill and Claire came and then the others."

"Mary and Andrew Bell? Are they related?"

"Yes, they're twins. Andrew takes the Anchor Boys and Mary takes the Brownies. Claire takes the Guides and Bill the junior section of the BB. There's no senior section."

"How did the meeting go? In the light of this murder did anything happen that was odd or unexpected?"

"No. Claire got a bit on the defensive about having to hand in her programme to the minister but she's a bit haphazard and the minister is I suppose ultimately responsible for every group which uses the church premises."

"So nothing untoward?"

"No. Colin Tait came along as Bill and I were leaving. He takes a youth club in the church hall, and the minister had asked him, via Mrs Hobson, to come and see him with the objective of getting the infant kids to come to Sunday school so he was there on two counts. I talked to Colin this morning and he didn't offer very much about his meeting and it's unlike him to be unforthcoming."

"So something was worrying or upsetting him then?"

I don't suppose it meant anything. Maybe he was just thinking about his next lesson. He has the infants' class and is a marvellous teacher. The wee ones love him to bits."

"Can you tell me where I could find Bill.. Mc..?"

"McFarlane. He works in the Clydesdale Bank, the one in town, in Hope Street I think but I can give you his address. His wife has just had their first baby."

I gave him Bill's address.

"Thank you. What about the Bell twins?"

"I think Mary is at Strathclyde University. I'm not sure about Andrew. I don't know where they live but Bill will help you there. I don't know if Claire works. She has four children. I don't know her address either but Mary will know, if you see her first."

"Thank you Mrs French. You've been very helpful."

He turned to his PC.

The Pulpit is Vacant

"Penny, we'll have a quick word with Mr Tait and then get back to the station. See if PC Selby has anything for us."

We said our goodbyes and I went back to relieve Mrs Hobson of my class. She was reading to them. I did not know how much the Inspector had told her so I just took the book from her and told her that the Inspector wanted to speak to Colin so maybe she could go along to his room now.

I thought about the minister as I read mechanically.

He certainly wasn't a well-liked man, not by his family anyway. Mrs Gentle was bullied, maybe not physically but certainly mentally and there was no love lost between him and Ruth and what about Ruth's boyfriend - Kevin - he couldn't have liked the man either. Still it was one thing not liking someone and another thing hating them enough to kill them.

"Miss you've missed out a paragraph."

One of my brighter sparks had been paying attention it seemed. I pulled my thoughts back into the classroom

At lunchtime the murder was the main topic of conversation because the police car had been spotted. Colin and I were bombarded with questions and once again Colin was unusually quiet. It was I who filled them in on the reason for the police visit.

The afternoon passed without incident and I got home around 4.30. Once again William appeared outside my door. Jill was in this time. She had a soft spot for William. Not quite old enough yet for boyfriends, she treated him like a younger brother so I asked him in again and gave them both milk and biscuits. Jill suited her new hair colour, an almost honey blonde, and she asked William if he liked it. He did. His older sister tended to ignore him he had told me and the others girls were younger than him so he was quite flattered to be asked his opinion I think.

I asked Jill if she had seen her Dad that day, them both being at the same school but she had not seen him except in the distance and she preferred it that way as it was not 'cool' to have a father as one of your teachers.

I busied myself getting the dinner ready but my mind was very much on the murder at the manse.

CHAPTER 17

Back at the station DCI Davenport went off to his own room, calling for DS Macdonald, and the others discussed the case. Nothing as exciting as this had ever happened in the time Frank and Penny had been at the station. The DCI came back out after a while and questioned the men who had been searching the manse grounds. Frank had little to report. After days of no rain the ground was hard so no footprints could be seen outside the lounge or any other windows. No windows had been forced. One window at the side was slightly open at the bottom but it had been a warm night. It was the bathroom window. Frank had asked Ruth Gentle about it and she said any one of the family could have opened it and not said.

"Right everyone. Into the incident room and we'll see what has to be done."

Penny, Frank and the other two PCs moved down the hallway to the large room where current cases were discussed. The Inspector called out to DS Macdonald to join them.

"Now the facts are that Reverent Gentle was stabbed by a sharp instrument, probably a knife, in his lounge, probably sometime between when his meeting with the youth workers took place and this morning when his daughter found the body."

"Sounds like a game of Cluedo," said Frank and received a glare from DS Macdonald. Davenport continued, "I haven't heard from the police surgeon yet. He was going to attend the post mortem himself and get back to me as soon as he could. He himself had no other pressing work to do but it will depend on how busy the pathologist is.

The people who need to be seen are, Bill McFarlane, Andrew and Mary Bell and Claire Davidson. We need also to interview Mrs Gentle and her daughter Ruth. Fiona, you take Frank with you and go back to the manse and talk to Ruth Gentle. Tell her I'll come myself in the morning to see her mother. Penny you come with me to see Bill McFarlane. Hopefully he will be able to give us the addresses of the Bells and Claire Davidson.

Elizabeth French had given the DCI Bill's address and soon they were pulling up in front of an end terraced house. The garden looked well-tended and at this time of year was a riot of colour from azalea bushes. Charles Davenport, himself a keen gardener, admired especially one flame coloured one almost at the front door. They rang

The Pulpit is Vacant

the bell and a neat, fresh-faced, fair-haired woman opened the door with a baby in her arms. Seeing Penny in her uniform, she looked alarmed but Charles Davenport was quick to reassure her.

"Don't worry Mrs McFarlane; we haven't come with bad news, for you and your husband anyway."

"Oh, thank God. Bill went out to get us a fish supper and I thought at first that he had been in an accident."

She led them into the lounge cosily decorated in browns and reds with pale walls and an old fashioned comfortable-looking settee and chairs. The TV in the corner was on and Noel Edmonds was hosting 'Deal or No Deal'.

"We're having an early meal tonight. We were both hungry after having been up so early with this wee man." She looked proudly down at her new baby boy.

"What's his name? "asked Penny, tickling him under the chin and getting a small grin for her troubles. She knew that at this age it would just be wind making him 'grin' but she felt absurdly pleased all the same as babies did not often take to her. Having no brothers and sisters of her own, she preferred teenagers and dogs to young children and babies.

"He's called Graeme," said Alison.

The noise of the front door opening and closing came to their ears and Bill came into the lounge, looking worried.

"I saw the police car. What's wrong?"

"Don't worry Mr McFarlane. It *is* bad news but not for you personally. There has been a murder. The minister has been murdered in his lounge between last night when you saw him and this morning when he was found by his daughter. I just wanted to ask you a few questions about last night."

"My goodness! Murdered! Sorry. Go ahead, Inspector."

"Detective Chief Inspector Davenport."

"Sorry, Chief Inspector. What did you want to know?"

"When you arrived, who was in the house?"

"Well the minister himself obviously and his wife because she saw us out."

"You left when?"

"Oh quite early because I wanted to be here to help Alison with wee Graeme."

"Did you leave on your own?"

"No I left with Elizabeth, Elizabeth French. She was there when I arrived and wanted to get home in good time as she had a lot of school work to do. She works at Southview Primary School."

"Yes, I know that. I've been to see her already."

"So you'll know that we left together," said Bill sounding a bit put out.

"Yes but we have to double check everything in a murder inquiry." The DCI smiled, putting Bill at ease again.

"Now when you left who was in the house?"

"Well there was the minister who showed us out, Mrs Gentle who had just arrived with some tea and a girl who I believe was their daughter. I forget her name."

"No one else?"

"Oh sorry, the Bell twins and Claire Davidson the guide leader were still in the lounge and Elizabeth and I met Colin Tait the youth club leader at the front gate. He was about to join them unless he changed his mind. He told us that the minister had asked him to come as he takes a youth club in the church hall."

"Can you tell me where the Bell twins and Mrs? Miss? Davidson live?"

"Mrs Davidson, Claire, lives at 32 Frederick Street, quite near the library," piped in Alison. We're quite friendly and go to each other's houses quite often. She's had four children so has been a good help to me."

"Sorry I don't know where Andrew and Mary live," said Bill, "but Claire will be able to tell you as she and Mary know each other quite well, being in charge of Guides and Brownies."

"Thank you both. You've been a great help. I don't suppose you know of any ill feeling between the minister and anyone else."

"I'm afraid not. The only thing I know was that he was quite rude to his wife and his daughter, his wife for bringing the tea in too late and his daughter for meeting someone he felt was unsuitable."

"Tell me more about that."

"Well he said he hoped she hadn't been seeing some "good-for- nothing" and she said she would see anyone she wanted to. I think he made some old fashioned remark about her having to do what she was told while she was living under his roof and then we left."

The DCI thanked them again, complimented them on their new son and he and Penny left.

It did not take them long to get to Claire's house but they were unlucky as only her mother was in with the children and she could not tell them when Claire would be home.

"She tells me nothing," moaned the woman. "She just invites me here to be a baby sitter."

The DCI asked her to tell her daughter to pop in to the police station as soon as possible and they left.

Deciding that they could do no more that day, Penny and Davenport made their way back to the station where Penny was introduced to Pippa who had been collected at school by another female PC.

"Sorry Pippa pet. I hope you weren't worried when I didn't turn up at school."

"No Daddy, I wasn't worried. It's happened before you know and anyway I enjoy getting a lift in a police car. You know that."

They hugged each other.

The Pulpit is Vacant

DS Macdonald told him that there was no more news from Ruth Gentle apart from the fact that she let slip that her mother might have an easier life now. Her mother was still sleeping and they would expect the Chief Inspector in the morning, hopefully not too early.

"Thanks everyone. See you all in the morning. Come on young lady, let's get you home. Would you like an easy meal tonight? MacDonald's?

CHAPTER 18

It was Thursday afternoon and DS Macdonald was talking to Penny about the meeting with Bill McFarlane. Nothing much had come from it that they did not already know and Penny must have sounded disappointed because Fiona Macdonald noticed.

"Don't get downhearted Penny. A murder often goes a bit cold but there's evidence out there waiting for us I'm sure."

DS Macdonald was a woman of few words on most occasions but in her short time at the station had proved herself to be on the ball as with her knowledge of Frank's racist tendencies earlier in the week.

Penny liked her and respected her already and it was nice to have a female superior in what was a predominantly male profession. She felt cheered by her superior's words.

There was a cursory knock on the door and Fiona Macdonald called out, "Come in."

DCI Davenport entered, nodded at Penny and asked his DS if she and one of the PCs would pay a visit to Colin Tait's house that evening and interview him again about his meeting at the manse on the night of the murder.

"He seemed very nervous when I spoke to him and I wondered if he told me everything."

Penny was disappointed when she said she would take Frank but realised that it was probably sensible to take a man along when it was a man who was being interviewed.

"The murderer must have pulled the knife out cleanly and Martin says this was very fortunate for him or her as in most knife murders the knife sticks in the ribs. It seems that our murderer was also lucky in that blood didn't spurt out. Anything else before you go?"

He gave both of them a warm smile and Penny thought again what a handsome man he was.

"I'm going out with PC Selby now. We'll probably have lunch together."

Davenport went into the main room of his area and spoke to Frank and shortly after this they left. Frank was following up on a breaking and entering of two local shops, one a delicatessen and the other a corner shop.

"Mr Jordan," he smiled at the dapper little man who faced them over the counter of the delicatessen. "I'm PC Selby. Can you give me some details about the robbery please?"

The Pulpit is Vacant

This was duly done and Davenport and Frank moved on next door.

"Mrs Mohammed, tell me about your robbery."

Mrs Mohammed gave a nervous smile and Davenport smiled back.

Interviews over, the DCI suggested that they stop off for some lunch and asked Frank if there was anywhere he could recommend.

"There's a nice pub down the next street...Sir." He remembered the Sir just in time.

"I don't drink on duty Selby and neither should you. I'm surprised you didn't know that," Davenport sounded surprised rather than annoyed.

"The last DCI didn't seem to mind," Frank sounded surly and the Sir was missing.

They found a tearoom. Frank felt silly sitting among a predominantly female clientele and he ate his scone and drank his coffee with bad grace. Davenport tried to get him to thaw out by asking him about his aspirations in the police force but all that got him was a diatribe about being passed over in favour of someone else.

"A black woman too," he said, in his disgruntled frame of mind, forgetting to whom he was talking.

"Maybe this is the time to say that I noticed the difference in your treatment of the two shopkeepers, Selby. You smiled and were polite to the man and abrupt and impolite to the woman. I hope you're not racist. I won't stand for that in my team."

Frank reddened and put his coffee cup to his lips to avoid having to reply. Davenport paid for the coffee and scone and they walked back to the car.

It was about 7.20 in the evening when DS Macdonald and Frank Selby paid a call on Colin Tait having first phoned Elizabeth French to find out his address. Colin lived in a first floor flat in the West End, quite near Byres Road and they had difficulty parking which put Frank in a worse mood than he had been in already with having an evening visit to make. He would have parked on a double yellow line normally as it was usually easy to convince a traffic warden that he could do that when on police business but he knew instinctively that DS Macdonald would disapprove. He did not share Penny's feeling for their superior officer. He liked woman slim and blonde or slim and brunette, not middle aged and mousy fair

They had to walk back two blocks to Colin's flat.

All the flats were occupied and the names showed a variety of nationalities as was to be expected in Glasgow's West End. The card bearing Colin's name had a scrawled C Tait and Frank wondered if he had just recently moved here. He was to wonder this again as soon as Colin opened the door. Dressed in immaculate cream Chinos and white short-sleeved shirt, his fair hair short and tidy, he was the epitome of neatness. He probably had not had time to get his card printed.

The Pulpit is Vacant

DS Macdonald introduced herself and Frank, saying that they just wanted to ask him a few more questions about his visit to the manse on Wednesday evening. Colin appeared nervous but readily agreed to answer their questions and led them through to what appeared to be a study, housing as it did a large desk, red filing cabinet and computer equipment. Colin waved them into the two chairs and perched himself on the desk and Frank wondered if his lounge was not yet furnished for visitors.

"Mr Tait. Tell me please about your visit to the manse on Wednesday evening," said DS Macdonald.

"Well the minister had spoken to my head teacher. He, the minister, wanted to know if I would help promote his Sunday school to my infant class. Mrs Hobson was all in favour and asked me if I would go to the manse when it was convenient. I was going that night anyway in my role as youth club leader. I was late because the traffic was held up on the Kingston Bridge."

Colin added, "I didn't want to try to get my wee ones to go to his Sunday school. I'm a humanist and don't really approve of structured religions. I could hardly refuse Mrs Hobson so I thought that I could maybe make the minister understand my predicament. Mr Tasker, the previous minister was very tolerant of all other faiths and my non-faith. I went along to Mr Gentle's church on his first Sunday here out of curiosity and the man was verging on fundamental so I was not looking forward to our conversation really."

"Ok Mr Tait, you've been very honest with us. Could you now tell us please who else you met that night and what transpired between you and Mr Gentle when you spoke to him?"

"I told the other man, your boss, that I met Beth French and a Bill McFarlane at the manse gate as they were leaving. When I got there there were five other folk in the lounge. One woman was the guide leader and the two younger ones, twins I believe, took the Brownies and the Anchor Boys. I take a youth club at the church and I love working with children but as with organised religion I don't like uniformed organisations much. I was in the Cubs myself and didn't enjoy it at all."

That's three people and you said five," Frank spoke for the first time. "Who were the other two?"

"Mrs and Miss Gentle who had come in with tea for the ones who had been there for some time. The minister asked them, rather abruptly, I thought, to pour out the tea and then leave us. His daughter flushed up but his wife just busied herself with pouring the tea then they both left. The look the daughter threw at her father was not a friendly one."

They had heard this before.

"The others got up to leave immediately they could after tea but the minister and I hadn't had

The Pulpit is Vacant

our conversation so I stayed on for about another half hour then Mr Gentle showed me out, telling me that it had been an interesting meeting. It might have been interesting for him but I felt as if I had been through a mangle. I felt like a job applicant rather than a youth worker and school teacher. He was determined to talk to my class even without my approval and I got the impression that he usually got what he wanted. He did try just before I left, to be a bit more sociable but I found his questions about myself intrusive rather than interested."

"So you think he was not on great terms with his daughter. What about his wife? "asked DS Macdonald

"She just looked in awe of him, a wee bit scared if anything."

"Thank you Mr Tait, you've been very helpful."

Frank thought he caught a look of relief on Colin Tait's face as he showed them out but when he mentioned it to DS Macdonald as they went down the stairs, she put it down to a natural nervousness at being interviewed by the police and relief that it was over.

The talk in the car turned to members of staff and Fiona Macdonald asked Frank how long he had been at the station. He had been there for four years, he told her.

Had he been in for any promotions?

"Yes the one which Salma Din got", he said trying to keep the resentment from his voice.

133

"Think you have to be female and black these days to get anywhere," he added, forgetting again to whom he was speaking.

"Ma'am or DS Macdonald when you are speaking to me PC Selby," she replied quite mildly. "I do hope you will give Sergeant Din a chance. Think of how you would feel knowing that you had been promoted over someone who would still be at the station, and you an Asian woman."

"Yes ma'am," Frank muttered and they drove the rest of the way back to the station in silence.

CHAPTER 19

"Well, what do we have so far?" DCI Davenport looked round the incident room. A blown up photograph of Robert Gentle's prone body dominated the room and the staff sat round about, some on seats and some perched on desks.

"Frank and I went to see Colin Tait yesterday." said the DS. "He said about his meeting with the minister that he went the day his head teacher mentioned that Mr Gentle wanted to see him as he was going that night anyway. He claimed that he was nervous because he was a humanist and having been to Mr Gentle's first church service he was worried about meeting a man whom he claimed was fundamentalist in his views."

"I thought it sounded a bit lame, myself," put in Frank, "and why did he go to the service in the first place? Was it just idle curiosity as he claimed?"

"Well I went too," said Penny. "I was curious to know what the new man was like but then I knew Mr Tasker and had been to one or two of *his* services."

"Why else would Colin be nervous of this man?" demanded the DCI.

No one could tell him or offer any ideas.

"The minister insisted that he was going to try to get Colin's wee ones to come to Sunday School in spite of Colin being against it," added the DS.

"Any other comments to make folks?"

"Well the daughter didn't get on well with her father by all accounts," said DS Macdonald. "I've read the reports and Bill McFarlane, Elizabeth French and Colin Tait all commented on Mr Gentle's attitude to Ruth and her attitude towards him."

"They might just have had an argument that day of course," said Davenport. "What about Mrs Gentle?"

"I think she was in awe of her husband," said Penny.

"She mentioned that he would be annoyed at the blood stain on the carpet, certainly," said Davenport.

"By what Ruth said to her Mum when we were having tea in the kitchen, I think he was quite definitely the boss in the house." That was Penny again.

"Good man," muttered Frank Selby.

"What was that PC Selby?" asked Davenport.

"Nothing, Sir."

The Pulpit is Vacant

Penny threw Frank a dirty look which did not go unnoticed by DS Macdonald.

"Did anyone find out about the son, the one coming from Australia?"

Silence.

"Well one of you get on to that. Find out when he is expected here or, if he's already here, when he arrived in the country. Penny, I want you to go back to the manse. See if you can find out anything about Ruth's boyfriend. He wasn't liked by Mr Gentle, so she said while I was there. Tell Mrs Gentle I'll come to see her myself later today."

"I'm on my way, Sir."

"Selby, I want you to inquire in the manse district. See if you can find out anything about the family. I know they've only recently arrived but you never know. We might hit it lucky."

"DS Macdonald, my room please."

Penny drove back to the manse. It was now early afternoon and she hoped that she would get Ruth on her own. She might open up to someone her own age if her mother wasn't around.

She was in luck. Ruth opened the door.

"Oh I'm sorry. Mum is still in bed. She isn't used to sleeping pills you see and they've knocked her out completely."

"That's OK Miss Gentle. I just wanted to ask about the rest of the family. Have you notified everyone?"

"Call me Ruth please. Come in. There is no one to tell except Philip and he should be here shortly as his plane was landing around 12."

Ruth had led Penny into the kitchen.

"Whereabouts in Australia did he live? Have you all been out to visit him?"

Penny's friendly manner hid the fact that she was trying to find out Philip's relationship with his father. Ruth seemed happy to talk. She went on, "Philip's been out there for about two years. He lives on the outskirts of Melbourne. I went to see him last September. I went to Brisbane at the end of May to work during my holidays from university and spent a few weeks with Philip before I came home. I'm in third year at Strathclyde."

"Doing what?"

"Oh, engineering."

"What about your boyfriend, Kevin isn't it?"

"Kevin's on the same course. That's where we met. He came out to Australia with me. Mum knew that he was there but we agreed not to tell my father."

"Didn't he like Kevin?" Penny slipped in quietly.

"Like him! He hated him. He wouldn't let him over the door here. Just because Kevin nearly got sent down for smoking hash! I mean hash is safer than smoking cigarettes."

"What about your Mum?"

"Oh she liked him on the occasions she met him on nights when my father was out and he came

The Pulpit is Vacant

here but she had to pretend she felt the same as my father. She never would stand up to or argue with him."

"How did Kevin feel about your father?"

"He took it better than I did. He said that all fathers felt that no one was good enough for their daughters. But it wasn't just that. My father just had to be in control. He wanted to rule me like he ruled Mum. There were times when I could have killed hi...Sorry. I didn't mean that literally."

Penny assured her that she understood and asked if Ruth's mother and father had visited Philip in Melbourne.

"Mum would have loved to have gone but Philip left home after a big row with my father so there was no way they wanted to see each other.

"What was their big row about?"

"I think I had better let Philip tell you that himself, if he wants to though it's hardly relevant when he wasn't even in the country at the time of the murder."

"No other relations to inform then?"

"No both my father and mother were only children, constable."

Penny left, telling Ruth that she had come to ask if there was anyone else who had to be informed and to say that DCI Davenport would come up to the manse later in the day to see Mrs Gentle.

As she drove back to the station Penny hoped that Ruth would turn out to be innocent of this murder though right now she was giving herself and her brother possible reasons for thinking that life would be better without him.

Frank Selby was doing a door-to-door enquiry of the houses near the manse. So far he had found very few people who had even seen the Gentles let alone knew anything about them. Only one woman who lived right next to the manse had seen Mrs Gentle get out of the car to open the gate and had seen her come out and walk down the road just a few days ago.

"Where might she have been going on foot?" asked Frank.

"Either the railway station or the local shop or the library," replied the woman. "There is really nothing else as being new she wouldn't be visiting any of the houses I don't imagine."

Frank went back the way he had come and went into the general store. He looked at the array of greetings cards on display while the woman serving attended to two customers.

When they were alone in the shop he asked about the minister's wife.

"A new minister moved into the manse up the road quite recently. I wonder if you've seen any of the family at all."

"Oh the poor man who was murdered!" Nan Brodie's eyes lit up. "Yes I've served his wife and his daughter but not him."

"Can you tell me anything at all about Mrs Gentle and her daughter?"

The Pulpit is Vacant

Nan Brodie took a deep breath.

"Well that poor woman was in awe of her husband. She always mentioned him. 'My husband doesn't like tinned vegetables; has to have fresh. My husband's fond of plain bread, doesn't like pan."

"What about Miss Gentle?"

"I overheard her talking to her father one day. I don't think she liked him."

"What gave you that idea?"

"She told him that she was thinking of leaving home to be with her boyfriend and he said she wouldn't leave home because of what he might do to her mother if she wasn't there to protect her. She said he was a cruel man."

"Was she - the daughter - afraid of him?"

"Didn't sound like it to me."

"Thanks Mrs ...?"

"Mrs Brodie - Nan Brodie."

"Is there anything else you can tell me?"

"Well there's a son living in Australia I think."

"Do you know anything about him Mrs Brodie?"

"Sorry, no." Nan Brodie looked disappointed as if she had failed somehow.

Charles Davenport poured himself and Fiona Macdonald a cup of coffee, grateful that he could bring in his own percolator and coffee and not have to drink the dirty water they called canteen coffee. He sat down and his left hand strayed to his ear lobe which he tugged gently.

"What do you think Fiona? Any gut reaction towards this case?"

"I'm afraid not Sir. I know that nine times out of ten it's a family member but by the sound of it Mrs Gentle is too timid and in awe of her husband and the daughter isn't hiding her dislike of her father. The son wasn't here."

"Well the worm might have turned in the case of Mrs Gentle and the daughter might be double - bluffing by making her dislike obvious."

"True. What about the boyfriend, Kevin?"

"Haven't met him yet so can't say. Then there are the Tuesday night visitors. All I know is that they didn't know the man before he arrived here and he could hardly have got himself hated within a few days of arriving surely?"

"No, it's not likely as you say. I know that Frank Selby thinks that Colin Tait was nervous of our questioning but I think it was just natural unease at being in the presence of two police officers. A lot of people get nervous in these situations."

There was a knock on the door and Penny entered.

"That's me back Sir from seeing Ruth Gentle."

"Get anything from her?"

"Well she did get a bit heated when she talked about how her father wanted to control her the way he did her mother and said she sometimes wanted to kill him but I'm sure that was just exaggeration, the way people often say that in the

The Pulpit is Vacant

heat of the moment. She did say that her mother would have visited her brother in Melbourne but that her father and brother had fallen out so no visiting was allowed though Ruth did go while she worked in Australia."

"Did you ask the reason for their falling out?"

"Yes, I asked what they had fallen out over but she was reluctant to say anything and said I should ask her brother when he arrived."

"What about the boyfriend?"

"Mr Gentle didn't like him when he discovered that he had smoked hash at university but it seems that Kevin wasn't as bothered about his being banned from the house as Ruth was. He just went when Mr Gentle was out."

Another knock at the door heralded the arrival of Frank.

"Any fresh news, PC Selby?"

"I met the shopkeeper of the local shop, a Mrs Nan Brodie and she was quite ready to gossip about the new family. Seemingly Ruth wanted to marry Kevin and persuade her mother to move in with them and the father threatened to treat Mrs Gentle badly if Ruth moved out. Apparently this Mrs Brodie overheard Ruth Gentle talking to her father."

"Right. Having heard all you have to say, I guess that Ruth Gentle is our strongest contender for murderer so far.

There was another knock on the door and another PC popped his head in.

"Sir, I'm just back from the airport. Philip Gentle came in on the 12 noon flight from Dubai on Tuesday."

The four in the room looked at each other.

"It seems that we have another contender: a son who by all accounts hated his father. I wonder if Ruth Gentle or her mother or both of them knew that he was already in Glasgow or if they really do think that he is coming in today. I think another visit to the manse is called for."

CHAPTER 20

Idecided that I had to go up to the manse and give that lovely little woman my condolences. It was not something I was looking forward to but I felt that it had to be done especially as they were so new here and had no friends yet.

Dinner over, I left Jill doing her weekend homework so that she could have Saturday and Sunday free and Jim doing the same thing with his marking. I had brought all my class's hobby notebooks home with me but I would not be able to settle until I had done my visit.

It was about seven o'clock when I walked over to the manse, opened the main gate and walked up the hill to the front door.

It was Mrs Gentle who opened the door. She was wearing severe black and looked almost pathetically pleased to see me and I was glad I had come. She invited me in and told me that she had been given sleeping pills by her doctor and had only woken up a few hours ago just in time to

Frances Macarthur

speak to the chief inspector when he came up to see her. She had found him very pleasant. I noticed that she did not take me into the lounge but into the kitchen and she explained that her husband had been found in the lounge.

I told her how sorry I was about her husband and asked who had found the body. She explained that it was Ruth and hastened to tell me that she was often asleep before he came to bed so she had not known that his side of the bed had not been slept in till the morning.

I asked her where she would live as the manse was no doubt a house tied to the job and she told me that they had bought a small house in Fife near where they had once lived and she would probably go there. She told me that Ruth would probably marry Kevin after they graduated and that she knew that there would always be a place for her with them too.

"What about your son?"

"How do you know about him?" she asked puzzled.

I had to tell her that Nan Brodie, the shopkeeper had told me but I said I didn't know how she knew and Mary Gentle seemed prepared to let it go at that.

"He arrived on Wednesday afternoon having travelled over from Australia. I haven't seen him for a few years and I'm sorry that he and my husband hadn't patched up their quarrel before the death."

The Pulpit is Vacant

This information came out in a somewhat breathless rush almost as if she had practised it and was saying something rehearsed as children did at school when they were guilty of something and trying to convince the teacher that they were innocent.

I didn't ask what the quarrel was about. It would have been intrusive.

She seemed quite willing to talk to me so I stayed for a while before leaving knowing that I still had a lot of work to get through that night.

As we went to the front door, Ruth came out of a room with a reddish-haired, well-built young man. She introduced him to me as her older brother, Philip, from Australia and we shook hands. She too told me that he had only just arrived in Glasgow on Wednesday afternoon. He gave me a charming smile and said he was pleased to meet me.

I arrived back home later than I had meant to but relieved that I had gone. Jim was still busy but Jill had obviously finished her homework as she was ensconced in front of the TV. How Jim could work with the TV on I did not know as I took myself off to the kitchen table with my pile of hobby notebooks.

Most of the children had talked about their hobbies so not much was new but their grammar and spelling did not live up to their enthusiasm for their hobbies so I had a lot to correct. William used his yellow notebook to take notes then he transferred special things into his hobby notebook so his hobby jotter was extremely neat and tidy although his spelling and grammar left a lot to be desired. I had not yet, as I had promised, taken home the yellow notebook. It might be interesting to see what he had invented about the war. He had a good imagination.

I enjoyed reading the boys' notebooks rather than the girls' because the former were, on the whole, more interesting as ten year old girls were only, it seemed, interested in boy bands and I got totally fed up reading about these and seeing the pictures stuck in most of the pages. Only Jacqueline Beaton had a different hobby. She played tennis and her notebook held pictures of Tim Henman and other tennis stars. Like William, she tended to be a bit of a loner and sometimes they sat together at the interval much to the delight of the other boys who tended to tease William about it but not in Jacqueline's hearing I would imagine, as she was sharp tongued and clever and could talk rings round most of the boys.

It took me till after midnight to finish correcting and reading the notebooks but I was determined to get them all done as Jim and I had promised to get all our school work done on Friday night so that we could have a day away with Jill. She had asked if she could bring Helen and we had agreed.

I got to sleep surprisingly quickly that night but woke in the middle of a nightmare in which

The Pulpit is Vacant

a huge bird was chasing William and Jacqueline and me round the manse garden. I woke in a sweat and must have shouted out because I woke Jim. I got up and made us both a cup of tea and we discussed where we would go with the two girls. If the weather was nice we decided to go to Tarbert Loch Fyne. It was so picturesque at the harbour there and there were plenty of places to have lunch. Luckily they weren't girls who had to be constantly amused. Both had new digital cameras and were quite happy to go somewhere scenically beautiful. Jill had taken some bird pictures for William to put in his hobby notebook and he was very proud of them. He had taken her up to his hide in the manse garden last year and had promised to take me one day too.

Jim fell asleep quickly but it took me some time to drop off. I hoped that I would not go into the same nightmare again.

CHAPTER 21

Saturday morning at the police station was quite quiet. Detective Chief Inspector Davenport had gone back up to the manse with DS Macdonald. Frank was writing up his interview with Nan Brodie the day before, at the same time chatting to Penny.

"Wonder what the new sergeant will be like. Wonder if she'll wear that scarf thing."

"Hijab."

"Aye that."

"Frank please try hard not to show any racism towards her, or any sexism come to that. I don't think the DCI would appreciate the first and the DS definitely wouldn't appreciate the second."

"I'm going to be surrounded by bloody women!"

Penny ignored that and they worked in silence for a while.

"Hey Penny."

He looked up from his computer.

"The DCI is called Charles and the DS is Fiona Macdonald. Charles and F Macdonald. Bonnie Prince Charlie - and his girlfriend was Flora Macdonald. That can be our nicknames for them - Bonny Prince and Flora!"

In spite of herself Penny was quite taken with the idea. She liked both her superiors but Frank had been clever working that out.

"Yes. Good one Frank but be very careful not to say it in their hearing."

She walked back to her desk and Frank reluctantly went back to his report.

Shortly afterwards, Davenport and his DS arrived back. He called his team into his room and told them about his interview with Philip Gentle. He had told him that he knew that he had arrived in Glasgow a day earlier than his Mother had said he would be arriving and he had admitted that this was the case. Asked where he had been, he said that he had visited some friends, not wanting to arrive at the manse until his sister was at home and thinking that she would be at university during the day. He had told the DCI that his mother had confessed that she had lied about when he was due to arrive as she thought he might be a suspect for his father's murder having fallen out with him some years before. He had agreed to back this up and Ruth had been convinced to do the same though, being an open, forthright person she was not happy about it and was sure they would be found out as indeed they had.

The Pulpit is Vacant

Asked what his relationship was with his father, he had admitted that they had had a very bad row before he left home years ago. Asked what the row was about he said that his father wanted him to be a doctor but that he did not want to enter upon years of studying, not yet anyway. He wanted to travel the world with some friends, working for his trip in the places they visited. His father had said that if he set foot on a plane he need not come home again as he did not want a layabout for a son.

Davenport was getting the picture of a very controlling man. He held the reins which led his wife to giving up her idea of a career in teaching; he tried to shackle his daughter using her love for her mother and he had tried to mould his son into what he wanted him to be.

What did they think, Davenport asked now. Had one of these three people snapped for ever the chains with which Robert Gentle was trying to bind them? All had had the opportunity. Ruth and her mother had both been in the house. Philip could have visited friends but left them and come over to the manse or in fact never been with friends at all and also been in the manse. And there was Kevin. Could he have tried to free the woman he loved from the prison she was in?

Frank, ever ready to venture an opinion was sure it was a man's work. Penny thought that a woman could just as easily have stabbed the minister but liked Ruth and Mary Gentle and hoped that it wasn't them. She even ventured that it might have been an outside job but nothing had been stolen according to the two women and so what would the motive have been?

"DS Macdonald, what about you?" asked Davenport.

"You've left out Colin Tait. I haven't met the others but I have met him and he is definitely nervous about something."

The phone rang and the DCI lifted the receiver, "Missing? Since when?

I'll send someone round to see her right away."

He put down the receiver.

"That was the desk. There's been a phone call from a Mrs Paterson saying that her son is missing. His bed hasn't been slept in.

Penny and Frank, get round to her house. I've written down the address."

The two constables left.

"What an induction to us in our new jobs Fiona - a murder and now a missing person."

It didn't take long for Frank and Penny to reach the Paterson house. It was quite near the manse to which they had been going recently.

Mrs Paterson answered their ring. She looked worn out and anxious and had a baby in her arms and a toddler clinging to one leg.

"I'm so sorry. It's probably nothing. William is often late home from school and I'm afraid with five younger than him I just let him come and go

The Pulpit is Vacant

as he wants. He's never given me one worrying moment and that's why I'm scared that something has happened to him."

"Does he have any older brothers or sisters? asked Penny.

"Yes, George and Arlene."

"Have you asked them, Mrs Paterson?" asked Frank.

"Well I've asked his sister Arlene, my oldest but she isn't close to William. He was.......Oh what am I saying... he *is* too quiet for her. George the next eldest is out looking for William. He's gone to the Old Muddy to ask some boys in his class if they've seen him but he isn't interested in football so I don't think he'll be there."

"When did you last see William Mrs Paterson?" Frank asked.

"He had his supper last night about nine o'clock then went into the room he shares with George and the two younger boys. He's working on something. I expect it's for school. George went to bed about eleven. He must have seen William then but when he came for breakfast he must have assumed that William had eaten his and left the house because it wasn't till lunchtime when I asked if he'd seen William that he said that he hadn't seen him since last night. I was busy with the younger ones and didn't realise that William hadn't had any breakfast."

She started to cry and the baby in her arms joined in obviously sensing her unease.

155

"Don't cry Mrs Paterson," soothed Penny. "I'm sure he must have a good reason for being out. It *is* only early afternoon and you know what kids are like. They forget the time if they get interested in something."

"Can you think of anywhere he might have gone?" Frank asked her.

"He sometimes went to his teacher's house. Mrs French is very good with him and he likes her daughter. Jill I think her name is."

"Right we'll go round there first and then come back. By that time George should be back."

It did not take long for Penny and Frank to discover that there was no one in at the French house. When they knocked at a neighbour's door she could tell them that the family had gone off in their car quite early that morning but when asked if there was a small boy with them she could not tell them.

Back at the Paterson house, George had come back having drawn a blank. None of the boys at the football game had seen William that morning.

"When you went to bed last night George, was William asleep or did you talk to him? Did he say he was going anywhere today?"

George's head went down.

"George. What is it? Tell me. Now."

Mrs Paterson grabbed her son's arm and shook him.

The Pulpit is Vacant

"George, you have to tell us. What did you and William talk about last night?" said Frank.

George was on the defensive.

"He was always going out at night, well, recently anyway."

"Going out? Where?"

"He went to the manse. He's always gone during the day, during weekends and sometimes early in the evenings too but recently he started going later on."

"Why didn't you tell me?" his Mum asked.

"Well..."

"Well what? George, tell me. It could be important."

"Well he gave me 50p for not telling you."

"Do you know whereabouts in the manse grounds he went?" Penny asked him.

"No I wasn't interested in his silly birds or his silly war games."

"What war games?" asked Frank.

Mrs Paterson told them about William's insistence on having only two inches of bathwater and of his refusing to have any sweets recently.

"I think it was a school project but I didn't pay much attention. I never did pay much attention to William. He's so quiet that it was easy to miss him if you know what I mean. With so many other kids it was nice not to have one to bother about. Oh God. What's happened to him? I'll never forgive myself if he's hurt or had an accident."

Penny asked if she had a recent photograph of William and his mother went off and came back with his school photograph from last summer.

"Do you think he might have gone away for the day with Mrs French?" asked Frank.

"No. *She* would have told me if he didn't think about it."

Penny and Frank left saying that they would go up to the manse and see if there was any evidence that William had been there. He might have fallen asleep in the garden or even just be talking to someone in the family there.

CHAPTER 22

The policeman and woman opened the manse gates and surveyed the slope leading up to the front door. On their right was a sloping lawn which would be ideal for sledging if there was ever any more snow in the winter. On the left, trees fringed the driveway.

"We'd better ring the station Frank," said Penny.

"OK You do it."

Penny phoned and was put through to the DS. She explained what had happened, told her that they were at the manse gates, and was given permission for them to search the manse grounds.

"You look in amongst these trees, Penny," said Frank. "I'll try round the back and the other side of the house.

Frank went off up the incline and was soon lost from Penny's view. He had hardly reached the house when the front door opened. Ruth stood there. Like her mother she was wearing black. She was dressed for going out.

"Hello, are you back to see us? Have you found whatever was used to kill my father? I was going to the shop but I'll stay if you want me."

"Sorry Miss Gentle. I haven't been at the station much today so I don't know about that. A wee boy has gone missing and we were told by his brother that he often came here to bird watch so we're searching the grounds. We should have asked permission first. I apologise."

"Oh dear. That's dreadful. Would you like my brother and me to help you? I was looking out for Kevin my boyfriend when I saw you both coming in the gate."

"Thanks Miss Gentle but the garden isn't that big and you have enough on your plate right now. We'll let you know when we've finished. I can't imagine he'll be here. I mean it's nearly - he looked at his watch -12.30 - he couldn't still be asleep even if he did manage to fall asleep here somewhere."

"Ok." She shut the door and went off down the driveway. He turned round and saw that a young man had just come in the gate. This must be Kevin.

Round the back of the manse the garden was quite overgrown but there were the signs of what had once been a vegetable patch and there was a mildewed rabbit hutch and a ramshackle hut. Frank peered into the hut but the musty cobwebs hanging from the roof were evidence that no one had been in there for some time.

Spiders scurried across the floor, frightened at being disturbed in their previously secure home. Though he would have died rather than admit it, Frank was scared of spiders so he hurried back out.

He went over to the rabbit hutch. A few blades of straw remained in one section and he could imagine the manse children from the past, feeding and playing with their pet. In the centre of the overgrown garden was a pond. It looked murky and full of algae. He moved over to the other side of the house but there was only a narrow path there and the grass was high and had not been trampled. He remembered all this from his first search of the garden a few days ago though then he had been concentrating on footprints in the earth by the manse windows. He could smell the warm, syrupy smell of honeysuckle but could not see where it came from

"Frank! Frank! Come quickly."

It was Penny and she sounded urgent.

He ran back round the house to where Penny was standing at a point in the trees almost in line with the front door.

"Oh Frank, that poor wee boy. I feel sick."

She moved away and was sick, retchingly sick on the driveway.

Frank dived into the shrubbery. It took his eyes a short while to become accustomed to the gloom and by that time Penny had recovered slightly and had come to join him. She parted some bushes and Frank could make out a small shape huddled over on the ground. There were binoculars hanging from the nearest tree and as his eyes became more acclimatised to the dark, Frank saw a blanket on the ground and a cushion. There was something small on the blanket. He got a clean handkerchief out of his pocket and picked the thing up. It was a pencil.

Penny said, "I bent down and saw his head. Look at it."

Frank knelt and peered down. He felt faint and sick but, determined not to show any signs of weakness, he swallowed and stood up.

"Someone's bashed the wee chap's head in."

Penny had been looking round and said, "Yes and with this I think." She pointed with her toe to a large rough stone, discoloured at one end.

"Wish we had a torch but I don't think there's much doubt that that's the murder weapon. Penny one of us will have to stay here while one goes back to the station for reinforcements and someone will have to tell the family. I spoke to Ruth Gentle and she knows we were looking for him but she's gone out to the shop."

"Please Frank. Let me go to the station. I don't want to be left alone here. Call me a coward if you want. I don't think we should tell the family before

The Pulpit is Vacant

we let the DCI know. There's Mrs Paterson to tell too, poor woman."

Frank, not too keen to stay with the body in this foetid, dark hole in the bushes assured his colleague that he would remain here but asked her to be quick. He hoped that Ruth would come back with Kevin. He would tell them and they could break the news to Mrs Gentle if they thought she could take the second shock.

Penny burst into the station startling the PC on charge at the desk. She ran down the corridor, through two lots of swing doors till she came to Davenport's room. She entered as she knocked and discovered him talking to DS Macdonald. They both look startled.

"Penny what is it?" Fiona Macdonald asked.

"Please Sir, Ma'am, we've found a body. I'm sure it's William Paterson's. His Mum gave us a photograph. I didn't see his face but I'm sure it's him. He's in the manse garden, in the bushes beneath the trees. We need a torch and someone will have to go and see Mrs Paterson..."

"Thank you Penny."

In spite of the seriousness of the occasion, Davenport had to hide a smile at this slip of a girl telling him what to do.

"Sit down and get your breath. Why didn't you use your mobile?"

"Oh Sir, we never thought. How stupid of us."

Frances Macarthur

"Fiona, will you stay here and get in touch with Martin Jamieson and the SOC team. If it is indeed William I'll phone you and I'd appreciate it if you would go round and break the news to Mrs Paterson. She'll need a woman with her."

Even in the midst of the horror of the occasion, Penny noted that DS Macdonald did not seem to resent being sent to comfort instead of being part of the team at the sharp end of the investigation. She must, she thought, try not to see sexism lurking round every corner!

Calling out to two PCs to accompany him and taking a large torch from his cupboard, Davenport left the station calling over his shoulder for Penny to come back with them and be the one to inform the manse family about what had happened if Frank had not already done that.

Frank's colour had returned and he was standing in the shelter of the trees but out of sight of the poor little body.

He pushed aside the bushes and Davenport went into the darkness. He shone his torch downwards and they heard the intake of breath as the beam found the beaten head. Flies were already settling on the matted hair.

"Well we'll need someone to identify the boy but it's a bit of a coincidence that two boys should be using the manse gardens as a den which this obviously is, seeing the binoculars up there and the blanket. Frank. Go with Penny and inform the

The Pulpit is Vacant

folk in the manse that a boy's body has been found and that we're treating it as murder."

Looking at Penny's white face he knew that she needed some action.

"When you've done that, both of you search the grounds for any evidence."

"Sir I was waiting for Ruth Gentle to come back. She's only at the local shop with Kevin. I thought this might be too great a shock for Mrs Gentle."

"That's thoughtful Selby. You're right. Wait and catch Ruth when she comes back."

Frank and Penny moved to stand in the driveway, neither being at all keen to see what Davenport had seen in the light of his torch.

"I'm sorry I left you Frank. We should have used our mobiles to get help. I felt such a fool when the DCI asked why we hadn't just 'phoned."

Frank gave a weak laugh.

"Silly us."

They saw Ruth and Kevin coming up the drive and moved to meet them.

Taking a plastic bag from his pocket the DCI put his hand inside then picked up the pencil which Frank had put back down.

What could the boy have been writing and what had he used for light? He scouted about, being careful not to move anything and found a small torch. What had he been writing on? Had he been writing at all?

165

He straightened up and came out of the murder scene.

If he wasn't much mistaken, this murder and the last one were connected.

CHAPTER 23

The police surgeon and the SOC team arrived together. Martin Jamieson came out of the little den looking angry and the SOC team took his place. As always, Martin was immaculately dressed in a pale grey suit with pink shirt and dark grey tie. Davenport had never seen him look untidy except for the lock of hair which kept falling over his left eye. His normally cheerful voice was hard.

"How could anyone do that to a little boy? What did he ever do to deserve that?"

"I think we'll find that it was the same person who killed the minister," replied Davenport. "Maybe the boy saw something the night of his murder or maybe the murderer just thought he had."

"Well he died from a blow to the head, probably from that large stone which has been left there. Again I will have to do tests but I would venture that it was last night sometime."

Frances Macarthur

"Thanks Martin. I'll expect a call from you later."

Davenport turned to the head of the SOC team, a man in his late thirties with slicked- back dark hair.

"Mr Parker. I haven't heard from you yet about my other case and now there's been another murder. When can I expect some information from you?"

Vince Parker stiffened, sensing Davenport's displeasure.

"Sorry Sir. I've been down South attending some interviews. I'll get onto both cases right away."

Frank and Penny joined their boss some minutes after Jamieson and Parker had left. The folk in the manse were shaken by the second murder but in their opinion did not need medical aid this time. None of them knew William Paterson; if indeed it was he who was lying there, although Mrs Gentle remembered his name as her husband had mentioned a visit from one of the schoolteachers asking if a boy called William could use the manse grounds for bird watching.

All they had found in the gardens was a scrap of paper which had been blowing around on the front lawn.

The inspector looked at it.

"Could it be part of a diary? 'Wednesday' spelt incorrectly. Don't suppose it's of any relevance.

The Pulpit is Vacant

It was probably blown there when the bins were emptied. When are the bins emptied round here?

"I think it might be Monday the same as us but I'll find out Sir," said Penny.

The little body was carried out of the shelter among the bushes, covered by the blanket

Frank was dispatched to the station to bring everyone up to date and Penny and DCI Davenport made their way to the Paterson house. Mr Paterson was now at home and was protesting that William was never in and he could not understand what all the fuss was about. The boy would turn up when he was hungry. A burly man with tattoos on both arms, he was refusing to believe DS Macdonald who had come to tell them about the body having been found. Mrs Paterson was sobbing her heart out. With her woman's instinct she knew that it was her son. She looked up when Davenport and Penny came into the room.

"I hope you'll prove me wrong Sir," said Davenport having heard the man's refusal to believe that his son could be dead and he went on to confirm what DS Macdonald had already told them, that a boy's body had been found in the manse gardens. Mrs Paterson let out a wail and Penny went to her and got her to sit down on one of the fireside chairs.

"I'll need you to come with me Sir, to identify the body if it is William."

Mr Paterson, still protesting that it would not be his son, left with Davenport. Minutes later he was standing looking down at the body which was now on a stretcher on the driveway. One of the SOC team pulled down the cover and Davenport saw the man stiffen.

"Sir?"

"Yes it's William. What bastard did that to him? I swear if I find the man I'll kill him with my bare hands."

"Come on Sir. You need to get to your wife. She'll need comforting and there are your other children to think of now."

Still muttering and now with tears in his eyes, Mr Paterson let himself be led back down the driveway.

DS Macdonald and Penny were with Mrs Paterson and some of her children in the kitchen but they let Mr Paterson lead her through to the lounge. Davenport joined his officers. They were left with George and the girl they presumed was Arlene who was holding the baby in her arms. Some noise from an adjacent room informed them that the other Paterson children were probably playing there oblivious to the tragedy which had fallen on their family.

"Please Sir," said George to Davenport, "Is William dead?"

"I'm afraid so son."

"Would he have been OK if I'd told Mum he'd gone out last night?"

The Pulpit is Vacant

"No son. Someone wanted him dead. They'd have got to him some other time. It's not your fault."

Arlene burst into sobs.

"I never had much time for him. He was so quiet you hardly knew he was there. He was a good boy. Never did anybody any harm. It's not fair."

Still crying, she went out of the room.

Davenport waited until Mr and Mrs Paterson came back into the kitchen and told them that he thought that William's murder might be linked to the recent murder of the local minister. DS Macdonald put her arm round Mrs Paterson who was weeping brokenly.

"I'm very sorry Mrs Paterson," said Davenport, "but if it's any comfort, William wouldn't have known anything. Death must have been instantaneous. Penny here will get you a cup of tea. We'll leave you now but someone will come back tomorrow to ask you some questions."

Mr Paterson showed them out. Penny made for the kitchen. She was getting used to tea-making.

Back at the station a meeting was called and the rest of the staff brought up to date. Penny joined them shortly. She looked as if she too had been crying. Even the blasé Frank looked upset.

"Right team, I'll sum up. Robert Gentle was stabbed to death with a sharp knife sometime between nine o'clock on Tuesday evening and 2am in the morning. He was facing his murderer so it must have been someone known to him, someone he had let in perhaps though no one else heard the bell later at night. William Paterson was beaten to death probably with a large stone sometime last night - the definite time still to be determined by the police surgeon. It would appear to me that the two deaths are connected."

There was a murmur at this.

"The boy is now known to have been in his den some nights unknown to his parents. He paid his older brother George to keep quiet about this. It seems likely that he either saw someone or something on the night of the minister's murder or that the murderer found out that William had been there and was afraid that he had seen something incriminating.

I want William's friends spoken to and I want to know where the manse residents were last night, oh and Colin Tait can be questioned too. I'm going home now and I suggest you do too. All leave is cancelled until these murders are solved."

CHAPTER 24

Sunday, like Saturday, was a lovely day, the sky azure blue and cloudless. Davenport had had to bring Pippa with him as his sister had made plans for Sunday and he would not let her spoil them. Pippa had brought her current book with her and was happily ensconced in DS Macdonald's room reading her twenty-second Chalet School book where a tomboy turns up at the school and finds it very hard to fit into an almost completely female environment. Her hobby notebook sat on the desk beside her as she was going to update it with this latest book, the Chalet School being her reason for living at the moment. She was always asking her dad if she could go to boarding school but he knew that this was just a phase.

Meanwhile Davenport's little team were in the incident room.

Martin Jamieson had rung in with the time of death for William - between 8pm and 12 pm on Friday evening. Now all the folk with any reason for killing Robert Gentle would have to be questioned about their whereabouts on Friday evening too. There were fingerprints on the stone but too smudged to be of any use.

"Sir," said Frank. "I went to the Paterson's house yesterday. William was in the Anchor Boys briefly but he didn't enjoy it and left. Andrew Bell only started helping about six months ago so he wouldn't know William and vice versa. Tricia is in the Brownies but in a church nearer her home. Mrs Paterson is fairly sure that William would have known neither of them. I asked for names of William's friends but seemingly apart from some girl in his class, he was a loner.

"Thanks Frank. Put that in your report please."

"Sir, I checked with the council offices and the manse bins *were* emptied on Mondays," said Penny.

"Right so the scrap of paper is unlikely to have come from the manse. Thanks Penny.

Now, Fiona, you and I will go to the manse and talk to the three folk there."

He popped his head round the door of DS Macdonald's room to say to Pippa, "Will you be Ok pet? You've got your book and I'll leave you some money for the coke machine. We won't be too long. If you want me, ring me on my mobile."

Engrossed in her book Pippa did not even look up. "Sure, Dad. I'll be fine. I *am* ten you know."

"What's she reading Charles?" asked Fiona as they set out for the manse.

The Pulpit is Vacant

"Oh one of her favourite chalet school books. She's onto number twenty something I think. Wonder how many there are."

"Oh I can tell you that," she replied, going a bit red in the face. "There are sixty-two. I have the whole set except for one. I'm also a member of the Chalet School fan club. Sad really isn't it, a grown woman still interested in a child's book."

She hoped he would not ridicule her for her childish hobby. She liked this man already and wanted his respect. He did not disappoint her.

"It's a bit like me still playing with my model trains when I get the chance," he laughed. "One day you must come round and see my layout."

"Makes a change from 'Come up and see my etchings'," she laughed too, then straightened her face as they reached the gates of the manse.

Philip answered the door and ushered them into the study, putting on the electric fire as the room was on the dark side of the house so a bit chilly in spite of the lovely day.

"Do you want to see me first or will I get my Mum and my sister?"

"We'll speak to you first Sir. Do you have witnesses as to where you were the night of your father's murder? Your mother said you hadn't arrived by then but you had, hadn't you?"

"Yes. She told me that she'd lied and I told her you'd find out easily enough. Don't be too hard on her please. She's tried to protect me all my life."

"I'll speak to her later, Sir and now, tell me again where you were please."

"Well I was with friends in the West End but they left and Eric and I went to bed at around 11. I was tired after my long flights and they had work to go to in the morning and we had drunk rather a lot as well. I slept on my own I'm afraid so have no proof that I stayed in bed. However, I did not murder my father. We didn't get on but I didn't hate him enough to kill him."

"Where were you on Friday night between 8 and 12 pm?"

"I was here. With my mother, sister and Kevin. Kevin stayed overnight."

"Thank you. Will you bring your mother in here now please?"

Philip left the room returning shortly with Mrs Gentle then returning presumably to where his sister was waiting.

Mrs Gentle looked embarrassed.

"I'm sorry about lying about when Philip arrived, Inspector. I stupidly thought it would prevent you suspecting him. I did it on the spur of the moment. Ruth told me it was stupid but she backed me up. She always protects me."

"OK Mrs Gentle but be honest with me from now on please."

"I will be."

"A factual question first. Tell me where you've stayed over the years please."

The Pulpit is Vacant

"We started married life in Edinburgh, there for two years then Robert went into the army and we moved to Aldershot for...six years. After that we went to Catterick, in North Yorkshire for another six years then Robert came out of the army. We moved to Montrose for the next four years, then Stirling for a bit less, three years I think, then to Killearn for another four years and finally here."

"Can you think of anyone in your past life who might have wanted your husband dead badly enough to kill him?"

"Not many people liked him. Inspector but I don't think he had any real enemies."

"Right, I'm sorry to have to ask this Mrs Gentle but what were your feelings for your husband?" asked Davenport.

Mary Gentle's face reddened.

"He wasn't an easy man to live with chief inspector. He always had to have his own way but I had got used to that. He did, I admit, make things difficult with his inability to accept other peoples' opinions. That's why we moved so often. Robert rubbed people up the wrong way and always wanted his own way which didn't go down well with kirk sessions. Also I must admit I came close to hating him when he told me not to contact Philip. I did though, contact Philip I mean, not hate Robert. That's what I always did - I agreed then did what I wanted without letting him know."

"So you kept in contact with your son?"

"I wrote to Philip and he wrote back care of Ruth's boyfriend Kevin. It was the same with Kevin. Robert forbade Ruth to have him in the house but my husband was often out at church meetings or visiting organisations so we merely had Kevin in then. Ruth could have left and married Kevin. Oh I know Robert hinted that he would make life unpleasant for me if she left but he was never physically bullying only verbally and I've lived with that for so long that I knew how to diffuse his anger most times. I certainly did not kill my husband chief inspector. This worm did not turn."

It was along speech and Davenport wondered if it had been mentally rehearsed. She seemed keen to stress that he had never been physically abusive.

He smiled.

"Thank you for being so frank with us Mrs Gentle. Now would you confirm where you were on Friday evening, please."

"Certainly. I was here all evening with my son and daughter and my daughter's boyfriend Kevin."

"Thanks, now if you would ask Ruth to come in here please, then we'll leave you in peace."

They had no time to discuss anything before Ruth came into the study.

"Miss Gentle. Honesty from now on please."

"I'm sorry about that. I don't know what made Mum lie. I suppose the mother hen instinct."

The Pulpit is Vacant

"We've been told that you had on occasion arguments with your father. Is this true?"

"It certainly is true. He was a bully. He bullied my Mum and he tried to bully me. I don't think he ever hit Mum but only the other night he slapped my face in front of one of the youth workers. I hated him, I admit it. But I didn't kill him. I must admit that I'm not sorry he's dead but it wasn't me who killed him though I can't prove it as I was in bed alone that night. She gave a rueful smile, "Not much chance of my sharing a bed in my father's house!"

"Did Kevin stay over on Friday night?"

"Yes he did. Mum likes him and with dad gone...."

She stopped.

"Thanks Miss Gentle for your honesty. Can you tell me where I could find Kevin?"

"Right here, Inspector. He's been staying with us since the murder. There are plenty of rooms as you can no doubt see."

"Ask him to come along then please."

Kevin came in minutes later and confirmed that he had been with the family on Friday night. He also denied having murdered Robert Gentle, saying that he and Ruth were in no hurry to marry so it had not been necessary to get rid of the man even though he could not in all honesty say he liked him. He seemed to belie the theory that red haired people have short tempers as he seemed placid.

Going down the driveway Charles and Fiona discussed the interviews which had just taken place.

None of the four interviewed had alibis for the night of the minister's death and all had motives, in spite of Mrs Gentle saying that she had come to accept her husband's domineering ways. They could all give each other alibis for the night of the second murder but three of them had lied before and could be lying again though Davenport did not think so and Fiona agreed with him.

"Do you think that he was physically abusive to his wife, Fiona?"

"Well she seemed determined to tell us that he wasn't which was odd as we had never asked about that."

"That's exactly what *I* thought."

Charles started up the engine but before he could put the car into gear, Fiona Macdonald voiced her idea of visiting Elizabeth French.

"Charles. You know that Pippa has her hobby jotter for school? I wonder if perhaps William Paterson had one too. They're not in the same class obviously but it might be a school thing, hobbies."

"Good idea, Fiona. Would you manage by yourself this time? I'd like to get back. Even though I know she'll be fine, I don't want to leave Pippa too long and I want to find out how Frank and Penny got on with Colin Tait if they're back."

The Pulpit is Vacant

"No problem. I'll be back shortly."

She jumped out of his car and made her way across the road and down the next avenue to where the French's white painted detached house was to be found.

It was Jill who answered the door. Fiona, telling her who she was, asked for her mother.

"Mum it's the police for you. Come in please. She'll not be a minute. She's doing the ironing upstairs."

At this, footsteps could be heard coming downstairs and Elizabeth appeared.

"Hello. Is there any news about the minister?

"Mrs French, is there somewhere private we can go? I've got some really bad news for you."

Elizabeth French led her into a pleasant book lined room. There was a TV in one corner and a stereo sound system in the other. It was obviously a family room as there was evidence of various peoples' hobbies lying around - a guitar no doubt the daughter's, a video of Tiger Woods, presumably the husband's and an open novel belonging to someone.

Elizabeth sat down in one of the armchairs: Fiona Macdonald took the other.

"We tried to contact you yesterday."

"We were away for the day to Loch Fyne with Jill and her friend Helen. What's happened?"

"One of the boys in your class I think, William Paterson......"

"Yes he's in my class. What about him? Has he had an accident?"

"He's been murdered Mrs French."

"Murdered! William? What for? Why on earth would anyone want to kill a wee boy?"

"We don't know but we wonder if he saw something on the night of the minister's murder. Can you tell me if by any chance he had a hobby notebook?"

"Yes our head teacher has rather a thing about hobbies so we are all encouraged to get our classes involved in writing and talking about their hobbies. William had a hobby jotter. I was marking it just the other night. He loves..."

She swallowed.

"He loved birds."

"We think he might have been in his den in the manse garden the night of the first murder and either saw something or was thought to have seen something."

"Where was his body found?"

"In the den."

"Oh poor Mrs Paterson. She'll be distraught. She's a lovely woman but with so many kids she obviously couldn't spare each one a lot of time. William often came here. He liked Jill my daughter. She'll be so upset."

"I wonder if I could see William's jotter if it's still here."

"Of course."

The Pulpit is Vacant

Mrs French went out and came back with a well-cared for jotter and handed it over to DS Macdonald.

"Thanks for your help Mrs French. I'll return it to you. I'm sorry to have to ask this but where were you on Friday night?"

"I was here with Jim my husband. We both spent the evening marking things for school so that we could have Saturday free for our outing."

"You understand that we have to ask anyone who could be involved in the first murder."

"Yes I understand."

"Thank you for the jotter, Mrs French."

"I hope it helps you to find out the monster that did this thing."

DS Macdonald thanked her again and left the house. She had a long walk back to the station but it would clear her head to have the walk.

A monster? Maybe. A scared murderer, certainly. She hoped that there would be no more deaths.

CHAPTER 25

I shut the door on the police sergeant and wondered how on earth I was going to tell Jill about William. I knew that I could not protect her from all of life's bad things but this was going to be really hard.

Deciding to put off the moment, I went to my bedroom. It was hard to believe that William was dead. He had been quite a big part of my life in school and out of school and I would miss him.

Who else would miss him? He had not been close to any of his siblings and I knew that he and his dad had not seen eye to eye, his father seeing him as a bit of a sissy and feeling disappointed when William did not want to come with him and George to watch Rangers play.

His Mum would feel awful as she had been too busy to spend time with him. Poor William was going to make more of an impact dead than alive. There were so many people who were going to feel guilty now.

I felt tears pricking at the back of my eyes and put my head down on the pillow which was soon wet with my tears. I should really go to the Paterson's' but felt reluctant to go right now. I had just consoled Mrs Gentle and did not want to go through it all again. That was selfish, I knew, then realised that before doing anything. I had to tell Jim and Jill.

Going downstairs I heard the back door shutting.

"Jill!" I called out.

"She's just left love," came Jim's voice from the kitchen. I went in to find him making a sandwich. "She's away to Helen's. What did you want her for?"

It was wrong to feel relieved but I was.

"Jim. You know that wee boy William who comes here quite often?"

"The one you asked the minister to let play in the manse garden?"

"Yes him,"

"What about him?"

"He's been murdered." Even saying the words sounded wrong. I had seen him only the other day. How could he now be dead?

"Who would want to murder a wee boy?"

"The police think he might have seen something or someone on the night of the minister's murder. They've taken away his hobby notebook, to see if he has written anything in there I expect."

The Pulpit is Vacant

"But you were reading it only the other night. Did you see anything unusual in it?"

"No."

"His poor parents. Imagine how they must be feeling. Think how we would feel if it was Jill."

I felt guilty then and decided that I would have to go even though I felt so much more upset this time. Somehow the minister's death had made things better for a number of people so could be half justified but William's death was going to hurt everyone, his family especially.

Standing outside the Patersons' door, at the bottom of an old tenement building a few streets away from my own house, I felt shivery. The evening was warm, a lovely May evening but I felt cold.

The door was opened by Arlene. I had taught her some years ago and had found her a grown up little thing at ten. She must now be in her teens. She asked me to come in and took me into the living room which was empty.

"I'll fetch Mum and Dad," she said.

I looked round the room noticing the bareness of the carpet and the lack of any ornamentation. This family had not had things easy and now this! The door opened but it was only Mr Paterson who came into the room.

"Hello Mrs French. Sorry my wife can't speak to you right now. She's too upset. It's really good of you to come. I know William was very fond of you and you were very kind to him."

Again I felt tears pricking my eyes.

"I just had to come and say how sorry I was Mr Paterson. I don't need to see your wife. Just tell her I came and if there's anything I can do just to ask."

I heard myself uttering the usual platitudes. What could I do? I knew that no one could undo the terrible crime that had been committed and all that would help them was time.

"The only thing which would help us right now is finding out the person who killed our son and seeing him put away for the rest of his life," said Mr Paterson, bitterly.

On this note I left.

When I got back Jill was still out and again I felt glad. Jim must have realised this as he offered to tell Jill for me and I gratefully accepted his offer. We went into our living room and started on the Sunday papers but I don't think I took in anything I was reading. A couple of hours later Jill came in and Jim took her into the kitchen. I heard her say, "Oh no!" then crying sounds. I heard her footsteps on the stairs.

"She knows now love." Jim came back in and picked up his paper.

"Thanks."

Two murders. I wondered if there had to be any more before this was all finished.

CHAPTER 26

Later on Sunday afternoon, Claire Davidson came into the station and asked the policeman at the desk if she could speak to the person in charge of the Gentle murder.

"My name is Claire Davidson and I was told to come to the station, "she explained.

Davenport was informed and came down the corridor to take her along to his room. He thought she looked very slim and boyish for a mother of four.

"Sorry to have to bring you down here Mrs Davidson but we missed you yesterday when we called at your house."

"I was meeting some friends. My husband's on the oil rigs so I don't get much time on my own but Mum has come to stay for a while so I took the chance to get out. Is this about the death of the minister? I read about it in the paper."

"Yes. Mr Gentle the new minister was found dead in his lounge on Wednesday morning. You were one of the last people to have seen him alive and I wondered if you could shed any light on who might have done this."

"I'm sorry Mr…"

"Davenport. Detective Chief Inspector Davenport. I'm in charge of this investigation."

"I'm sorry. I only met the man that night and although I had an argument with him, I certainly didn't want him dead."

"What was the argument about?"

"He wanted us to present him with our programme for the following session and I don't have time for that sort of thing. I have four children to look after and a part-time job at the doctor's where I am one of the receptionists and I've always managed without forward planning."

"Did he accept that?"

"No he did not. He told me that the Guides used the church premises and he was responsible for all activities taking place there. As if we didn't have enough bother with Child Protection red tape!"

"Did you part on friendly terms?"

"Well not exactly friendly. I agreed to do what he wanted but not with very good grace I have to admit. He went on to talk to Mary Bell about the Brownies and she was happy to do what he asked as was her brother Andrew but then I imagine that Bill McFarlane will do his programme plan for him as he's in charge of the BB."

The Pulpit is Vacant

"Would you not have to do it for the Brownies Mrs Davidson?"

"I suppose I should but Mary is a competent girl and the Brownie syllabus is very flexible so she knows I would leave it to her."

"Did Mr Gentle accept this?"

"He did. He would see that Mary was a girl easy to please so he could influence her work more so than he could mine."

"So you thought he would be a manipulator then, someone who likes to be in charge?"

"I certainly did."

Robert Gentle was not coming across to Davenport as an endearing person.

"Did the three of you leave together?"

"Yes we did. I live quite near the Bells so we walked back together."

Davenport asked her for Mary Bell's address and she gave it to him.

"Was there anyone else there when you left?"

"Yes a guy called Colin Tait. I met him a couple of times at the church halls. It seems that the minister had asked him to come up to the manse, to discuss his youth club I think."

"You didn't hear their conversation?"

"No. Mr Gentle showed us out before they started talking."

"Just one more question Mrs Davidson. Where were you on Friday evening?"

191

"Friday evening? I thought you said the minister was murdered the night of the meeting."

"Yes he was but there's been another death and we think they're connected."

I was at home with my mother and three of the kids. My eldest son was at the BB. Who was killed this time?"

"A wee boy who might have seen the murderer."

"That's terrible. His poor parents must be in a terrible state."

"Well thanks for coming Mrs Davidson."

Davenport conducted her back along the corridor and left her at the main door, going back to his room.

The stories of the youth workers all seemed to tally and the only discordant note was the nervousness of Colin Tait although Claire had not mentioned it. Why not? Had she been too annoyed about the meeting to notice other peoples' behaviour or just not a perceptive person? Who had mentioned Colin's nervous demeanour? He would need to read through all the notes again to find out.

Back in his room, he picked up the reports. He read that Mrs French had reported Colin as being a bit 'unforthcoming' when she asked him about his meeting with the minister. DS Macdonald had described him as 'nervous' but had thought that normal under the circumstances.

Colin had explained his reluctance to meet with the minister as being unwilling to go along with the minister's religious slant on youth work and his reluctance to try to get his wee ones to go to Sunday school and no one could blame him for being unforthcoming about the meeting they had had. Davenport imagined that once again the minister would have brooked no arguments and would simply have stated his intention of talking to the two different age groups as long as the head teachers of both primary and secondary schools agreed.

Was he reading too much into Colin's manner or was Colin indeed hiding something?

The only people left to interview were the Bell twins though Davenport was sure that they would have nothing more to add. He decided to tie up this last loose end himself. It was only a short car ride away and once again he was lucky as both Mary and Andrew were at home though Andrew when he came to the door looked dressed for going out. His denim trousers looked new and his shirt freshly ironed.

Davenport introduced himself.

"Oh hi! We were expecting someone to call round but not a bigwig!" laughed Andrew. "Do you want me to get Mary or do you want to speak to us separately?"

"You're obviously on your way out Andrew so I'll speak to you first then you can get Mary for me please."

As he suspected, he learned nothing new from Andrew who had just been wanting the meeting to end quickly so that he could meet his friends for a couple of beers. He had noticed no atmosphere except when Claire had been reluctant to write up a syllabus.

"I don't think the minister was used to being argued with; he looked quite startled when Claire tried to stick to her guns."

Andrew left the room, returning with Mary. Both had short fair hair and as far as possible with different sex twins they looked identical even down to the dimple which each had on the left cheek.

"Bye Inspector." Andrew left the room.

"Miss Bell…"

"Please call me Mary. I get nervous when someone calls me Miss. Makes me feel like I'm back at school somehow."

"Right, Mary. I hope this isn't a bad time to come and see you."

"No it's fine. I'm studying for my exams next week. Andrew has them too but he doesn't need to study. He's brilliant, lucky thing. Guess he got my share of brains along with his own." She laughed.

Davenport liked her. He hoped that Pippa would turn out to be as delightful as this young girl.

"As you may know I'm interviewing everybody who was at the manse on the night of the minister's murder. Can you tell me if you noticed anything at all, any atmosphere?"

The Pulpit is Vacant

"Well, the schoolteacher was edgy. She was keen to get away. So was Bill McFarlane but then his wife's just had a baby. He probably wanted to get back to help her. The man who arrived late looked as if he didn't want to be there at all. He looked rather upset when we got up to go."

Mary was obviously more tuned in to peoples' moods than her brother.

"Did you meet any of the family?"

"Mrs Gentle and her daughter came in with supper. Mrs Gentle seemed timid and the daughter was quite red faced as if she'd been arguing or excited about something."

"Thank you Mary. We should get you into the police force with your good eye for things,"

She laughed.

On the way back to the station, Davenport thought again about Colin Tait. Another witness had noticed his discomfort at being in the manse. Was there more to this than just reluctance to discuss his infant class and his youth club?

CHAPTER 27

Monday morning at the station was hectic, so much so that Salma Din's arrival did not create the stir it might otherwise have done.

At about ten o'clock, Penny was told that DCI Davenport wanted to see her in his room and she knocked and went in to find a beautiful young Asian woman sitting there looking very smart in her police uniform.

"Penny, this is Sergeant Salma Din. Salma this is Constable Penny Price. Penny's been here for a few years as has her colleague Frank Selby who is out at the moment with DS MacDonald. Penny will introduce you to the others in her section, won't you Penny?"

"Of course, Sir." Penny smiled and Salma Din smiled back, relieved at meeting such an obviously friendly constable.

It had taken her a long while to be accepted in her last station and she had been a bit reluctant about applying for promotion elsewhere but maybe here things would be different.

She and Penny left the DCI's room, Penny chattering as they went.

"Where were you before you came here?"

"Over in the West End, Dunbarton Road station," replied Salma.

"Did the DCI tell you about our two murders?"

"A little, to explain where the DS was as she had hoped to be here to welcome me."

"She's quite new too and so is the DCI. He only came last week. There are lots of new brooms around here."

"You'll be kept very clean then," said Salma and they both laughed.

Penny went on to warn her about possible racist comments from Frank Selby.

"If it's any consolation he's also sexist. Otherwise he's a good colleague."

"I've learned to handle folk like him over the years, Penny," said Salma, "at school and at work. Who knows, maybe between us we can convert him from being the racist MCP of the station."

Penny went on to bring Salma up to date about the two murders and added, "I'm to go later to question a man called Colin Tait. He teaches at the local primary school here and takes a youth club at the church one night a week and he was at the manse on the night of the first murder. As the DCI is sure that the two murders are connected and

The Pulpit is Vacant

Colin is one of the possible suspects, then he will have to give us details of where he was on Friday too."

"I wonder if I'll be getting involved too or if I'll be left covering other things," Salma mused out loud.

She was not to be left in doubt for very long. The DCI called her back into his room shortly afterwards.

"Salma, I'm going with Penny to interview Colin Tait shortly. Perhaps you would get to work with some of the other PCs to do a door-to-door enquiry round the manse area when they come back from another search of the manse grounds. They'll show you where to go. Perhaps you might also have a word with the owner of the convenience store near the manse. Her name is Nan Brodie and she keeps her eyes and ears open, by all accounts."

"Yes Sir."

"We want to know if anyone was seen going into the manse grounds on Friday night. There are two entrances to the gardens. Also find out if anyone saw the boy, William Paterson going in. The main entrance is at the bottom of the driveway and the other, smaller gate is at the side. Both are overlooked by some houses and there's faint chance that someone might have seen something."

Salma went back to Penny delighted to be involved.

"What about the PCs I'll be working with?" she asked.

Penny knew what she was asking without being told.

"Oh they're fine. They're both family men with no promotion ambitions. They'll probably be fatherly rather than racist. I should have said that another problem with Frank is that he applied for your job."

"Oh great!" said Salma. "Racist, sexist and passed over. What a combination! Still, to be forewarned is to be forearmed."

At that point the DCI came into the room and then he and Penny left for Southview Primary School

Once they had spoken to Colin Tait, nearly everyone except a few PCs on the case would have seen him and they could compare notes.

It was lunchtime at the school. Charles stopped to speak to his daughter in the playground. She was with a dark-haired girl and a slightly older boy and seemed to have settled down and made new friends already. His move would have affected her worse if she had been older he thought. She had had quite a bit of upheaval with the divorce, her mother going to stay in England and now a new school but she was sensible for her years.

They stopped at the head teacher's room first and they talked a little about the murder. Mrs Hobson had told the children at Assembly

The Pulpit is Vacant

and they had been on the whole excited rather than upset. William's brothers and sisters had not been present and William had not had any friends except Jacqueline Beaton. She had been very upset and had been taken home by the school auxiliary once Mrs Hobson had ascertained that her mother was at home.

Mrs Hobson went off to get Colin Tait from the staffroom and returned with him. She opened the door of a little room beside her own and told them they could use it to interview Colin in.

This time instead of being nervous, Colin was annoyed.

"Look, what is this? I can understand that I might be in the frame for the minister's murder but surely not for William Paterson's!"

"Well Mr Tait, we suspect that the two murders might be connected as the boy was found in the manse gardens and it stretches credulity that there are two homicidal maniacs roaming the South Side."

The DCIs tone was brisk, bordering on cool and Penny wondered if he did indeed suspect this nice-looking young man.

Colin was immediately contrite.

"I'm sorry. I guess you have to question us all again in that case."

"Where were you on Friday evening Sir?"

"I was out at the cinema just off Byres Road."

"Alone?"

"I'm afraid so."

Was it Penny's imagination or did Colin look a bit furtive when he said that?

"There's no one to give you an alibi then?"

"Sorry. No."

At this point the school bell, signalling the start of afternoon school, rang.

"Would it be suitable if we came to your house this evening, Mr Tait? I don't want to disrupt your school day."

"I'll be in," was the almost curt reply.

Penny wondered what more the DCI wanted to ask him and was delighted when he took her into his confidence on the way back to the station.

"I agree with DS Macdonald, Penny. There's something not quite right with Colin Tait."

"He certainly looked a bit uneasy when you asked if he had anyone who could confirm that he was at the pictures, Sir."

"I'd like you to come with me this evening Penny. Are you free?"

Penny said yes. She was delighted again. She was sure she would learn a lot being with this man.

CHAPTER 28

Back at the station it was very quiet. The police constable at the desk informed Davenport that none of his team was back yet.

"When they do get back Penny, we'll meet in the incident room and compare notes."

So saying, he strode off to his own room and Penny was left. She went down to the canteen for a coffee and some lunch and was soon engaged in banter with PCs from other departments. They asked her about 'her' murder and she felt quite important being able to tell them what had happened so far.

It was about twenty minutes before she was back in her own part of the station and Salma Din was back.

One of the PCs had found someone who had seen William Paterson or at least a small boy answering his description, walking up the hill at the side of the manse that evening but could not tell them at what time. Apart from that the only piece of information had come from Nan Brodie who said that she had seen Ruth Gentle and a young man. They had come into her shop at about 7 o'clock.

"They were laughing and happy," reported Salma to Penny, "but she didn't know where they were going. They could have been going home or going out. She was quite put out that they wouldn't tell her where they were going. She loves to gather information I think. She certainly asked me a lot of questions about myself and I found myself telling her everything."

"What did they buy?" asked Penny.

"That wasn't any help. Ruth bought stamps and the young man bought an Evening Times."

"I just thought if it was chocolates they might have been going out but if it was bread and milk they would have been going back to the manse," Penny explained.

"Yes that's why I asked. Stamps and a paper isn't much of a clue, "replied Salma and they smiled at each other.

Penny had just started to tell Salma about her visit to Colin Tait at the school when voices announced the arrival of DS Macdonald and Frank Selby. Penny told them about the meeting in the incident room and she introduced Salma to them both. DS Macdonald apologised for being out when Salma arrived and shook her hand. Frank gave a muttered, "Hello" and went off down the corridor.

Soon they were seated in front of DCI Davenport who had a flip chart on which were written the names of the Gentle family, Colin Tait and Kevin. Frank supplied Kevin's name which was Grant. Davenport added the names, Elizabeth French, Bill McFarlane, Claire Davidson and Mary and Andrew Bell.

"I asked Miss Gentle Kevin's name when we were there this morning Sir," Frank said as he was writing.

"Right, Fiona, take us through the whereabouts of the family on Friday night."

According to each one, questioned separately, they were all together in the manse all evening. Mr Grant stayed overnight

"In other words, none of them has an alibi as they could all be shielding one of them," said Davenport. "Penny and I talked briefly with Colin Tait and he too had no alibi, having been at the cinema alone. Salma, any luck with the house-to-house and the woman at the shop?"

"One woman saw a boy the victim's age walking up the hill which leads to the side gate of the manse but she can't remember the time. Mrs Brodie at the store saw Miss Gentle and the man she presumed was her boyfriend when they came in for a paper and some stamps."

"So they did go out."

"That's not very suspicious Sir. Going out briefly to the local shop could slip anyone's mind," said Fiona Macdonald.

"Nothing else?"

"No Sir."

Davenport tugged at his left ear lobe. His team were beginning to recognise this as a habit of his.

"Well it seems as if we're no further forward though maybe if we visit the homes near the manse in the evening, someone who is at work now might have something to tell us."

He turned to his DS.

"Fiona. Get that arranged will you. I'm going over to Colin Tait's flat with Penny shortly. There's something that young man is hiding, I'm sure of it. Whether it's got anything to do with this case or not I'm not sure but I mean to find out."

He gave a grimace.

"Not getting very far are we? Let's hope that the murderer doesn't give us another victim in the effort to keep safe."

In a house in the city, the murderer was about to have another sleepless night wondering exactly the same thing - to keep safe would there have to be another murder?

CHAPTER 29

D S Macdonald went into her room and started reading William's hobby jotter again. Something was troubling her but she could not put her finger on it. She decided to sleep on it. There was no rush to give it back to Mrs French.

Davenport popped his head round her door.

"Right Fiona, that's Penny and I away to see Colin Tait. Get off home yourself after you give instructions about this evening's house to house. Anyone not involved can go home too. I want everyone back here bright and early in the morning."

"Will do. Hope you have some luck," she replied.

It took Davenport and Penny about an hour to get across the city as it was the rush hour. The Kingston Bridge was hectic as usual and Davenport was quiet as he manoeuvred the car into the lane for Charing Cross. Penny, who was much more used to the city traffic than her boss, realised that

Frances Macarthur

the bridge was hard work on someone used to quieter streets. He had come from somewhere in Ayrshire she thought. She kept quiet for once.

As they went up Gibson Street he asked her for directions and she directed him up past the university and down to Byres Road. She remembered a parking area up to the right quite near the entrance to the subway and directed him there. They were lucky to get a space and were soon walking down then across Byres Road to the street where Colin Tait lived.

Penny rang the bell at the close mouth and they were invited to come up. Colin was waiting on the landing for them. He looked much more relaxed than he had done at school. Penny had taken a liking to this young man when she had seen him briefly at the school with Davenport but had not had much time to really look at him then as they had only had a quick word. He was gentle looking and very neatly dressed in black trousers with a pale blue open-necked shirt. Had he worn a tie when she saw him at school? Probably, as he struck her as a rather old fashioned, correct sort of person.

He led them into the living room. It was furnished in a minimalist style, wooden floors and large cream settee and big comfortable - looking chairs with a few big cushion seats in shades of blue and black. There was a bookcase under the window and a TV in the corner. Nothing else. It was light and airy.

The Pulpit is Vacant

"Do you live here by yourself, Mr Tait?" asked Davenport.

"Most of the time but sometimes my cousin comes to stay and sometimes friends stay over. I became popular with folk when I moved into this flat so near to the university and the trendy eating places." He laughed.

"Well Mr Tait. I need to know more about where you were on Friday night. You said you were at the cinema. Would you tell me what you saw please?"

Penny wandered over to the bookcase. Being an avid reader herself she was always interested in other peoples' books. Colin obviously liked science fiction which didn't interest her at all. Books by Ray Bradbury dominated the shelves. She glanced down at the bottom shelf and picked out a copy of Palgrave's Golden Treasury remembering it from her school days. Opening it she read on the inside cover; "From Colin to Hilary with love". Maybe this was the cousin and she had obviously lent it back to Colin to read.

Davenport was now asking Colin if he had met anyone while he was out that night. The answer was in the negative but Colin did not seem disturbed by his lack of alibi.

"Did you know William Paterson Sir?"

"Yes Chief Inspector. I studied Biology and Botany at university and was also interested in birds and animals so he often came to ask me if he could have a look at my bird book. I keep it at school with other reference books so he would sometimes come into my room at the interval or lunchtime."

"How did he strike you, Mr Tait?"

"He was a timid kind of boy but got quite animated when he got onto the topic of birds. He wanted to show me his hide in the manse garden but with living out the West End it never happened though I believe that Beth French went once to see it."

"Do you know if he ever took any of his school mates?"

"He only had one friend I believe, a girl I saw him with occasionally. I don't know her name but Elizabeth would know it I expect."

"Well Mr Tait, thanks for your time. I'm afraid we have to keep you on our list of possible suspects so if you can think of anyone who might vouch for you on Friday night please let us know. Also it would help to know if anyone saw you leave the manse grounds the night of the first murder or if anyone saw you come home and could verify the time you got here."

At this point Penny thought she caught a look of...what? Hopelessness? Despair? But it was gone almost as soon as it came.

Colin Tait came with them to the door.

"I hope you find out who did these murders, Chief Inspector. It wasn't me but only I know that."

The Pulpit is Vacant

Penny had found Colin Tait likeable this second time but then she liked Ruth Gentle and Mrs Gentle too. She almost hoped that it would turn out to be Philip Gentle but what if she liked him too when she met him?

"Sir, do you really think it could be him?"

"I don't know Penny. For a nice young man he seems to lead a very solitary life. He never has anyone to vouch for him."

"He did mention friends staying over and the book I was looking at was for a Hilary from him. Maybe she was his girlfriend and they've split up."

Once again Davenport had to concentrate on his driving, leaving Penny to her thoughts. In this way they reached the South Side and Davenport asked for directions to Penny's flat.

"Quite near the scene of the crime, young Penny. What were you doing on Friday night?"

They laughed.

CHAPTER 30

"Terrible din in here."

Frank's words as he came into the canteen on Tuesday lunchtime caused a stir of bafflement as only Salma and Penny had been talking. It dawned on Salma first but Penny wasn't far behind.

"Very funny Frank," she said sarcastically, looking sideways at Salma and hoping that she wouldn't be hurt by this pun on her name. Salma smiled back and shook her head as if to say that she was unconcerned.

"What is?" enquired Frank with an air of innocence.

"Leave it Penny. I'm used to things like that. I don't let it bother me anymore," said Salma, smiling at the girl who had risen to her defence. "I've heard that pun many times."

It was lunchtime on Tuesday. Three days had passed since William's murder and they were no further forward. Still only five names seemed to be in the frame, the Gentle family, Kevin Grant and because of his nervousness, Colin Tait. It was hard to see the timid Mary Gentle in the role of double murderess, thought Penny and knew that the others shared this opinion and surely Ruth and Kevin could have married without having to kill Ruth's father. Colin Tait was a gentle creature. In Penny's eyes that left Philip Gentle and because she hadn't spoken to him it was easy to cast him as the murderer. Maybe he had come home to tell his father that he was going to do something he would have disapproved of - go into business instead of to university, marry someone unsuitable. Who? Another man perhaps. That would have caused a rumpus but why come home in that case? Why not just stay in Australia? Penny found herself posing this question to Salma.

"Salma, why might Philip Gentle have had an argument with his father on the day he came home?"

"Planning to marry an Aborigine," Salma volunteered mischievously.

Penny laughed.

Frank, sitting on the other side of the canteen glowered down at his plate of pie, beans and chips. He and Penny had always sat together for lunch and now here she was, laughing and joking with the new sergeant.

Meanwhile Fiona Macdonald and Charles Davenport were sharing a pub lunch in one of the

The Pulpit is Vacant

Southside's pubs. Away from the station, Fiona showed a softer side and they were discovering shared interests. Both played bridge, playing with friends rather than at a club although Charles was going to have to travel some distance now for his game unless he could make up another foursome nearer to his new home. Both played golf, Charles with a handicap of fifteen, Fiona with twenty-four. There was a police golf competition in the autumn and they thought that they might partner each other. Charles was still a member at Troon but was thinking of moving to one nearer his home in Newton Mearns. Fiona had suggested a few clubs and was beginning to hope that he might join hers. She found herself drawn to this handsome, friendly man, yet she had only known him for two weeks and because of her past experience she was against station romances. She laughed inwardly at herself for even entertaining the thought that Charles Davenport might find her attractive or desirable.

For his part, Charles found his companion relaxing to be with. She seemed calm at work, fair towards her colleagues and now here, outside of work she showed a sense of humour too.

She wasn't pretty in the usual sense of the word yet her soft brown eyes attracted him and he suspected that underneath the rather severe clothes she wore to work there lurked a pleasing rounded figure. He laughed at himself. She was probably in a relationship and anyway station romances were not advisable.

Pippa's mother was a stunning brunette with a volatile temper, not made less volatile by his anti-social working hours. Rows had become almost commonplace and their home a battleground. Now that they were divorced, they had again become friends and he saw her when she came to take Pippa down South or when he took his daughter down for the holidays.

He had almost demolished his pie, beans and chips and she was pushing away the remains of her ploughman's lunch.

"Back to the sweat-shop, Fiona," he said. "We haven't discussed the two murders. You can tell me what you think on the drive back."

It was only a short drive but it didn't take long for her answer.

"Not a clue Charles."

"Exactly. That's what we need, a clue," he quipped back but both knew that already the trail was growing cold.

Charles parked his car in the staff car park and together they walked into the station. It was a large building, housing a number of departments, a modern piece of architecture quite unlike the old buildings from which they had both come. Neither of them noticed Frank Selby watching them from the canteen window.

CHAPTER 31

Davenport was fuming. He always thought of himself as a competent man but the meeting he had just experienced had made him feel like an errant schoolboy. He had been summoned to his chief constable's room in what they all nicknamed 'the penthouse', the suite of rooms at the top of the large building which housed the Southside police force. He had been kept waiting for about ten minutes, the secretary being very apologetic but unable or unwilling to explain the reason for the delay. Her phone rang and he could hear a loud voice at the other end.

"Go in Sir," the woman said. "Mr Knox is ready for you now."

The man behind the large oak desk looked like a bulldog. He had a flat face and what appeared to be no neck. His face was florid and scowling. He made no move to rise though this was their first real meeting, Davenport having only glimpsed him in the distance. Neither did he ask Davenport to take a seat.

"Well man! What's happening with these two murders? Any suspects yet?"

"Not really, Sir."

"What do you mean, not really? You either have or you haven't."

"What I meant Sir was that there are people who could have committed either or both murders but so far we have no proof."

"It's a week since the first murder, man. A murder trail goes cold after a week. You surely know that."

"I'm confident that we'll find out who did both murders Sir."

Grant Knox rose from his seat and started pacing the floor behind his desk.

"I'm being hounded by the press, especially now that a child has been killed."

"Do you want me to handle them, Sir?"

"Are you suggesting that I can't cope Davenport?"

"No Sir but I know how far we've got so I would know what information to give them."

"The only information they need to have is that we are confident of making an arrest soon."

"Is that wise Sir?"

The man's face, already red, became almost purple.

"Are you daring to tell me how to do my job man?"

The Pulpit is Vacant

Davenport was silent, realising that if he spoke he might infuriate this man even more. He thought back to the chief constable he had served under for many years at his last station, a fair man who had come up through the ranks and knew what the job of DCI entailed and he wondered how many years Knox had put in as a working policeman.

"Right I'll see the press later today and tell them that an arrest is imminent. Make sure that you have a name for me as soon as possible. No police leave until then you understand. None."

"Yes Sir."

Knox sat back down and began to shuffle through some papers on his desk and Davenport realised that the interview was over. Barely containing his anger, he left the room and made for the elevator.

"Bloody man lives in cloud cuckoo land," he muttered as it descended.

He went into his own room and shut the door, almost slamming it. Fiona in the room next door heard it and wondered what had happened. He always left his door open as he liked to be available to all his staff and he had never shown any sign of temper in the time she had known him. After their very enjoyable lunch together and their discovery of shared interests, she had been about to speak to him about maybe organising a bridge game sometime but thought that this was not a good time. She returned to her thoughts about the case.

219

Who could have killed the wee boy? The minister appeared to have been somewhat of a control freak so it was possible that he had tried to control someone who snapped and lashed out but what reason could anyone have for murdering William Paterson? It could only have been because he or she thought the boy had seen them on the night of the murder.

She heard her boss's door open and he stood framed in her doorway.

"DS Macdonald, would you come into my room please."

Fiona rose, straightened her skirt and went next door. Davenport was standing looking out of the window. He turned and gave her a weak smile.

"You must have heard my door slam Fiona. Sorry. I've just had a meeting with the chief constable and he infuriated me."

"Don't worry I've met the man. He interviewed me when I put in for a sideways move. He made me feel very small and foolish. I could almost hear him saying, "Stupid emotional woman.""

"I was lucky and was seen by his deputy, Solomon Fairchild, a very likeable man. Think I might ask to see him about this case."

Charles suited the action to his words and made an appointment to see the assistant constable later that day in his office on the floor above Davenport's section of the large station. He was not kept waiting

The Pulpit is Vacant

this time. Solomon Fairchild was, like Knox a large man but his face was almost cherubic, pink and smiling.

"Charles, it's nice to see you again. Have a seat. How are things doing at the sharp end?"

"Not too well, Sir. We're hoping for a breakthrough in our two murders."

"Coffee or tea? I'll get that organised then you must tell me all about it."

"Coffee please, Sir."

Fairchild rang through to his secretary and asked very pleasantly for two coffees to be brought. They chatted while they waited about how Charles had settled in and Fairchild asked about how DS Macdonald and Sergeant Din were doing. Davenport was happy to tell him that both seemed to have settled in well.

"Met your young PC, Penny Price isn't it? She's an attractive youngster. She chatted to me in the lift one day."

"That's our Penny, never one to stand on ceremony."

"On a more serious note, how is Selby getting along with Sergeant Din?"

Charles hesitated.

"I know he can be racist, I don't miss much, you know. Clamp down hard on him. He could lose his job if it continues."

"Yes, Sir."

"Now Charles, how can I help you?"

"Well Sir I've just had an interview with Mr Knox and..."

"Is this about the press statement?"

"Yes, Sir."

"Well you may or may not be pleased to know that Grant has passed this onto me to deal with. He leaves tomorrow for a trip to the USA, a fact-finding trip which will take him to four cities and will last about three weeks."

Charles could feel a grin spreading over his face.

"I was worried Sir as he said he was going to tell them that an arrest was imminent."

"I take it that that is untrue?"

"Yes, Sir."

"Very well I will tell them that the investigation is proceeding and leave it at that. Grant can be...a bit hasty sometimes."

Charles knew that he would say nothing more against his superior office and respected him for that.

He took his leave, thanking the assistant chief constable for his time.

CHAPTER 32

There were times when Charles Davenport really missed his wife's presence and tonight was one of them as he had to attend Parents' Evening at Pippa's school. In the middle of this enquiry into two murders, he would have welcomed a quiet evening at home but he would never let his daughter down and she was really keen for him to go and see her classroom and the things she had up on the wall.

Saying cheerio to his sister who was again helping out, he got into his car, thinking that he had been at this school only recently to see Colin Tait.

He had been given a letter telling him that he could come any time between 7 and 8pm and he hoped that by coming early he could get away faster. Mrs Hobson did not like the children to accompany their parents so he asked the janitor, on duty at the door into the school, which classroom Miss Kennedy taught in and was directed to a list on the wall. Miss Kennedy was in Room 7 on the ground floor. Elizabeth French's room was upstairs but Colin Tait's was room 4.

The young girl who welcomed him was a surprise as Pippa had said that her teacher was "old but quite nice Dad". He should have remembered that to a child anyone over eighteen was old!

"Hello. Miss Kennedy?"

"Yes."

"I'm Pippa Davenport's father."

She smiled.

"What a lovely daughter you have, Mr Davenport and how sensible for such a young age. She's settled in really well and has even tamed the class bully."

It transpired that the bully had tried his tactics on young Pippa and been put in his place, with the result that the boy wanted to sit with her in class.

"He's older than she is as he was kept back a year. I think she'll be good for him."

Charles pulled his left earlobe. His team could have told her that meant that he was pleased or puzzled. In this case he was delighted.

"Yes she keeps me in order too." He grinned. "Does she have any problems with any subject?"

"Well probably her weakest subject is Maths but I wouldn't say she was poor even at that and her English is excellent. She gave us a really good hobby talk recently."

The Pulpit is Vacant

"Is this part of the curriculum for her age group? It seems quite a difficult concept for eight year olds."

"Mrs Hobson wants them to have a try at it from the age of eight upwards to get them less nervous of it by the time they come to secondary school where they have to give a solo talk as part of their standard grade exams in fourth year."

"I see."

"We don't expect much from them at Pippa's age but hers was really good, very professional with the cue cards. Was that your idea?"

"Yes it was. I think she would talk all night about The Chalet School. Maybe it won't be so easy for her the next time when she has to choose another topic which she told me she has to do. So is there anything I can do to help with her Maths?"

"I know it's frowned on these days and don't let Mrs Hobson know I said it, but you could get her to learn old fashioned tables. And I've told the class they can use the same stimulus for their second talk but their last one will have to be on something new. Some of them found the talk very difficult so I wanted to make it as easy as possible the second time."

Charles said that he thought that that was fair then he winked.

"The tables will be our secret. Now I see a queue forming at the door so I'll get away."

"Have a look round the room before you leave Mr Davenport. Pippa has a few pieces of work on display. She would be upset if you didn't see them."

Charles left feeling pleased with what he had heard and seen. Pippa's written work looked very good for a child her age and the essay on the wall had been very imaginative.

It didn't take too long to get home at this time of the evening and he was able to say goodbye to his sister and see her off before 8-30 pm. He told her what a good report Pippa had got and also praised his daughter who was delighted and went happily off to bed. When she had left he wanted to talk about it to someone else and on impulse rang Fiona Macdonald.

They chatted about Pippa for quite a while and managed to keep off the subject of the murders. When she hung up the 'phone, Fiona went back to her book, feeling delighted that Charles had wanted to let her know about Parents' Night. She gave herself a mental shake. She really must not get too attached to either Pippa or her dad.

CHAPTER 33

DS Macdonald walked into the station on Wednesday morning just in time to hear, "Dreadful smell of curry in here."

At first she was puzzled. She had a keen sense of smell but could smell no curry. Then it dawned on her. At that point she saw Penny Price cross the room, hackles raised, saying, "Frank Selby. Stop that. It's blatant racism. Give Salma a chance for goodness sake!"

"Penny, leave it. It doesn't bother me, really it doesn't," said Salma.

"PC Selby, my room. Now." Fiona Macdonald's tone was icy.

Looking like a schoolboy caught with his hand in the biscuit jar, Frank left the room.

"I wish she hadn't heard, Penny," said Salma. "I would rather handle things my own way. This telling-off will only make him dislike me more."

"But the DS can't be seen to ignore racism Salma," Penny responded.

Frances Macarthur

"Remember I got the job he wanted *and* I'm female too," said Salma. "He'll be against me on three counts."

"He's got a good sense of humour," Penny told her, "but it often gets him in trouble and this will be another black mark against him."

"*Black* mark, Penny? Nice pun."

They grinned at each other.

At that moment Frank re-entered the room looking thunderous. He came up to the girls and muttered a most ungracious, "Sorry Salma" to which she replied," No problem Frank." He nodded abruptly and went across the room. Penny went back to her own desk too. There had been a few houses broken into the night before and she and Frank were due to visit the house owners concerned. She must have a talk with him and try to make him see that it was important for team morale that they all got along with each other.

As they left the station she tried to get him in a better mood by using his nicknames for their bosses.

"Frank. Flora Macdonald and the Bonnie Prince went out for lunch together yesterday. Think anything will come of those two - getting together I mean?"

Frank brightened a little.

"Yes I saw them coming in together today as well. That would be something - a station romance eh? I thought you might fancy him yourself Penny Farthing."

The Pulpit is Vacant

At the use of her old nickname Penny felt relieved. Frank was getting back to his usual sunny self. He might be racist and sexist but she had always liked him and enjoyed working with him. She risked asking him about his interview with the DS

"Seems racism is almost a hanging offence... well...I could lose my job, she said."

"It's not worth it then, is it and Salma's a nice girl."

Penny dropped the subject after that. It did not take them long to get the details of the break-ins. Three large houses in the Newlands area had been entered last night. Two had been deserted; their owners away on holiday but the other one had been burgled while the owners slept.

Penny and Frank were pretty sure it was the work of someone well-known to them and were confident that after the fingerprint expert was let loose on the houses, they would be able to pin the robberies on the man whom they suspected.

On the way back to the station, Penny spoke of how nervous Salma was and how she felt guilty having got the job he wanted. Frank grunted. He came, Penny knew, from a background of racist parents. They were white and Catholic and hated everyone who wasn't the same and they had passed their prejudices to their children. It was not going to be easy for Frank to shake off the shackles his mother and father had tied him with but surely once he got to know Salma he would see that she was a nice person.

Glad that her parents had been free thinkers and thinking she had done enough for now, Penny changed the subject to the two murders. She wanted it to be Philip Gentle if it could not be someone unknown whereas Frank said he would put his money on Kevin, Ruth's boyfriend whom he thought was almost too genial and accepting of Robert Gentle's opinion of him and his refusal to give their marriage his blessing.

"Would the wee boy, William, have known them, even if he had seen them," Penny wondered out loud.

"He could have described them Penny."

In the manse, one of their suspects, Kevin, was talking to Ruth.

"We wished him dead, Ruth. Remember that night in the garden, the night he was killed. I said I wished he was dead."

"I know you did Kevin," said Ruth, "and we both felt the same way but it was only our way of saying that we wished he would stop interfering in our lives and in Mum's. We would never have committed murder. I was just furious and Mum had obviously been ordered to bake for the meeting and she's been so busy since the move. Dad never does anything to help. Saying I wished him dead too, when I came back out to you was only our way of saying that we wished he would stop interfering

The Pulpit is Vacant

in our lives and in Mum's. We would never have committed murder."

"I know my love but I for one am sure to be a suspect."

"What about me Kevin? Stabbing is a woman's type of thing rather than a man's."

"A man could just as easily stab someone Ruth. They might think we killed William because he saw us."

"Saw us where? He couldn't have seen into the lounge could he? When the youth workers left the curtains were closed. How could he see the murder?"

"That's a good point Ruth. If he couldn't see into the lounge then he must have seen someone getting into the house and that wouldn't be you because you were already in and probably getting ready for bed and I had left quite a while before the youth workers. Your Mum was indoors too and Philip hadn't arrived."

"We're assuming that the boy *did* see someone. Maybe the murderer just worried in case he did.

Kevin stopped and ran his hand through his already rumpled red hair. He often did this in times of stress and it always made Ruth feel motherly towards him, as if she wanted to protect him from harm.

"This is getting us nowhere Ruth. I believe that it wasn't you....."

"And I believe that it wasn't you or Mum so that leaves Philip and I don't want to believe that it's him so who else is there?"

"One of those folk who visited the manse that night?"

"But why?"

"No idea Ruth. I'm baffled and I imagine that the police are baffled too.

CHAPTER 34

Kevin was correct. The police were baffled.

DCI Davenport had called a group meeting once again. An enlarged photograph of William Paterson was now alongside that of Robert Gentle. Police officers hate above all else the murder of a child, especially such a nice wee lad as William, and the mood was very subdued. There was a lot of muttering which subsided as Davenport took his position in front of them.

"We have three main suspects, people who were at or near the scene of both crimes, namely, Mary and Ruth Gentle and Kevin Grant. Also Philip Gentle was in Glasgow earlier than we at first thought and he could have come to the manse before he said he did.

On the first occasion, there were also the youth volunteers, Claire Davidson, the Bell twins, Colin Tait, Bill McFarlane and Elizabeth French though when they left the manse Robert Gentle was alive. One or more of them could have returned later that night to kill the minister but there seems to be no reason for one of them to commit the murder of a man whom they had never met until that night. Apart from those I've mentioned, there could have been a complete outsider but he or she took nothing if that was the case and nobody disturbed the murderer as the body wasn't discovered till the next morning."

"What about the murder weapon, Sir? Any thing there?" This came from Frank.

"There has been no sign of the murder weapon. The kitchen knives from the manse kitchen were sent to the lab and discovered to be clean. I heard from Vince Parker of SOC this morning. There was a full set. It seems a bit over the top to check yet the knives of all the youth workers but we will do if any of them should become suspect."

"What about William's murder weapon?" asked Penny before Davenport could draw his breath.

"I'm just coming to that PC Price. Be patient. The stone found at the site was used as we suspected but because of the roughness of the weapon, there were no fingerprints found on it. There were no footprints as the ground was too dry and hard."

"Why on earth would anyone want to kill a child like William?" asked one of the older men, a father himself. There was a lot of muttering at this.

"Obviously William posed a threat to the murderer of Robert Gentle so he must either have

The Pulpit is Vacant

known the person or have been able to describe him or her. The latter is unlikely as it would have been too dark for seeing clearly. It's much more likely that the person was known to the boy and he recognised a familiar walk or shape or both. William was in the gardens in the days before the murder so would have seen the Gentle family and he knew Colin Tait and Elizabeth French from school."

He paused.

"Of course he may not have seen anything but the murderer thought he might have and killed him in case.

He paused then continued, "I really can't see a motive for one of the Bell twins or Claire Davidson killing Robert Gentle."

Penny then mentioned that if the murderer had walked in front of a lit window then he or she would have been seen quite clearly by the boy but the general opinion was that it was more likely to be someone the boy knew than an outsider whom he had seen that night. Surely the murderer must have known too that William used the bushes as a hide-out else they would not have known where to find him. Robert Gentle could have told his family that he had allowed the boy to come into the garden. Ruth could have told Kevin. William might have talked about it at school or to his family who had mentioned it to someone else.

DS Macdonald spoke up.

"Probably the least likely to be recognised would be Philip Gentle as he'd only just arrived and he hasn't got a distinctive walk or anything else very noticeable."

"You're right. And what possible motive could he have had for murdering his father? They had fallen out but he could have stayed away or left again. He didn't need to kill him. Any other ideas folks?"

Penny volunteered the fact that they still had not worked out the reason for Colin Tait's nervousness and the DCI agreed that this was something they should work on finding out.

"We've mentioned that Philip Gentle didn't have anything special to be recognised by. What about the others?"

No one had the answer to this. The only one who stood out at all was Bill McFarlane who was well over six feet tall.

"Elizabeth French Sir," said Frank. "She's William's teacher and will probably know him really well. Maybe she can help us out rather than harass his parents right now. We could talk to his classmates too and maybe his brother George who was the nearest in age."

Penny smiled at him. He was showing his caring side and she hoped that Salma had noticed.

It was agreed that DS Macdonald and Penny would visit the primary school the next day and that the DCI and Frank would seek out George

The Pulpit is Vacant

away from his home. Fiona could return William's jotter at the same time. She still could not pinpoint what it was that was niggling in her mind about it.

The rest of the team were to be out and about in the manse area again asking residents if they had seen anything at all untoward on either of the murder nights. Quite a lot of folk had been away from home when they had gone round the houses the last time.

Everyone hoped that the murderer now felt secure and would not need to kill again.

CHAPTER 35

Thursday morning dawned bright and sunny and hot for mid-May. The manse gardens were at their best, full of azalea bushes and rhododendron of varied colours. Mary Gentle stopped to admire one particularly beautiful bush of deep pink azaleas , and, smelling honeysuckle, ventured round the uncultivated side of the house in search of the source of the scent. There, amongst the overgrown tangle of knee-high grass and weeds was the honeysuckle bush, yellow flowers pale here out of the sun.

"I must get to work round here," she thought then almost immediately came the realisation, "but I won't be here much longer."

She lifted her face and felt the warmth easing the rigidity of her shoulders through her thin white blouse.

It was so long since she had had to think for herself and it was quite scary yet at the same time challenging in an exciting way. She could go and stay in the house in Fife which Robert had chosen for them to live in after his retirement or she could sell that house and choose one where *she* wanted to live.

She picked up some small branches and twigs which had fallen from a tree and laying them on top of each other she made a tiny bonfire. She took two suspender belts and some flimsy underwear from the carrier bag she had brought with her and added them to the little pile. She struck a match and set fire to the heap. The little flame blazed up and the thin clothes wrinkled at the edges before melting in the heat. When the fire had built up in strength she added more bits of branch, the dog's lead and collar and a whip and thick belt. She had to relight the fire a few times and add more wood and the carrier bag and she was glad that none of the bedrooms overlooked this side of the house. When at last she had nothing but a pile of ash, she walked back to the house feeling almost light-headed with relief.

Some of Robert's punishments had been mental not physical. He had often made her wait some days wondering if she was to be physically punished. She could not burn the evidence of that and she knew it would be some time before her mental scars healed but today she felt happy.

She went inside and made herself tea and toast. She finished off two cups of tea and a full slice of toast and marmalade. She hated thick marmalade

The Pulpit is Vacant

with all the bits of peel but had always bought this kind as it was Robert's favourite. She would buy some Robertson's shredless marmalade now. She picked up her shopping bag and went out into the May sunshine, down the driveway and out through the main gates. She felt a shiver of unease as she passed the bushes where the young boy's body had been found but her light-heartedness returned a she passed through the gate.

She met nobody on the way to the store and there was nobody in it apart from Nan Brodie.

"Good morning, Mrs Gentle," she welcomed her first customer of the day.

"Mrs Brodie isn't it?" enquired Mary.

"That's right but everyone calls me Nan."

"Please call me Mary," said that lady now, experiencing a little frisson of pleasure at the realisation that there was no one to reprimand her for being too friendly with the local folk. She could call Mrs French Beth now if she wanted to.

She was sorry that she would have to leave this area but wait - she did not have to leave if she did not want to. She could sell the house in Fife and buy one here and she could learn to drive and use Robert's car or buy a smaller one. Robert had pooh-poohed her suggestion that she learned to drive, making her feel inadequate as he often did. He had also pointed out that she seldom went anywhere without him, making her realise how few friends she had. Surely she could manage to

Frances Macarthur

drive. A whole vista of a self-planned future rose up in front of her. She could travel a little. Robert's pension would be hers and if she was careful and made some money on the house sale and spent less on a house here, she could maybe afford to see some places she had only read of. She would love to visit Greece. Robert had had a suspicion of all things foreign and had insisted that they holiday in Britain. This meant of course that they had a healthy bank balance.

She hummed to herself as she filled her wire basket and then realised that it would not do to be seen as happy so shortly after her husband's death.

Certainly Nan Brodie found it odd till she remembered the conversation she had heard between the minister and his daughter. The woman was quite right to feel happy!

"That'll be eleven pounds and twenty-eight pence, Mary," she said and smiled at her.

"Good morning, Nan. I'll stop for a chat sometime but I'd better get back and get breakfast started for my daughter and son."

Nan Brodie watched her go. If it had not been for the death of William Paterson, the murderer might have done quite a few people a favour, she thought.

By the time Mary got back to the manse, Ruth and Philip were up and although still not washed and dressed were ready for breakfast. Ruth smiled

The Pulpit is Vacant

when she saw her Mum put shredless marmalade and pan bread on the table but said nothing.

"Mum do you think the police will be here again today?" asked Philip.

"Don't know dear but I expect so. I expect that we'll be seeing quite a lot of them till these murders are solved."

"Mum, doesn't it worry you? I mean they probably suspect one of us," said Philip.

"No dear, "she replied placidly. "I know it wasn't one of us and that's all that matters."

Philip, leaving the breakfast table to go for a shower, wished he had her serenity. He knew that by hiding the fact that he had come to the manse earlier than expected, he had made the police suspicious of him and he also suspected that Ruth, who was open like their Mum and hadn't hidden from the police the fact that she hated her father, was also likely to be a suspect as was Kevin by dint of being Ruth's boyfriend. The police maybe also suspected his Mum because they would have guessed by what had been said that Robert Gentle was a bully. The quiet little mouse could have decided to fight the cat back.

There was no way he was going to tell his Mum any of this but he was unsettled as he went for his shower.

Ruth was thinking along the same lines but naively reasoned that it would not take the police long to realise that Mary Gentle could not have harmed a fly let alone her husband. She realised that she, her brother and Kevin would be suspects but she trusted in British justice to clear the innocent.

In another house in the city, the murderer was hoping that the police and British justice would be baffled and that the crime would go unpunished.

CHAPTER 36

Jim French sat at his desk in school waiting for his first year class to arrive. When they had first come to the school in August, they had been apprehensive and well-behaved on the whole but now that they had been at the 'big' school for three terms, they were a bit of a handful for some young teachers who had not been tight on discipline. Why did new teachers always think they could start off being friendly and expect discipline to follow that?

Jim had reaped the benefit of keeping them in check from the start so he could still keep them in order yet be his natural, humorous self on occasion. Children are funny. Only the other day when the classes were having their annual photograph taken, he had been called to the hall because this class wanted him to be in their picture. He had thought that they must dislike him for his strictness but obviously not!

The first of the class arrived noisily at the door.
"Quiet now," said Jim.

The rest followed and were soon seated. He got one of the first arrivals to hand out books and folders.

He was reading with them Joan Lingard's book "The Twelfth Day of July" and they had reached the part towards the end of the novel where the Protestant and Catholic children were facing each other across the no man's land street which divided the two rival factions.

Jim always started this book by telling the class that they did not know if he was Catholic or Protestant and this kept them from voicing any bigoted views that they and their parents might have. It was a non-denominational school so took in pupils of both persuasions and he did not want any sectarianism rearing its ugly head.

If it had been a 'better' school he would simply have given them the book home to read and they would have got the message quite quickly but because he couldn't let the books out of his sight, he was reading it with them and the danger of this slow read was that bigoted opinions might be fed before the message got across.

"During the 'face-off' in the book, stones started being thrown and Jim had just reached the part where Brede, one of the Catholic girls and one who was against any fighting, was hit on the head by a thrown brick and knocked unconscious.

The Pulpit is Vacant

This sobered up most of the children, including those on the Protestant side of the street.

Jim was enjoying reading this part which would he hoped make some impact on the staunch Protestants and devout Catholics in his class, when he heard muffled sobbing from near the middle of the class.

He stopped reading and looked in the direction of the sobs.

"Sir, it's George Sir," said the boy sitting next to him. "He's crying Sir."

Jim moved quickly towards George and said to him to come outside for a minute.

Once out in the corridor, he asked what the matter was.

"Our William, Sir," hiccupped George." He was killed like that, with a brick and it's all my fault."

"Come on George. Why was it your fault?

"Sir I should have told Mum or Dad the first time he went out at night but I took fifty pence off him instead and kept quiet."

"George. William would have done the same if you had asked him not to say anything and anyway he was dangerous to the person who murdered Mr Gentle and that person would have got to him somehow and found him somewhere else."

"Do you think so Sir?

"Yes."

"But William wouldn't have been in the manse garden on the night Mr Gentle was killed if I hadn't kept quiet. If he hadn't been in the garden then he wouldn't have seen the murderer in the first place."

There was no answer to this child's logic and Jim felt very inadequate.

"William loved his birds Sir. He wouldn't have harmed a fly. It's not fair that he's dead."

At this point the period bell rang. Jim went into the room and dismissed the class. As they filed out on the way to the next subject, looking curiously at George who was one of the 'hard' men in the class, Jim decided to take George to his Guidance teacher. It might be better if he went home feeling as upset as he did. He might also be teased by the other boys if allowed back into class right away. Hopefully by the next day the incident would have been forgotten

George had one more thing to say,

"Sir I wonder what happened to William's yellow notebook. I'd like to have it. Would Mrs French let me have it?"

"I'll ask my wife George. If it's not at home then it must be in school. I'm sure the police would let you have it but I imagine right now they will want to read anything William wrote in it recently.

Later that same day, Penny and DS Macdonald visited the primary school. Having first okayed it with Mrs Hobson, they were escorted by an auxiliary to Mrs French's classroom. Fiona Macdonald handed over William's hobby jotter then asked if they might speak to anyone who was particularly friendly with William.

The only person being Jacqueline Beaton, the DS asked if they could have a word and, mindful of Child Protection regulations, both she and Penny went with her outside.

"Jacqueline, don't be frightened. We just want to ask you a few questions about William."

"OK."

"Did you know where William went when he did his bird-watching?"

"Yes. He went into the manse gardens."

"Did anyone else know this?"

"Well some of the boys must have known because some of them went to play there once and they teased him about hiding in the bushes."

"Thanks Jacqueline. Did William ever talk about Mr Gentle and his family?"

"He told me when the minister said he could keep going there. He was pleased that he was allowed in again."

"Did he ever mention Mrs or Miss Gentle?"

"No."

"Do you know if William had told any of the teachers where his den was?"

"Well he had asked Mr Tait to come and see it and he was so proud that Mrs French had said she would come sometime but don't think she had or he would have told me."

Frances Macarthur

They thanked Jacqueline and Penny stayed outside while DS Macdonald went back into the classroom.

"Mrs French. Do you know if William knew any of the youth workers?"

"I don't know. He did know Colin but I'm afraid I don't know about the others. Certainly his family weren't churchgoers. At least William wasn't because we talked about church when we were doing our war project and very few of the class went to Sunday school or church. I was half thinking of taking them in little groups if their parents would let them go. Church became an important part in peoples' lives during the war. Sorry. I'm waffling. No I'm sure William wouldn't know any of the youth workers except Colin - and me of course."

Thinking it a waste of manpower for two folk to go looking for George, Frank was delegated to do it and was standing near the Paterson's' house waiting for George to come home from school when George came out of the house..

"Hi George, I'm PC Selby. Not at school today?"

"I was sent home early. Can I see your ID?"

"You certainly can young man."

Frank handed over his card and George studied it carefully.

"What d'you want?"

"Do you know if William talked about his hide-out in the manse to anyone?"

The Pulpit is Vacant

"Don't be daft. He didn't even tell Mum and Dad and he only told me because he needed me to leave the window open for him. Why would he pay me not to tell if he was going to blab about it himself?"

The young lad had a good point there.

"Do know if he ever went inside the manse for any reason?"

"Don't think he would. He always took what he called his rations with him and anyway he mostly went at night recently. He was all wrapped up in his war project and he said that going at night made it seem more secret."

Frank thanked George and drove back to the station. All that he had learned was a bit negative but it was better than nothing he supposed. It seemed unlikely that William knew the Gentle family except by sight and he probably had not seen them very often either.

When he shared his findings, or lack of them with Penny, she confirmed his suspicions telling him what they had learned at school.

Frank went along the corridor to tell the DCI.

It seemed that only Colin Tait and Elizabeth French would be recognised clearly by the young boy.

CHAPTER 37

I found school quite harrowing these days. Everything seemed to remind me of William. I missed his intense gaze when I spoke to the class and his eagerness to learn as well as his eagerness to please me. I missed his immersion in our war-pretend times. I could have struck Fred when he said, "Miss we'll have to have a pretend funeral for William. How will we say he died?"

"What on earth do you mean Fred?" I found myself barking at him. He looked a bit taken aback at my obvious anger but plodded on nevertheless.

"Well Miss, we had funerals when one or our war-time houses was hit by a bomb so now William's war family will have to have a funeral for him. Maybe we could say he was run over by an army tank or hit by a piece of.....what d'you call it?"

"Shrapnel," provided Liam his eyes lighting up.

"Don't be stupid." This came from Jacqueline. "A little boy wouldn't get hit by shrapnel. He wouldn't be on the battlefield."

"Who're you calling stupid?" Liam was on his feet.

"You!" she retaliated.

Unable to think of any retort to that, Liam clenched his fists.

"Calm down Liam. We are not going to have a funeral for William because his death wasn't make-believe and it would be too upsetting for some of the class."

"And for you Mrs French," said Jacqueline. "I know you were fond of him."

She smiled and at me and I found myself smiling back.

I realised that at their age boys were on the whole ghoulish and loved stories of blood and guts. They had not got close to William as Jacqueline had and I must try to be understanding.

Promising them that I would think about how we could account for William's character being absent from now on in our war theme scenario, I managed to steer them into learning to write a letter correctly and soon they were composing thank-you letters to various friends or family members although not without the usual protesting that they would 'phone, not write.

There was a tap on the door and Mrs Hobson entered.

"Mrs French," she said. "Could I have a word with you in private?"

The pair of us went outside.

The Pulpit is Vacant

"Your husband has just rung the school to ask if you would take home William Paterson's notebook. His brother would like to have it."

"That's fine Mrs Hobson. It must be his hobby notebook he means. You know, the one you want every child to keep. He kept notes on the birds he saw. I gave it to the detective sergeant but she returned it. I must have it somewhere, either here or at home."

"Well, let his brother have it."

"I was going to give it to his parents.

"Well make sure someone gets it. Maybe give it to Mrs Paterson and ask her to let George have it when she's read it."

We were speaking quietly but I could almost see the ears pricking up in the classroom which had gone very quiet. I was glad when she left.

At the interval, I put William's jotter into my briefcase and promised myself that I would go round to the Paterson house that night.

As I drove home my mind was in turmoil. Thoughts of William and his death mingled with other worrying thoughts. Jim and I had been having talks about Jill. We had decided to tell her that we had adopted her. She was old enough to know and we thought that maybe it would take her mind off William's death. I was so worried that she would feel that we had lied to her. Maybe this was not the right time to spring something big like this on her. Jim thought it was the right time and

I would just have to trust his judgement which was less clouded than mine was at the moment.

"Have you finished your homework, Jill?" I asked when she came downstairs for her usual supper of oatcakes and cheese.

"Yes Mum. Why? Is it important? I want to phone Helen."

"Helen can wait. This is important. Your Dad and I want a chat with you."

Nervously I wound my hair round my forefinger.

"What is it Mum?"

"Your Dad will be here in a second. We'll tell you together."

"You're getting divorced. You're separating. You're..."

"Calm down love. Look here's Dad now."

At that moment Jim came in from the kitchen carrying plates of oatcakes and cheese for us all.

We sat down.

Jill looked from me to Jim and back again.

"What is it? You're scaring me."

"There's no easy way to say this love," said Jim, "so I'll just come straight out with it. Mum and I couldn't have a baby of our own so we chose you."

I shut my eyes, afraid to look at Jill.

"D'you mean I'm adopted?"

"Yes."

"Cool."

"Cool?" I squeaked.

The Pulpit is Vacant

"Yeah. That means when I'm older I can look for my real parents. We were told in school last year that the law lets you do that now. I'll have two sets of parents. We've been reading a book at school and there's this girl in the book who had great fun finding her real Mum. Her real Dad was dead."

Her face fell.

"I hope my real Dad's not dead."

Children never fail to surprise. We had agonised over this moment and now Jill was seeing herself as some sort of heroine in a story!

Jill looked at Jim who was looking a bit sad.

"Dad, you'll always be my Dad and Mum you'll always be my Mum. Don't worry. Now can I go and tell Helen?

"Of course pet."

She almost ran from the room and soon we could hear her excited voice from the hall.

We looked at each other.

"Well that went better than I'd hoped," said Jim "Not half."

I grinned at him. So much had gone wrong recently that it was strange to be feeling happy.

257

CHAPTER 38

The day of the funerals dawned bright and sunny. Robert Gentle was being cremated but Mr and Mrs Paterson had asked their elder children what they wanted for their brother and perhaps feeling guilty at having largely ignored him in his life, both George and Arlene wanted William buried so that they could visit his grave.

There were quite a few people at the crematorium. Mary Gentle, knowing that her husband had made very few friends in their travels, had been going to ask for the small chapel in the grounds of Lynn Crematorium but her daughter and son had persuaded her into having the larger one, the St Mungo Chapel as although he had not been popular in his other parishes, probably quite a lot of his new church here in Glasgow would come and they had been proved right in their choice as about forty attended, one being DCI Davenport.

The officiating minister had spoken with the family the evening before and he gave a short history of Robert's life. One hymn, 'Will Your Anchor Hold', one prayer, the committal and a final hymn, 'Abide With Me' and they were back out in the sunshine. Mary invited the guests back to the manse for some refreshments and the cars set off.

In another part of the city, cars were pulling away from the Paterson's' house.

Arlene and George, looking grown-up and smart in their black clothes, accompanied their mother and father. Tricia had begged to be allowed to go but her mother had won her over by telling her that as she was the oldest being left at home, she would have to help the baby-sitter with Jean and Gemma the twins, Robin aged three and baby Sam.

There was a brief service at the funeral parlour then the cars moved off to the local graveyard. The coffin had William's name around it in white flowers and also one in the shape of an eagle. It had been William's dearest wish to see a golden eagle. They had read this in his hobby jotter. His mother, in the car travelling behind the hearse, started to cry at the thought that he never would see one now. Her husband took her hand.

At the graveside were many friends of Mr and Mrs Paterson and quite a few parents of his classmates. Children were not expected at graveside burials but Jacqueline was there with her Mum and Dad. She carried a single red rose which

The Pulpit is Vacant

she hoped to be allowed to place on the coffin. She had seen this done in a film a few weeks previously.

Elizabeth French, her husband and daughter were there as were other members of the family, aunts, uncles and grandparents, and neighbours. Colin Tait had come too. No one spoke as the white coffin was carried to the grave by Mr Paterson.

DS Macdonald and Penny were there and behind the groups nearer to the grave, a late arrival walked up - Ruth Gentle - who wanted the family to be represented. She knew that Kevin and Philip would help her Mum who was surprisingly calm.

The minister spoke of William's short life. He prayed for the family at this very difficult time.

Penny, listening to what was being said, was also watching those standing round the open grave. Colin Tait or Elizabeth French could be a murderer.

She looked at them.

What on earth could be the reason for one of them to kill the new minister? It surely must be Philip Gentle. William Paterson's death was easier to understand as that would be to keep the murderer safe but why on earth would one of them want Robert Gentle out of the way, permanently?

"Ashes to ashes; dust to dust....." intoned the minister and William's parents and Arlene and George threw handfuls of earth onto the coffin which now rested in the small hole in the ground.

A hymn was sung, William's favourite from his Sunday school days, 'Jesus Loves Me'

Near to Penny, Elizabeth French was sobbing and her husband put his arm round her and led her away, their daughter following them.

As Jacqueline and her family passed the grave, her Mum gestured at the rose and looked inquiringly at Mr Paterson who smiled and nodded. Given a nudge by her Mum, Jacqueline dropped her rose into the open grave.

The family were last to leave the graveside and when Penny looked back, the white flowered W.I.L.L.I.A.M was resting by the side of the grave. It would be placed on the grave until a headstone could be raised.

Ruth, not wanting to impose on the family, left as quietly as she had come. She would be needed at home to help cater for the guests

Robert Gentle's ashes would be scattered in the Garden of Remembrance at the crematorium as Mary and he had never discussed their funerals, surprisingly enough and she did not know if he had a favourite spot.

Back at the manse, Mary stood at the window, a cup of coffee in her hand. With the funeral over, she felt that freedom beckoned. She wished she could confide in someone about what life had been like at times but was almost ashamed now at her submissive behaviour. She could have left Robert once the children had left school. Never mind, it was all over now - but at what a cost!

CHAPTER 39

It was Saturday morning and Charles Davenport was spending the first part of the day with his daughter. They had been going to go to the park but it was wet and windy, a complete contrast to the day before. He knew he was lucky that Pippa could always amuse herself

"Dad, how do you spell Wednesday?"

"Capital W.e.d.n.e.s.d.a.y," he called back. "What are you doing?"

He had been reading in The Herald about how police were still no further forward in making an arrest for the double killings on the South Side and Pippa had been writing at the table in the kitchen.

"Writing up my hobby diary for school. I've finished my book and want to write up the last few days. I've to talk about it in school next week."

"I thought you had to talk about something else this time."

"Miss Kennedy changed her mind about that, thank goodness."

"Sorry pet, she told me that at Parent's Night. I'd forgotten."

She wandered through to the living room and sat on the floor at his feet. He rumpled her fair hair which was not in its usual pony tail.

"What will you talk about love?"

"All the main characters -Tom Gay, Daisy, Miss Wilson - you know the people that are in the book most. And then I've to tell about any exciting things which happen."

"Tell me one of the best bits."

She snuggled back with her head against his legs. "Well Tom Gay - she's a female who wants to be a boy, thinks she's locked bugglers....."

"Burglars Pippa."

"Yes burglars, in a room but she's really locked Miss Wilson, the headmistress and the matron and two other people in there."

"How long do you have to speak for?"

"About five minutes."

"Why don't you write something out and practise on me tonight?"

"We're not supposed to read something out Daddy. remember."

"Well you write out what you want to say and I'll bring some more white cards from work and you can write wee notes to remind you what you want to say. That helped you the last time. That's what I do if I'm making a speech. Is anyone else using reading as a hobby?"

The Pulpit is Vacant

"Oh yes, quite a few of the girls and one boy. They used their books last time too."

"Were the talks interesting?"

"Some of them."

She went back out to the kitchen.

Just then the phone rang. It was Fiona Macdonald. She had had a chat with one of the PCs who had been making door to door enquiries and wanted to tell him the outcome.

"Come over for an early lunch Fiona. You can fill me in and we can go back to the station together."

Charles went back to the Herald, finished it then picked up The Guardian which was his newspaper of choice. He felt he had to keep abreast of Glasgow's news so bought The Herald but he preferred The Guardian for world news and for the crossword. It was usually compiled by Araucaria on a Saturday and he often kept it for the evening when Pippa was in bed.

He decided to make a start on it while waiting for Fiona to arrive.

"Bearing a grudge at beer (6)". That was an easy one he thought as he fitted 'bitter' into 1 across.

He was well on his way to finishing the acrosses when the peal of the doorbell heralded the arrival of his colleague.

Dressed in her workaday black slacks, shirt blouse and black fitted jacket she was a pleasing sight. Although she did not have to wear uniform

Frances Macarthur

to work she always dressed formally, rarely in casual clothes and he wondered fleetingly what she would look like dressed for a night out.

"Come in Fiona."

"Hello Charles. Hello Pippa."

Pippa had come from the kitchen curious as to who the visitor was.

"Hello... I don't know what to call you," she said in a child's forthright manner.

Fiona looked at Charles.

"It's up to you Fiona," he said.

"Well then, Fiona will be just fine," said that lady. "What's in the jotter Pippa?"

"I'm writing up my talk on "Tom Tackles the Chalet School""

"Oh I'd love to see that. I'm a fan of the Chalet School too. Did your dad tell you?"

Charles looked sheepish.

"Sorry. I forgot."

"What's your favourite book, Fiona?" asked Pippa excitedly. She had never had anyone to share her favourite books with before.

"My favourite is definitely the one where Jo has to grow up when she's chosen to be head girl. It's 'The Chalet School and Jo', I think. I have the whole set except one "Redheads at The Chalet School.""

"The *whole* set! Daddy, Fiona's got the whole set of the Chalet School books except one."

"Yes I heard."

"I'm going to have the whole set too. I've got up to this one." She looked at the spine of her book. "Number twenty-two this is."

"Well if you ever can't find the next one just come to me," Fiona said. She grinned at Pippa who grinned back then took her into the kitchen to see what she had written so far. Charles had done four more clues when Fiona returned to the living room, leaving Pippa to finish off her talk.

"What have you got to tell me about the house to house?"

One of the PCs had reported one person seeing someone opening the side manse gate on the night of William's murder. The lady had had toothache and been up to take a pain-killer around 12.30 am. Unfortunately it had been too dark to see clearly but the figure was of average height, could have been a tallish woman or smallish man and was wearing trousers and an anorak-type jacket with the hood up.

"Not much to go on there, is there?" said Charles gloomily.

"Well, Mary Gentle is small and Kevin Grant is well over six feet. Ruth on the other hand is quite tall for a woman and Philip is on the small side for a man."

"Claire is tiny but Elizabeth French, Mary Bell, Andrew Bell and Colin Tait are all under six feet. Bill McFarlane's tall. I think," added Charles.

"Yes he is. I remember noticing that at the William's funeral. So if we go by this one sighting we're left with Ruth and Philip Gentle, the Bell twins, Mrs French and Colin Tait. Doesn't narrow the field much, does it?"

"Better than not narrowing it at all. What about motive?"

"None on the part of the youth volunteers. Ruth could have murdered her father in a sudden rage at him trying to come between her and Kevin or she might have snapped at him bullying her mother as he seems to have done on occasion. Philip could have done it for the second reason as well."

"Not really strong motives, are they Fiona?"

"No, they're not."

"Let's get back to work. I think we need to see if we can find out more about our youth workers, apart from Claire Davidson who is tiny. The person who went in by the gate is more likely to have been someone from outside the family who would all have been home at that time I imagine. I'll drop Pippa at my sister's on the way there."

Something was tickling at the back of Fiona's mind as Pippa, clutching her jotter, got into the back of her father's car, leaving the front passenger seat for Fiona. If she stopped trying to bring it to the front of her brain it would most likely get there of its own accord when she was least expecting it.

CHAPTER 40

After school on Friday, I went to do the weekly shopping at Morrison's in Newlands. My mother had come up to live with us some years ago and we had often done this weekly shop together on a Friday afternoon after school. She had died of a brain tumour two years ago and I still missed her. She and Jim had got on well and I knew that Jill still missed her gran. The first inkling we had had of the tumour was the morning she had asked for the 'white stuff you put in your tea'. She had gone downhill quickly after that. It had been so sad to see her lose her sharp brain. I remembered the day I had found her wandering in one of the aisles at Morrison's with no idea what she wanted, Mum, who was the best bridge player I had ever met.

Mum had never liked Peter, neither had my Dad but that had been our only disagreement and they had both taken to Jim and spoiled Jill terribly when we went to Hastings to visit them. They had both agreed not to mention Peter though Mum had thought it wrong to start married life with a secret. Dad had died suddenly about five years ago, in his beloved garden and I had persuaded Mum to come and live with us quite soon afterwards.

I would have liked to have had Mum to talk to now about all that had happened.

I had decided to go to the Paterson's after the shopping, well, after I had taken the shopping home. Jim called this Friday ritual, 'going for the messages', which had always intrigued me and I remember Jill's excitement at doing this for the first time and her disappointment when no messages transpired!

It always intrigued me that folk had their own shopping routines. I know I never went down the aisles which sold spices or pet food and I seemed always to buy the same kind of chocolate biscuits. I loved looking at the items of the person in front of me. Often there were things which I had never used.

It was about five thirty by the time I was driving up our street. I had to pass the manse, a place which had twice become a murder scene and I turned my head and looked to the left so as not to see it as I passed by.

I wondered how long it would be before Mary Gentle left and how a new minister would feel about living in a house where there had been a murder and working in a garden where a small boy

The Pulpit is Vacant

had met his end according to DS Macdonald at the funeral.

I tried to console myself with the thought that Mary would be able to live her own life now, that Ruth Gentle and Kevin Grant could marry whenever they wanted to and that Philip Gentle could follow his heart without offending his father. I did not know what has caused the rift between father and son but it was over now.

I tried to make myself believe that William had been saved any bullying, maybe an unhappy marriage, illness...I caught myself up short. I was being ridiculous. There was no way I could put an optimistic slant on the cruel murder of a young boy!

As I walked up the path, carrying bags of groceries, my mind flew back to the time just recently when William had helped me pick up my spilled tomatoes. In some ways it seemed ages ago; in others it seemed as if it were yesterday.

The path needed weeding I noticed. Jim did most of the gardening but I usually did the weeding of the path and the back patio. I must get down to it at the weekend.

The phone started ringing as I opened the door so I put the bags down in the hall and answered it, hoping that my remaining bags would be safe in the open boot. We lived in quite a quiet street but these days nothing was certain.

It was Colin Tait.

"Beth, Colin here. I couldn't get a chance to speak to you today at school. Have you heard if the police are any further forward with the murders?"

"Colin. Give me a minute to shut the car boot."

I put the receiver down on the glass-topped hall table, ran down the path, grabbed up the last three bags, shut the boot, checked that the car was locked and having put the bags on the floor with the others, picked the phone back up.

"Sorry Colin. No. I haven't heard a thing. The funeral was awful wasn't it? It was good of Mrs Hobson to let us both off. Jim got off too - but then you know that - thank goodness as I needed him there."

"Yes Beth, the coffin looked so small and the eagle-shaped floral arrangement was so sad."

"Look Colin, 'fraid I'll have to go and get on with the dinner. I'll let you know if I hear any more. Will you do the same for me?"

"Of course."

I hung up and went into the kitchen and put away the shopping I had bought. There was no rush for the dinner but I just couldn't take talking any more about William's funeral or his death. Now what? I could make a start on the dinner as I had told Colin I was about to do or I could visit the Patersons with William's hobby notebook.

I decided on the latter.

I had meant to go a few days ago but had put it off.

The Pulpit is Vacant

I walked there and went briskly to the door and rang the bell before I could have second thoughts.

Arlene opened the door. She, like William, had been a bit of a loner when I knew her at primary school. I think she had to help out a lot at home with the younger children and found her peers a bit juvenile with their skipping ropes and dolls.

"Hello Mrs French. Is it Mum you want?"

"Yes please, Arlene. Is it an awkward time? I can always come back."

"No, it's OK. We've had our dinner. George and I can get the washing-up done."

"Thanks Arlene."

She disappeared into the house and it was not long before Mrs Paterson arrived at the door and invited me in. She looked careworn and very, very sad, her eyes red and puffy from crying. We sat on the worn settee.

"I know this will upset you," I said to her, "but George has asked for William's hobby notebook and I thought you'd like to see it first."

"George!" she called and he came immediately.

"Mrs French has brought William's notebook."

I handed the jotter over.

"It's not that one I want Miss. (I had not taught George but he knew me from Arlene and more recently from William). I want the yellow one where he put in his war things when he went out at night."

"Sorry George. This is the only one I have."

273

He took it, looking a bit down-hearted and left for the kitchen.

"Thanks Mrs French. I appreciate you bringing it. I'll read it after George. How I wish I'd made time for him when he was here!"

I said that it was nothing, gave her my commiserations once again and left, glad to have got the visit over.

CHAPTER 41

It was Monday morning and Penny was thinking about Colin Tait. A good-looking young man like him probably had a girlfriend, yet there had been no mention of one and he appeared to live alone as there were no feminine things in his flat - mind you they had only seen the main room and the hallway. She mentioned this to Salma who had never met him.

"Maybe he's old-fashioned and his girlfriend still stays with her parents or with friends. Not all young folk live together, Miss Price." Salma put on a mock severe voice and Penny laughed.

As if he could thought read, DCI Davenport came into the room and asked Salma to go across to Colin's flat that evening.

"I want you to ask him if he knew Robert Gentle when he lived in Sussex. It's a long shot but worth a try and it will give us another opinion on the young man who is the only one of the youth workers showing any signs of nervousness and the only one apart from Mrs French whom William knew. I want you also to look at his kitchen knives. If he has a set see if any are missing."

"OK Sir. Can I take Penny with me if she's free?"

"I am free Sir. Can I go?"

"As my old English teacher always said to me, not *can* I but *may* I?" he laughed. "There's no reason at all why not."

Penny, having been given directions to Salma's flat in Bridgeton, went across to pick her up after her evening meal with her mother and drove them over, across the Kingston Bridge which was busy as usual. There was probably an easier route but Penny was unfamiliar with Bridgeton and Salma was not au fait with the route either. When they were safely at Charing Cross, Penny asked Salma if she knew this side of the city,

"Not very well. I don't do much socialising Penny. I tend to go home to my family and stay there."

"What family do you have?"

"Mum, an older brother who lives down in London, two younger sisters and a young brother. One of my sisters is a teacher. Dad died a few years ago. What about you Penny?"

"I'm an only child. Mum's a widow too but she has a male friend, Jack, whom I like so I get out and about quite a lot and come over here quite often. There are so many eating places in Byres

The Pulpit is Vacant

Road. Maybe we could come across together - if you'd like to that is?"

"I'd love to Penny."

Salma wondered if, for the first time since primary school, she was going to have a good friend in Penny. She hoped so.

As usual it was hard to find a parking space but Penny eventually manoeuvred the car into a tight space between a battered old Morris Minor and a motorbike in one of the side streets.

They walked through to Colin's street.

"Funny that Colin's nameplate is just a scribbled name," said Penny when they reached his close. "I noticed that the last time I was here."

"Why's that odd?"

"Well, he's such a neatly dressed guy and his flat was extremely tidy."

"Maybe he's just arrived."

"Don't think so but that's something we can ask. Maybe we should talk to his neighbours too - find out as much as we can about him."

They rang the bell. No one answered.

They rang the bell of the flat across the landing from Colin, explained that they were police officers and were buzzed in.

It was a woman in her early twenties who met them on the landing.

"Police? What's the matter?"

"No need to worry Miss......"

"Livingstone. Carol Livingstone."

"No need to worry Miss Livingstone. I'm Sergeant Salma Din and this is PC Penny Price. We'd like to ask you a few questions about your neighbour Colin Tait."

"Colin! He surely can't have committed a crime. He's such a lovely guy and a perfect neighbour. He waters all my plants when I'm away and they don't have noisy parties unlike the folk above me."

"How long has he lived here?" asked Penny.

"Well I've been here two years almost and they were here when I arrived. That's all I know."

"*They*," said Salma. "I thought he lived alone."

"No Hilary lives with him, though come to think of it I've only seen Colin recently. Maybe they've split up."

Thanking her again for her help, the two policewomen went back down the stairs.

"I think we should wait in the car for a wee while to see if Colin comes home. Save us another journey. Do you mind Penny?"

"Not at all. I had nothing special to do tonight. Hilary. She gave him a poetry book. I saw it in his bookcase when I was last in his flat. Wonder why they split up."

They sat in companionable silence for about ten minutes then Penny spotted Colin in the wing mirror coming along the road with another young guy. They got out and greeted him and suggested going back to the flat with him. The other young guy gave Colin a quick wave and continued down the street.

Once in Colin's hallway, Penny went towards the living room and the other two followed her.

"Sorry to bother you again Mr Tait. My name is Sergeant Din. PC Price you've already met. My boss DCI Davenport wanted to know if you had ever met Robert Gentle before either in Scotland or down in Sussex when you lived there. It's a long shot but we have to ask."

"No Sergeant. I only met him once, on the night he died. I had seen him once before that but it was at his first service and he didn't talk to me then."

Penny, watching his face closely, thought he was quite happy to answer this question. He seemed almost ready for it and showed no surprise. Was that normal? Or was she looking for things?

"One more thing," continued Salma. "We spoke to your neighbour Carol Livingstone before you arrived home and she mentioned that you shared the flat with a girl called Hilary yet we thought that you lived alone."

"We split up recently. Hilary moved out." Colin said tersely. His face, so relaxed a minute ago was now closed up. "Can't think why that would interest you."

"Sorry Mr Tait. In a murder investigation even personal affairs tend to get brought into things."

"Yes I know. I'm sorry too. Afraid I can't really help you. All I can repeat is that it seemed tense in the manse that night."

"I'm also sorry to ask but can I see your kitchen knives?"

Colin led them into his kitchen which also had a dining area at one end. He opened a drawer under the sink. All his kitchen utensils were there, among these some knives.

"Sorry. I don't have one of those wood blocks with knives. I have three of varying sizes. Here they are. Why don't you take them with you? I can buy some more."

Salma thanked him and not being able to think of anything else to ask they said their goodbyes.

They sat in the car once again and Penny shared her feeling that Colin was prepared for the "had he met Robert Gentle before" question but that he was really uneasy when the talk became more personal.

Salma agreed with her about the latter but put it down to the fact that the split with Hilary was recent and still raw.

They were still no further forward. Could they eliminate Colin Tait from their suspect list?

CHAPTER 42

Salma Din and Penny Price would not have been so ready to dismiss Colin Tait as a suspect if they could have heard the telephone conversation taking place not long after they left the flat.

"Hilary. It's me, Colin. Your mobile must be going out of range or something. I can hardly hear you. Can you hear me OK?"

"Yes Colin. How did it go with the police? Just as well I made off when I saw them."

"The police know about you. Carol told them we shared the flat. They assumed you were a girl."

"What did you say?"

"I said that you had moved out recently and that we had split up."

"Quick thinking. We'll make a criminal out of you yet."

"It's not funny."

"Sorry but it's not that great for me either having to move back in with my parents. I can't tell them why and they've assumed that our relationship has broken down and are saying they told me so. When can I come back?"

"Not until this thing's over."

"I don't know why I had to move out in the first place."

"I've told you this umpteen times. I didn't trust Robert Gentle to have that knowledge of us and he might have found out. I knew him in Yorkshire, for a short time when I was at the barracks at Catterrick and let's just say he wasn't nice to know then. I doubt he'd changed. A leopard doesn't change its spots. I don't want the police to know about you or about the fact that I knew Robert Gentle."

"So I'm with my parents until this case is solved?"

"Please Hilary. This is hard for me too."

Having hung up the phone, Colin sat with his head in his hands. How he had hated Robert Gentle and how shocked he had been when he saw in the parish church magazine that Robert Gentle was to be the new minister. He had gone along to the first service hoping against hope that it would not be the same man. It was and he had not mellowed over the years if his sermon was anything to go by.

Then had come the news via the session clerk that the man wanted to meet with all the youth workers. Added to that, Mrs Hobson told him that the minister wanted to see him with regard to his infant class children coming to Sunday school.

The Pulpit is Vacant

He could have simply given up his youth club work but he could not abandon his job.

He had gone along - late - in the hope that the meeting would be about to close and he would only have to be in the man's presence briefly but that had backfired too. Beth French and Bill McFarlane had already left. He had talked to them at the gate and then had hesitated for quite a while before going up the path, wondering if he could go home and plead illness, then realised that he would have to meet the man sometime and when he got to the door the others were on their feet, holding empty cups and making excuses for leaving so soon.

He had been trapped by politeness into accepting tea and a piece of cake and once in the trap he had been held there.

His hopes that Robert Gentle would not recognise him were shattered immediately.

As he laid down his cup on the floor, at his feet, the minister said,

"So Colin, we meet again."

He could see his new, happy life collapsing round him like a house of cards and had begun to plead with Gentle, saying that he was a reformed man and would he please let bygones be bygones.

Gentle had just smiled, like the cat which had found the tin of evaporated milk with the lid off.

Oh he would have loved to have put his hands round the man's neck and squeezed till the life drained out of him or smashed his smug face in with whatever came to hand but he found himself pleading again. What did the minister have to gain from dredging up his, Colin's, past mistakes?

"Surely you understand that the school authorities have to know and I could hardly let you continue with the youth club under the circumstances."

"But they don't have to know," he whispered brokenly, knowing that it was pointless.

Determined not to break down completely, he staggered to his feet and ran to the door, luckily meeting no one on his way there. He had run down the path and got into his car.

What could he do to stop Robert Gentle interfering in his life once again he had wondered.

CHAPTER 43

"All written reports to be on my desk by the time you leave tonight." These words by DCI Davenport made a few of his uniformed staff realise that lunchtime would have to be forgone if everything was to be ready in time. Penny, conscientious to a fault, had her report ready and she knew that Salma had too as they had discussed this on the way home from seeing Colin Tait.

On the other side of the room however, Frank's face told a different story. He hated writing out reports. English had never been his best subject at school and he struggled to put into words the interviews he did. He seldom took notes and when he did they were so badly scribbled that making them out took ages.

Seeing his look of despondency, Penny went across the room.

"Right Frank, talk me through what you've done or heard recently."

Frank looked relieved.

He started telling Penny about his chat with George and as he talked, Penny wrote. He had a good memory.

"You've learned about as much as we did from William's teacher and classmates."

"I know. We don't seem to be getting much further, do we?"

Penny handed him what she had written and he took it gratefully and went off to type it out on the computer. He was OK with this. He had done well in IT at school and loved anything to do with computers. He knew that Penny's syntax and spelling would be correct so all he needed to do was type up what she had written. She had helped him out with things like this before.

"Owe you a drink, Penny. Are you free tonight?" he called across the room.

"OK, Frank. See you in the local after work."

"How about I pick you up later and we make an evening of it?"

"Is this a date, Frank?" Penny teased.

He blushed faintly.

"It is if you want it to be."

"Wow, a sell- by date."

Laughter rippled out in the room. One of the older PCs quipped, "Good one Sarge."

Across Frank's face different feelings flitted, surprise chased by anger chased by reluctant appreciation of the pun.

"Nice one Sergeant Din. That's us quits I think."

The Pulpit is Vacant

Once Frank had typed up his report, he and the other PCs grouped round one desk to compare notes. The door to door had revealed nothing else apart from the one sighting of an average-sized person going in the gate early in the morning. The visit to the school had thrown up nothing new but had maybe eliminated some of the youth workers just as the conversation with George had done.

They all congregated in the Incident Room where they handed over their reports before leaving.

"Meet in here tomorrow morning - at nine o'clock sharp," said the DCI with a stern look at Frank.

They all filed out, leaving Charles and Fiona alone.

As they walked down the corridor, Frank whistled "The Skye Boat Song." Penny nudged him. "No harm in whistling is there?" he asked.

"What if they catch on to why you're whistling that tune about Bonny Prince Charlie?"

"Unlikely."

In Davenport's room, the senior policeman and woman looked at each other in surprise.

"Wouldn't have pegged Selby for a Scottish song person," said Davenport.

"Me neither. I'd have guessed heavy metal."

"No point in hanging around tonight Fiona. I'll take all the reports home with me and summarise them before the meeting tomorrow."

Frances Macarthur

"Do you want to photocopy them and I could read them through as well?

"What a good idea! Two heads are better than one. If you don't mind and haven't anything better to do this evening, that'll be great."

He handed her the reports and she left for the room where the photocopier was kept.

As he was putting on his jacket, he caught himself thinking how nice it was to be able to share his workload with this woman. His wife had never understood the intricacies of his job and always wanted him to put off work to spend time with her and Pippa.

He had the best of both worlds now. He had an amicable relationship with his ex-wife, Fiona to share work with and the undemanding love of his daughter who seemed to accept the fact that he wasn't there for her all the time.

The DS caught up with him as he walked to the door and handed over the reports.

"Tell Pippa I'm looking forward to hearing about her talk once it's over."

"Will do. Goodnight Fiona. Happy reading!

CHAPTER 44

It was Tuesday afternoon, a fortnight after the murder of Robert Gentle. As promised, Charles Davenport was holding a brain-storming session in the incident room.

"We have all seen Colin Tait now. Do we agree that something is making him uneasy?"

Choruses of "Yes Sir" came from around the room.

"Salma, you and Penny were the last to see Colin Tait. Tell us what happened please."

"Well he denied having met Robert Gentle before that night. Seemed quite calm when I asked him but when I asked him about his girlfriend Hilary with whom he had been sharing his flat, he was definitely edgy. Wasn't he Penny?"

"Yes Sir. His face went all tight. I was watching him closely while Sergeant Din spoke to him. I think he was prepared for the first question but wasn't prepared for the second one."

"Why on earth would he be reserved about having a girlfriend?" asked Davenport.

"He hasn't got one now Sir. She doesn't share his flat any more. He said that they had split up recently."

"Well that's nothing new. Relationships end. There's nothing shameful in that. Getting back to the investigation, could this Hilary be involved in any way?"

"Maybe she helped him commit the murder Sir and he's keeping her out of the way in case she breaks down and tells us."

This from Frank who had a fertile imagination, thought Penny.

However, Davenport did not dismiss this idea of Frank's.

"We'll not rule out that idea, Selby. He must have some reason for not wanting this Hilary being mentioned or coming on the scene. Any more ideas on this folks?"

Silence came into the room and remained until Salma said, "Could she be someone he's ashamed of. Maybe someone his parents don't approve of so he's keeping her secret."

"People don't give a monkey's about what their parents think any more. Well not in *Western* culture anyway." Frank was dismissive. He had put a heavy emphasis on the word 'Western'.

The DCI decided to let that go. Salma replied quietly, "It was only an idea."

The Pulpit is Vacant

"I don't think it can be that. I mean we wouldn't tell his parents, would we?" said Penny.

"I really think we need to find this Hilary, even just to eliminate her from the enquiry," said Davenport. "Colin was out very late that night. Maybe there were bloodstains after all. No that won't do. We were told that it was a clean job and there was very little blood on the carpet and *that* had seeped from the body rather than spurted."

Frank, looking pleased that his idea had found favour, pressed the point.

"She might just have woken up when he came in and saw how upset he was and he thinks she might put two and two together if we questioned her."

"Frank, as this was your idea, how about you going over to Byres Road and doing some scouting around - in local shops, cafes etc. See if you can find out if they've been seen together and where she lives now. I don't want to scare Colin off so that he warns her and she clears off totally, otherwise we could just put pressure on him to tell us her whereabouts."

"Certainly Sir, can I take Penny with me?"

"Good idea but wait till we've gone over a few more points. Do you agree that we can rule out the Bell twins and Bill McFarlane? William didn't know them and they don't have any distinguishing features, well none that would be noticed in the dark and Bill McFarlane is too tall to be the person seen by our only eye-witness."

"Sir, was it a light night that Tuesday? Is it possible that the lad could have seen a stranger closely enough to recognise them again?" DS Macdonald spoke for the first time.

"Can anyone remember if it was a full moon that night," asked Davenport.

One of the older PCs said that he had a diary in his jacket pocket which he thought had the moon's phases in it and he left the room. He came back, opening the diary as he entered the room.

"It was a quarter moon that night Sir."

"Anyone know if it was cloudy?"

No one spoke.

"Well it couldn't have been very bright if it was only a crescent moon. I still think the murderer believed that he or she would be recognised and I am willing to remove the Bells and McFarlane from our suspect list. Anyone disagree?"

Nobody did so he continued.

"Did someone hear William in the bushes? Did anyone know of his hide-out? Frank, you spoke to George. What did he say about this?"

"He said it was a secret place so why would William tell anyone about it?"

"Yes but Jacqueline Beaton knew about it," said Fiona Macdonald, "and she said some of the boys might have seen him in the bushes when they played there."

The Pulpit is Vacant

"Right, Jacqueline and some young boys are not suspects but could they have told any adults?"

"Unlikely. It's not something of great importance is it?" said Frank.

"So the only people who would know about William being in the bushes are Robert Gentle, his wife and daughter, if he told them, and possibly Colin Tait when he spoke to William about birds."

"What about his teacher, Mrs French? Could he have told her? " asked Frank.

"Jacqueline said that Colin Tait knew about the den but hadn't gone to see it and that Mrs French had promised to go but she didn't think she had done yet or William would have told her.," said DS Macdonald.

"Right. Salma, will you go to the French house tonight and ask Mrs French if she ever went to William's den or ever told anyone else about it."

"Yes Sir."

"Also ask her if she knew Robert Gentle before he came here."

"Will do, Sir."

"Right team, let's summarise. We're ruling out for just now the Bell twins, Bill McFarlane, Kevin because he's very tall and Claire Davidson because she's very small. That leaves us Ruth, Mary and Philip Gentle, Elizabeth French and Colin Tait. Any feelings about any of them? Fiona?"

"My money would be on Philip Gentle. He did lie about when he arrived in Glasgow."

Frances Macarthur

"Salma?"

"Colin Tait. His manner is furtive."

"Penny?"

"Same as Salma, Sir."

"Frank?"

"I agree with the DS."

The other two PCs settled on Colin Tait and on that note the meeting broke up, Frank and Penny to go to Byres Road and then on for their drink together later in the evening, Salma to do some thumb twiddling until she knew that school was over and Elizabeth French would be at home. Mrs Hobson would not take kindly to another interruption in the school day.

DS Macdonald and DCI Davenport went into her room to discuss the person *he* placed top of his suspect list.

"Well Charles we didn't hear your favourite for the role of murderer. Are you hedging your bets?"

"Would I do a thing like that?" he laughed. "No. My money for the moment is on Colin Tait though Philip Gentle would come a close second. I just can't see either Mary Gentle or Elizabeth French killing that wee boy and I've taking a liking to Ruth Gentle. She seems transparently honest."

"Right then, what jobs do you have for us Charles?"

"Let's play truant. I want to pick Pippa up from school today. Come with me. She thought she might have to do her second talk today and I'm

The Pulpit is Vacant

sure she would like to tell you all about it. I make a mean spaghetti Bolognese which you're welcome to share."

"You're on."

Fiona was delighted. Going home to her empty flat was not enticing and she had no reason to stay at work having completed all her paperwork in readiness for the meeting today

Salma, looking up from the thumb-twiddling, watched them go. If she wasn't much mistaken the DS and DCI were getting quite fond of each other. She hoped that Penny wouldn't be disappointed. Penny hadn't hidden her liking for Charles Davenport.

CHAPTER 45

Byres Road was busy, very busy as the university students made their way to family houses, bedsits or eating places. Mingling with them were the working parents hurrying home to their families and other men and women making their way to the numerous bars or to evening classes.

The Oxfam shop was crowded, always a popular place for those not in a hurry anywhere. Penny persuaded Frank, once he had parked the car, to go in on their way to Colin Tait's house. She had finished reading Elizabeth Elgin's "Where Bluebells Chime" and was hoping to find a copy of "Wind-flower Weddings", the next book in the war saga she was enjoying so much. The girl at her library in Pollokshaws had told her that the book had been withdrawn for reprinting and she was really hoping to find an old copy. She had tried the charity shops in Shawlands to no avail.

Frank, not a reader, except for The Daily Record and The News of the World was idly scanning the non-fiction shelves for a book on second hand cars as he was hoping to buy one soon when he heard a voice he thought he recognised.

"No Hill, you can't come back yet. It's not safe. Please don't go on..."

The voice tailed off and as Frank rounded the bookshelf it was just in time to see a man who looked like Colin Tait exit the shop. Frank went out too and looked up and down the street but in the sea of humanity washing up the street in both directions, he could see no Colin Tait and a girl.

At this moment Penny joined him on the pavement.

"No luck. They had two of her books but not the one I want. What are you looking for Frank?"

"I'm sure I heard Colin Tait's voice. He was talking to someone called Hill, telling her that she couldn't come back yet as it wasn't safe. I was trying to catch a glimpse of them but the crowd was too thick."

"Come on. Let's ask around in some of the nearby bars. Maybe we'll find them both or failing that get some gen on them."

Some time later, having drawn a blank in every bar and restaurant, Frank was ready to give up and go back to the Southside for his date with Penny. Penny, remembering a meal eaten in a restaurant with a Scottish title, serving Scottish food in a lane off Byres road, suggested that they try there; one

The Pulpit is Vacant

last attempt before they gave up. Frank reluctantly agreed.

They went into The Bothy. It was as busy as Penny remembered it had been when she had met her friend there.

"Table for two?" inquired a young girl wearing a mini kilt.

Frank had thought about suggesting to Penny that they have meal there but he had picked up a menu and been shocked at the prices.

Not wearing their uniforms which they had changed out of thinking that they'd be able to mingle more easily in plain-clothes, Penny and Frank had to produce their warrant cards.

"How can I help?" the pleasant-faced girl asked.

"We're looking for a couple. He's fair-haired, attractive, in his early thirties. I don't know what she's like I'm afraid but he's a schoolteacher," said Frank.

"They live round here," added Penny. "It's a long shot as they probably eat at home. He's called Colin and she's Hilary."

"He calls her Hill," added Frank.

"I'm sorry," said the girl. It doesn't ring any bells with me. Do you want me to ask the others?"

Penny and Frank said that would be fine and the girl went off, returning about five minute later with a young lad in his late teens.

"This is Ted. I'll leave you with him. He thinks he knows them."

Frances Macarthur

With a swirl of her short kilt, she moved off to show another couple to their seats.

"I'm sure I've heard someone being called Hill, only recently. In fact I think it was last night. That's right, it was early so quite quiet and they were arguing when I took their meal over."

"Arguing about what?" asked Frank.

"Sorry, I don't remember and they stopped when they saw me."

"Can you describe the girl at all?"

"Girl? There was no girl. They were both men, one fair-haired and one very dark."

"Men? Both of them?"

"Yes. Men"

"Thank you very much for your help," said Penny,

Outside in the lane, they looked at each other excitedly.

"Hill," said Frank, "Hilary. That can be a man's name too can't it?"

"So Colin Tait was sharing a flat with another man, one who gave him a poetry book. I guess they must be......"

"Poofs."

"Frank! Homosexuals please."

"They're poofs to me."

"There you go again, sexist, racist and now homophobic. Is there anyone you *do* like?"

"You."

"Well I've gone off *you* Frank Selby."

The Pulpit is Vacant

"No date tonight then?"

"No and not till you smarten up your act."

Penny stomped off to where they had left the car, her excitement over having found out that Hilary was a man dampened a bit by the crassness of Frank's attitude towards homosexuals.

Excitement bubbled up again as they drove back to the Southside on the M77. She could hardly wait to tell the DCI this bit of news but it would have to wait till the morning. Frank agreed about this.

Across the city, unaware that Hilary had been found out, Colin had managed to persuade him against coming home just yet. He knew that his relationship with another man, anathema to someone of Robert Gentle's principles, would have given him a possible motive for murder to keep his love life under wraps if somehow the minister had found out. The authorities would not like a homosexual teaching infants, nor churchgoers like such a man running a youth club. He was no paedophile and had no police record but that would not have counted for much had his secret come out.

Yes, he had had a motive for murder and he wanted no one to know.

CHAPTER 46

Salma Din had sat for some time in thumb-twiddling mode. She wanted to give Elizabeth French time to get home from school and if she was a conscientious teacher, she probably stayed behind after school to tidy up and prepare for the next day. Salma's sister Shazia was a fledgling primary teacher and she was never home much before 5 pm. Salma's long, shiny black hair was escaping from the clasps which kept it up and back from her face so she went along to the ladies cloakroom to sort it.

At ten minutes after five she was walking up the French's path. Someone was obviously a keen gardener as the front garden was a riot of colour with azaleas and rhododendrons. A rich perfume wafted up from an especially beautiful reddish orange azalea.

She rang the bell.

A young girl answered the door. She was clutching a sandwich in one hand.

"Hello, you must be Mrs French's daughter. Jill isn't it?"

"That's right."

Jill looked past Salma to the police car parked at the kerb.

"Police? Is it Mum or Dad you want? Dad's not home yet and Mum's just arrived. She's in the kitchen starting dinner."

A voice called from inside, "Jill who is it?"

"Police, Mum!" she yelled back.

"Come in," Elizabeth French said coming into the hall wiping her hands on a kitchen cloth.

"Sergeant Din, Mrs French."

They shook hands then Elizabeth French led Salma into the lounge asking Jill to keep an eye on the potatoes.

When they were seated on a comfortable brown leather settee, Salma told Elizabeth that they were trying to find out who knew about William's hideout in the manse gardens.

"Well, I knew. I had promised William that I would visit him there sometime but you know what it's like. You mean to do something and never get around to it. I never did go."

"What about Colin Tait? Had he been there?"

"I don't think so. He was busy enough with planning lessons for his wee ones. He did chat to William from time to time about birds but I'm sure he never went into the hide-out but you'll have to ask him yourself."

The Pulpit is Vacant

"Did William talk in school about his den?"

"No, not even when he was doing his hobby talk. He might have told Jacqueline Beaton, the only child he ever had much to do with but that's all. My daughter Jill knew about it as did Jim my husband because I'd talked about it but they never saw it either. I'm sure."

"One other thing," said Salma. "We're asking everyone concerned in this case if they had ever met Robert Gentle before. Had you ever seen him before he came here Mrs French?"

"No I hadn't."

"Do you know if anyone else had known him before?"

"Well Bill hadn't. At least I don't think he had. He made a comment about him being Gentle by name and not by nature which sounded to me as if he had only just met him."

"What about Claire Davidson and the Bell twins?"

"Well Mary and Andrew grew up here. My husband taught them in secondary school and they were at my school though I never taught them so if they hadn't been anywhere else I doubt they'd have met him before. I don't know about Claire I'm afraid."

The sound of the front door opening and shutting reached them.

"That'll be Jim my husband," said Elizabeth. "Jim, I'm in the lounge!" she shouted.

A tall dark-haired man, in his early forties, Salma surmised, came into the room.

"I was held up again with the local councillor. They're trying to close my school," he added. "Half my life is taken up with meetings these days."

"This is Sergeant Din, Jim."

Jim and Salma shook hands.

"She's come to ask if I knew anyone who had been to William's hide-out."

"You were going to go you said, Elizabeth," Jim said.

"Yes I've said that but I never got around to it. I don't suppose you ever saw it."

"Me? I'd heard you talk about it but I didn't even know the boy, love so why would I have gone to see it?"

"I also asked your wife if she had ever met Robert Gentle before he came here."

"And that was a negative too," Elizabeth laughed but it was a nervous laugh.

Salma wondered why Elizabeth French looked intently at her husband as she said that.

"I'm a jealous husband. I guess you noticed how my wife was quick to reassure me that she had never met the minister before."

Jim's laugh when it came was also a bit forced, Salma thought.

She thanked them both for their time and was leaving as Jill came along from the kitchen to tell her Mum that the potatoes were ready.

The Pulpit is Vacant

"Jill," said Salma. "Did you ever go to William's hide-out in the manse gardens?"

"No."

It was probably nothing; people did tend to get nervous when they were involved in a murder enquiry but she would mention to either the DS or the DCI the fact that both Elizabeth French and her husband had reacted when Mrs French had been asked if she knew the minister previously.

Meanwhile Charles Davenport and Fiona Macdonald were sitting with Pippa over plates of spaghetti Bolognese. Knowing that both Pippa and Fiona would be happier if the meal was less formal, they were all sitting at the kitchen table.

They had gone, in Charles's, car to the school and Fiona was delighted when it was obvious that Pippa was pleased to see her.

She had hurled herself into the back seat, throwing her Barbie satchel in before her and was chatting excitedly before Charles had the car up to third gear.

"I did my talk today Dad. The teacher said it was good again and my pals liked it too. I think some of them might start reading the Chalet School books now."

"Wait till we get home pet and while I'm getting dinner ready you can tell Fiona all about it."

He set about his easy meal and could hear Pippa and Fiona in the living room.

"Right Pippa, what did you tell them in your talk? Did you read from notes?"

"Daddy gave me wee cards to use again. I had headings on them. When I forgot what I was going to say I just looked at them but I didn't need them often."

"Well done. That would make it sound more natural. Did you talk about the people in the book?"

"The characters," said Pippa. "We have to call them characters."

"Sorry. Go on."

"Yes I talked about Tom Gay and Bride Bettany and Joey of course. She's in all the books, well all the books I've read so far."

She looked at Fiona inquiringly.

"I think there's only one book she's not in, as far as I can remember Pippa."

"Then I talked about my favourite bit which was when Tom made a smashing house and people at the fair had to guess its name which was Tomadit -Tom made it. I had chosen a part earlier in the book the last time."

"Do you get marks for your talks?" asked Fiona. "When I was at school we didn't do talks."

"We get a grade. E is the best and A is the worst though no one ever gets an A."

"What did you get, Pippa?" asked Charles as he came in with a big steaming casserole dish of spaghetti.

The Pulpit is Vacant

"An E," she announced proudly. "I have to do another talk later in the year but that'll be harder as I can't talk about the same thing."

"Have you got the next Chalet School book yet?" asked Fiona.

"No."

"It's called, 'The Chalet School and Rosalie'. Remember if you can't find it, I have it and you can borrow it till you get your own."

"That's great Fiona. Isn't it Daddy?"

Davenport agreed that it was indeed great and for the rest of the evening until Pippa went to bed, the talk centred round what Pippa's next talk could be. Fiona suggested that she came into the station one weekend then wrote about what police do. Pippa thought that this was a great idea. She wanted to produce pictures this time to hand round while she was talking and Charles agreed that she could take his camera with her.

Pippa comfortably tucked up in bed, Charles and Fiona settled down in the living room with a drink, Charles with his favourite Whyte and Mackay whisky with water and Fiona with a gin and tonic. They had already decided that they both needed a drink so Fiona would get a taxi home. She could walk to work the next day and he would drive her to his house after work to pick up the car, a nuisance but she really felt like a drink tonight.

Talk naturally turned to the two murders. Fiona put forward a case for Philip Gentle being the murderer.

"He could have come home to find his father abusing either his mother or sister. I know Mary Gentle said he never hit her but Ruth said he had slapped *her* on the face and anyway Mary wouldn't tell us if it gave Philip a motive. Ruth is so transparently honest that she probably didn't think how it would look when she said he had hit her."

Charles agreed that this could be the case but said that his money was now on Colin Tait. There was a mystery surrounding him somehow.

Getting nowhere, they agreed that it was pointless to continue talking about the murders.

"How do you think Salma is settling in Fiona?" asked Davenport.

"I think she's quite happy. Penny seems to have taken her under her wing which is good. There's been a bit of racism from Frank. I had to get him to apologise to her the other day. Don't imagine that would help but I couldn't let it go."

"What did he say?"

"He said there was a dreadful smell of curry in the room."

"Should I have a word with him?"

"No leave it. I think Penny will come down on him hard if she hears him and it would be better

The Pulpit is Vacant

coming from her. Frank will only get aggrieved if you say something too."

"I must shadow him again when this case is over. I've gone along with Penny once and don't need to do it again but I must do it with the others and Frank is worth watching. I noticed a difference in his treatment of a Pakistani shopkeeper. Penny coped very well, I might add."

"Yes. She'll be an asset to the force. She's quick-thinking and she cares about people."

Charles got up to pour them another drink and the talk turned to golf.

CHAPTER 47

Penny lay awake from 4am, unable to sleep for thinking about what she and Frank had discovered last night. They had agreed to go together to speak to the DCI. She opened her bedroom curtain and watched as the black of night turned to the grey of dawn and then to the pale blue of early morning. The birds had been singing for hours.

Her euphoria of last night had evaporated. She had liked Colin Tait and had been sure that this gentle, fair-haired young man was not capable of murder, especially the murder of a young child. Now it appeared that, as well as opportunity, he could also have had a motive though what she did not know. Why did he need to hide his homosexuality now when he had shared a flat openly before?

It was time to get up.

She had arranged to meet Frank in the canteen at 8.30. Neither of them wanted to steal a march on the other and break the news to the boss without the other one present.

In the canteen, Frank, early for probably the first time in his life, was sitting tucking heartily into a plate of scrambled eggs on toast. She sat down across from him, having picked up a bacon roll.

They ate quickly.

Penny knocked on the DCI's door and they went in together when they heard his, "Come in."

"Morning, Penny. Morning, Frank."

"Morning, Sir," they chorused.

"Sir," said Frank. "We went over to the West End yesterday as you asked us to and we've found out something important about Colin Tait."

"What is it?"

"His flatmate Hilary is a man Sir," Penny burst out.

Davenport went to the door and called down the corridor.

"Right everyone. Incident room. Now."

When everyone had assembled he told them the news.

"That explains why his nameplate was scribbled," said DS Macdonald. "I thought with him being such a neat person, it was odd for him to have a rough and ready nameplate. Obviously the other one had Hilary's name on it too. When we discovered that he had shared the flat he would be delighted that we'd assumed Hilary was a woman."

The Pulpit is Vacant

"Well. All this looks very suspicious," said Davenport. "Surely only a guilty man would go to all this bother to stop us finding out that he was a homosexual."

"And it gives him a motive," said Penny who had had time to work this out. "If Mr Gentle knew of his liking for young men, he could have got him sacked from his job probably or Colin thought he could but how would Mr Gentle have known?"

"I think I'll visit this young man again, tell him what we now know and see what he says this time," Davenport said. "Any other news for us? Salma you were seeing Mrs French. Did anything transpire there?"

"She hadn't been to William's hide-out though she had been invited by the boy. Never got round to it she said. She didn't think that Colin Tait had been. I got the idea that the hide-out was a very private place that only special people like the teacher he was obviously fond of knew about. One schoolgirl might have known but who would she tell? Mr French and their daughter knew but neither had been to it."

"What about knowing Robert Gentle before?"

"That was a bit strange. She said she hadn't met him before then when her husband came in and she told him what I had asked, she seemed nervous. He made a joke about being a jealous husband and he laughed but it seemed a bit forced. Probably nothing."

"Yes people often get stressed during murder enquiries but we'll bear it in mind. Thanks Salma."

Davenport left. If he went quickly he could get to the primary school in time for the interval and not have to disturb Colin Tait during class time.

He was lucky. The bell rang just as he was pulling into the car-park. He made his way to the head teacher's room. Out of courtesy he would have to let Mrs Hobson know that he was in the school. He was surprised that he had got as far as her room without being challenged. After the Dunblane shootings, schools had tightened up on security.

When he was seated in her room he mentioned this and she was quick to point out that there was a colour coded pass which was different for every week but that the janitor was off sick and the office secretary had had to go home suddenly as her elderly mother had taken ill. He told her that he wanted to speak to Colin Tait again.

"Is he a suspect chief inspector?"

"Not more so than anyone else but there are one or two things I want to clear up with him."

Mrs Hobson pointed him in the direction of the staffroom and he made his way there. He knocked and entered.

There were three people in the room, one of whom he had never seen before. One was Pippa's teacher, the other Colin Tait.

"Mr Tait, is there anywhere we could have a quiet talk?"

The Pulpit is Vacant

Colin got up and led him out of the staffroom and into a small adjacent room housing a photocopier, a table and two hard chairs.

They sat down.

"Now Mr Tait, you have been less than honest with us."

Colin paled.

"You let us think that you lived alone when you have been sharing a flat with a young man called Hilary."

Colin was startled and rushed in, "Who I share a flat with has nothing to do with the murders."

"Well in that case why were you not open about you and Hilary?"

"Isn't it obvious? I'm a primary schoolteacher, an infant class teacher. If it got out that I was homosexual, my job would be in danger."

"How did you get through the Enhanced Disclosure check?"

"I'm not a paedophile, Inspector. I haven't had any dealings with young boys, so I have nothing to declare and there is no history for them to find out."

"Ok. Now that we know, do you have anything to add about the nights of the two murders?"

"I was with Hill both nights. One night we were in the flat once I got home from the meeting and the other night, as I said, we were at the pictures in a cinema just off Byres Road."

"I can't understand why you didn't tell us about your partner even if just to give yourself an alibi. I think there is still something you're not telling us, Mr Tait. I'd advise you to tell us the whole truth now. Things look bad for you already so don't make things worse."

"I've nothing more to say." Colin was adamant.

"Well in that case, I want to see you down at the station. My car is outside. Let Mrs Hobson know and meet me outside.

He left Colin staring after him.

CHAPTER 48

Mary Gentle hummed as she prepared breakfast for herself. She was having her first driving lesson this morning. She should have felt nervous but she did not. She felt excited and almost like a teenager again.

Since admitting to the police that she had lied to them about when Philip had arrived home, she had felt almost free. She hadn't realised the shackles that had bound her in her life with Robert until they were removed.

Ruth came down first. She only ever had cornflakes for breakfast. She was in a hurry as she was meeting Kevin in town.

"Good luck," she kissed her mother.

"Thanks dear. Take care."

Philip came downstairs about nine o'clock and wolfed into the bacon and eggs and tomato that Mary put in front of him. He had decided to pack up some of his books this morning. Although living here would now be much happier, he had told his mother that he wanted to return to Australia and make his life there and she was happy for him that he had made up his mind what to do with his life.

What should she wear for the lesson wondered Mary? Trousers might be best. She would wear one of the nice pairs that she had bought yesterday when she and Ruth went into town. One pair was light grey and the other navy. Robert would have hated them and she would never have worn trousers when he was alive as she hated unpleasantness and kept the peace by always wearing a skirt or a dress, a 'frock' Robert had called it, much to Ruth's annoyance. They had stayed in town for their meal and had come home then gone almost straight out to meet Kevin at one of the wine bars which apparently were quite new on the Southside. She had had her hair done, a blow dry they called it. It made a change from the curly set which she usually had. Her mousy fair hair had been given a rinse as well and she hardly recognised the woman who had looked back at her out of the mirror when the stylist had finished with her hair.

Ruth had put on a little make up for her before they went to meet Kevin. He had given a quiet wolf whistle, not loud enough to embarrass her and she had been secretly thrilled at his response.

Well it was time to go down to Shawlands, to the driving school on Kilmarnock Road. She threw a light jacket on over her pale blue jumper which went very well with the navy trousers, picked up

The Pulpit is Vacant

her bag and, saying goodbye to Philip, she left the house.

It took her less than ten minutes to reach the driving school and five minutes after that she was seated in the passenger seat of a red Fiat Uno. The instructor explained the gears to her and the pedals then drove away from the kerb. After about five minutes when they had reached the quieter streets of Newlands, he stopped and they changed places. The lesson passed without a hitch. Mary enjoyed sitting behind the wheel and felt that she had done reasonably well for someone who was not technically minded.

"Well done Mrs Gentle," the instructor said and Mary who had had scant praise during her married life, felt a glow of satisfaction.

She decided to look in at the estate agents of which there were a few in Shawlands.

She was looking for somewhere in this area she had decided. No one had really known Robert and her as a couple here and it could be a fresh start. The only drawback - how could she be so callous as to see two murders as a set-back, she wondered - was that she would be associated with a crime but then she would be associated with it wherever she went.

The estate agent showed her pictures of some flats but she really wanted a small garden. She loved gardening. It had been the best thing about living in a manse.

He showed her some houses but she felt that they were too big and would be too expensive. She did not yet know what she would get for the house they had bought in Leven. It was quite near Lundin Links golf course as Robert had been a keen golfer. Maybe that would be a selling point. She hoped so.

Thanking the estate agent for his help and promising to come back once she knew what she was getting for the Fife house, she went back outside.

"Time for a coffee," she thought.

There were plenty of places to choose from and no rush. Again that feeling of freedom surged through her. She had all afternoon and only Ruth and herself to make a meal for. Ruth had promised to be back around six. She and Kevin, now that their exams were over, were going to look for summer jobs. Kevin had been born and brought up in Glasgow and wanted to stay here and Ruth was happy to do that now that her Mum was going to stay here too. If they passed their exams they both hoped to go on to do honours. If they could not get rooms together she hoped that she could stay with her Mum.

Mary went into Costa Coffee and ordered a latte. She sat down at a table at the back and taking out her notebook, she began to write down what she wanted from a house - a lounge, two bedrooms, preferably one ensuite, kitchen and bathroom

The Pulpit is Vacant

and a small garden. She realised that what she was looking for was a modern flat on the ground floor, maybe one of those retirement flats though she would quite like a dog so it would have to be one which allowed pets. Another thing Robert Gentle had been adamant about was that they were having no pets, not even when the children were small.

Her latte arrived. She closed the notebook and sat back feeling very relaxed. She sipped her drink then, when it was finished, decided that she would do some shopping, probably at Nan Brodie's store, on her way home.

It took her only five minutes to get to the store. Picking up her basket, she thought about what they would have for dinner tonight. No need now for fresh vegetables. She would probably keep using them but for tonight she was going to make an easy meal. Ruth would not mind. Picking up a bag of frozen chips and a bag of frozen peas, she wondered what to have with them.

"Mary. How are you?"

Elizabeth French had come into the shop.

"I'm fine," said Mary gaily, then realising how bad that would sound, she apologised.

"Sorry Beth. That sounds awful considering the circumstances but I've just had my first driving lesson and I feel quite proud of myself."

"Don't apologise. I could see how it was with you and Robert. You're entitled to feel a bit free."

Mary blushed. How timid she must have looked to other people seeing her with her husband. They could not know the reason for this and she did not know Elizabeth French well enough to enlighten her. She thought to herself, 'If you only knew the half of it' and wondered if she would ever be able to tell anyone what she had gone through with Robert. Certainly not Ruth or Philip but maybe a friend if she ever had a close enough one to share secrets with.

Nan Brodie listening to their conversation, stored it all up for her circle of gossip-loving friends.

CHAPTER 49

DCI Davenport said nothing to Colin Tait as they were driving to the station and as that young man was experiencing mind-numbing fear, he said nothing either and the journey was made in silence.

When the car was safely parked in the staff car park, they got out, still silent and made their way to reception.

"Is there an interview room free?" demanded Davenport.

"Yes Sir, they're all free," the policeman on duty replied.

"I'll be using Room One. Ask DC Macdonald to join me there please."

Entering the room, the DCI walked over to the recording machine, switched it on and said into it, "DCI Davenport. Interview with Colin Tait. May 15th, 2.39pm"

He sat down at the table which along with four utility chairs, was the only furniture in the room and motioned to Colin to sit across from him.

Silence.

After what to Colin seemed ages but was probably only a few minutes, the door opened and DS Macdonald entered.

Davenport switched on the recording machine.

"DS Macdonald entering the room at 2.42."

Trying to give the young man some space, the DCI sat with his hands on his knees. DS Macdonald leaned back in the chair.

"Mr Tait I am going to ask you again. Why did you omit to tell us that you had been, on the evenings of both murders, with your flatmate Hilary?"

No response.

"What is Hilary's surname?"

"Mason."

"How do you spell Hillary ? One L or two?"

"Just one. It's the way a girl spells it but his Dad didn't know that when he had the birth registered."

"Mr Tait. You said that you were afraid that you would lose your job if it was known that you were having a homosexual relationship with Mr Mason but was this not better than being accused of murder?"

No reply.

"Colin. There's something you're not telling us."

The Pulpit is Vacant

Colin sat with his head in his hands, and then he looked up.

"I want a lawyer."

"You are perfectly within your rights to have a lawyer. Do you have one of your own?"

"Yes."

"Davenport spoke into the tape machine.

"Interview ending at 2.53."

He and Fiona left the room.

A few minutes later a police constable arrived and escorted Colin to a cell.

"What do you think Fiona? Is he guilty?"

"My gut feeling is that he isn't. He's scared stiff, that's for sure but I think it's being in this unknown situation and thinking he might be accused of murder that's scaring him."

"So what else is he not telling us? Why the refusal to speak?"

"He must think there's something else incriminating that we might find out. Could he be protecting Hilary?"

"It's possible. But what motive could Hilary have?"

"Maybe Hilary or Colin himself for that matter knew Robert Gentle before he came here."

"That's a possibility, Fiona. I think I'll take that line of questioning if his lawyer can get him to speak."

They went back to Davenport's room where they had a coffee. About half an hour later a call

Frances Macarthur

from the desk told them that Colin Tait's lawyer had arrived.

They went to the desk. A pleasant-faced young man in a smart dark suit was waiting there.

"John Swift, Inspector. I'm Colin Tait's lawyer and his friend too. What's he being questioned for?"

"It's in regard to a double murder. He claimed to being on his own on the nights of the murders but now we find out that he was with his boyfriend Hilary Mason on both nights. We can't get him to say any more. Maybe you can explain to him that he can't be in any more serious trouble than he is now if he tells us something else incriminating. He could be shielding Hilary and if he is and Hilary *is* involved then he would be an accessory. It would be better for him to be honest with us now."

"I can't imagine either of them committing murder but I can see that it looks black for Colin especially if he insists on remaining silent."

"Thanks for seeing it our way Mr Swift."

"Is there somewhere where I can talk to him?"

"Certainly."

This was arranged and once again Davenport and his detective sergeant went back to Davenport's room. They were not there long before there was another call from the desk that the lawyer was waiting to speak to them.

"I've spoken to Colin, Inspector and he understands that nothing he tells you can make you suspect him any more than you already do. He is willing to talk to you now."

Charles asked the constable standing at the desk to bring Colin back to the interview room and the three of them went along there to wait for him.

Davenport went through the ritual once again of informing the tape machine who was in the room, the date and the time which was now 4.02pm. He mentioned that there was now a lawyer named John Swift present.

"Now, Mr Tait. Will you please tell us why you hid from us the fact that you were in a relationship with Hilary Mason in whose company you were on the nights of both murders?"

"I'm sorry chief inspector. John has made me see that things couldn't be bleaker for me than they are now. I had better start at the beginning. "I went into the army when I left school."

Davenport's surprise must have shown in his face because Colin went on:

"Yes I know. I'm not the army type. I didn't want to go but my father- probably trying to 'make a man of me' - he put a sardonic emphasis on the phrase -persuaded me that I should. I hated it from day one. I was bullied by the other boys except one, a young man called Lewis, who was, like me, a gentle boy totally unsuited to army life. We became friends to much ridicule from the others.

Davenport made sympathetic noises. He could well imagine the hell the two quiet, timid boys would have gone through.

Colin continued: "I decided to go to the chaplain. I thought he would listen to me and perhaps find some way to help us. As you might have guessed" - DS Macdonald had started when he mentioned the word chaplain - "it was Robert Gentle I went to see."

"And he wasn't sympathetic?"

"Anything but. He described us as shirt lifters and poofs and said that maybe some time in the army would cure us.

"Decidedly unhelpful."

Fiona Macdonald's voice was quiet but Davenport caught the sympathy behind her words and wondered if she too had been bullied at some time in her life.

"We were not having a relationship, Inspector. We were just good friends. I didn't realise my leanings towards men until I left the army."

"Where did you go after the army, Colin?"

"I wasn't welcome at home. My mother was in awe of my father and my older brother and would not put up a fight when my father said he was ashamed of me and didn't want to see me again. My brother had been in the army before me and felt that I had brought shame to the family name."

"So if not back home, where?"

The Pulpit is Vacant

"I came to Scotland where I worked in pubs and saved to get to college. I shared a flat with three girls. I had saved money from my army days so that, plus my wages from the bar work, helped me pay for the accommodation and for the college fees. I went to Jordanhill, got a BEd and started primary teaching.

"Was Southview your first school?"

"No, I taught in a school in Bearsden at first but realised that I wanted to work with infants so went back to train for my Froebel qualification. I came here three years ago and have taken the infant class every year since then. I like the innocence of the very young child inspector."

"How did you meet Hilary?"

"He was the brother of one of the girls with whom I shared the flat. He was my first and only partner."

"So let me guess. Robert Gentle recognised you?"

"Yes."

"Was it that night you went up to the manse?"

"Yes. I went to his first service. I recognised his name and hoped against hope that it wasn't the same man but it was.

When he called the youth workers to a meeting and then asked Mrs Hobson if he could meet the infants' teacher, I was forced into going to see him. I went late in the hope that I wouldn't have to be there for long but that went wrong as Bill and

Elizabeth had already left and the others got up to go as I came in so I was in a one-to-one situation with him."

"Did he recognise you right away?"

"Probably but he is, or rather was, a cruel man, so he let me drink some tea first then he said, 'So we meet again Colin.' "

"How did you feel then?"

"I felt sick. I admit Sir that I felt murderous. I wanted to choke the life out of him, wipe the sneering look off his face but, and I know this will be hard to believe, I did nothing."

"What else did he say?"

"Something about the school authorities having to know."

"What did you do then?"

"I heard myself pleading with him then realised that I was letting myself be bullied again and I ran to the door, let myself out and fled. I'm not a brave man."

Colin sounded disgusted with himself and Fiona Macdonald felt pity for him. As Davenport had rightly guessed, she had been bullied at school and had determined never to let it happen again as she was sure Colin had too only to be defeated by someone to whom bullying came as second nature.

"And you thought that if we knew all this it would make you a suspect Colin?" she said quietly.

"Yes."

The Pulpit is Vacant

"You see if you had returned that night, William Paterson could have recognised you," said Davenport

"I couldn't have killed that wee boy Inspector and I got home very quickly that night. I needed Hill and his reassurance. I got home about 9.30. I drove very fast I'm afraid. Once I'd calmed down, I realised, of course, that I wouldn't be sacked for being a homosexual but at the time it seemed quite believable."

"Are you trying to make me suspect you, Colin?" Davenport laughed. "Well you've been honest now". He spoke once more into the tape machine, "Interview ended at 5.31pm."

He switched off the tape.

"Go home Colin. I can see you feeling murderous towards Robert Gentle but I can't see you bashing in the head of William Paterson. I could be wrong. Remember that you are still a suspect so don't leave the country."

He laughed to soften the command.

Colin, looking as if he had been in a fight with Mike Tyson, left the room with his friend and Charles and Fiona went back to Charles's room once again.

"What a thoroughly nasty man, Robert Gentle was," said Fiona. "I hope that Colin Tait can get through this with his reputation intact. If he's proved innocent does the fact that he's homosexual have to come out?"

333

Frances Macarthur

"It'll be hard to keep it quiet but let's see how we get on with our next suspect. I'm going to call Philip Gentle in for questioning tomorrow. Would you come with me to see Hilary? It shouldn't take long."

"No problem. I'm going out to play bridge tonight but not till 8pm."

They arrived, parked with difficulty and made their way to Colin's flat. It was obvious that he had only just arrived before them as he still had his anorak on.

"I expected you Inspector. Come in."

They went into the living room and Hilary rose from the settee.

"Hello. I'm Hilary. I'm so glad that this has come out into the open. It's great to be back home."

Dark haired and quite short, he was the antithesis of Colin.

"Mr Mason. Can you confirm for us that Colin was with you on the evenings of May the 6th which was a Tuesday and May the 9th, a Friday."

"Well we go to the pictures once a week and we went on Friday that week."

"What did you see?"

"It was a French film called "La Vie Noire". We went to the GFT just off Sauchiehall Street."

"And after that?"

"We came straight home. We were home by about 10.30 which was lucky as Colin got a phone call minutes after we got back."

The Pulpit is Vacant

"Mr Tait you never mentioned that."

"Sorry I forgot. It was a college friend phoning to remind me of a reunion next week."

"We can check that Sir. Thank you. Where does your friend live? What's his phone number?"

Colin supplied this information. Fiona wrote it down.

"And on the Tuesday, Mr Mason?"

"On the Tuesday I stayed in and was here when Colin came back from the meeting. There was a good film on TV that night, an old Charlton Heston one. I forget the title right now. After Colin told me what had happened we watched the film. I don't think we took much of it in."

"Any phone calls that night?"

"Sorry, no. Our neighbour, Carol, popped in but only briefly around nine to borrow some milk."

"Thank you for your help Mr Davis."

They called at Carol Livingstone's door to check and she had gone in for milk and she had seen both men.

The two police officers left. Charles took Fiona back to the station where she got into her own car and drove off. He went upstairs to his office and wrote up the meeting with Hilary Mason, brief as it was, and then drove off to his sister's to pick up his daughter.

It had been a long day.

CHAPTER 50

Thursday morning was another miserable, wet day, more like March than May. Penny stood on the steps of the station and shook her umbrella. She had brought a cheerful one, red with white polka dots on it, to keep her spirits up as she had felt a bit down last night after hearing about Colin being brought in for questioning. She liked the young man and hoped that he was innocent of both crimes especially the murder of wee William.

The constable at the desk told her that a meeting was scheduled for 9am in the Incident Room. She had had breakfast at home but realising that she had time for a cup of tea she went down to the canteen in the basement of the building.

Salma was seated there, nursing a mug of tea in her hands and looking thoughtful.

"Hi Salma," said Penny. "Wonder what the meeting's about."

"Probably to bring us up to date about the interview with Colin Tait yesterday," replied Salma.

"I hope that Frank will be on time today," said Penny worriedly.

"Why don't you give him a ring to speed him up?" suggested Salma.

Penny's eyes lit up. What an idiot she was! Of course that's what she should do. Taking out her mobile phone she rang his number.

"Hello."

"Frank it's me, Penny. Get a move on. There's a meeting scheduled for 9 o'clock. You don't want to be late."

"Thanks Penny, you're a pal."

"It was Salma's idea to ring you," Penny told him.

"Oh. See you soon." He rang off.

Nine o'clock saw them all seated in the Incident room. Frank had arrived out of breath at five minutes to nine. The DCI took the floor.

"DS Macdonald and I interviewed Colin Tait yesterday. He admitted to having known Robert Gentle years ago at Catterrick. Colin is a homosexual and Robert Gentle knew that. Colin didn't want us to find out either that he was homosexual or that he knew Robert Gentle as he thought that would give us a reason for suspecting him.

It seems that the minister recognised him at the meeting that night and taunted Colin."

"What a horrible man!" Penny could not help interrupting.

The Pulpit is Vacant

"Yes Penny. You're right. He was a bully and now we know a homophobe who would have reported Colin to the Education Authorities."

"Was he not right Sir? We don't want gay men teaching our kids, do we?" Frank sounded indignant.

"Not paedophiles Selby but Colin was in a relationship with another adult and I don't think would have harmed a child. He loves the wee ones he teaches."

Frank looked sceptical.

"So you're ruling him out Sir?" This came from Salma, sounding pleased. She, like Penny, had liked the young man.

"Well we can't rule him out completely but he does have an alibi now as he was with his partner at the time of both murders."

"But surely you can't believe what a p....what his partner says Sir? Would you believe a husband or wife if they gave their partner an alibi?"

"That's why I'm saying we can't rule him out completely, Selby."

Penny wanted to shut Frank up but she wasn't sitting beside him. Surely he must realise that the DCI was annoyed with him as he kept using his surname instead of calling him Frank as he usually did

"I'm going to ask Philip Gentle to come to the station this morning. He's the other one with no firm alibi. Salma I'd like you to be with me at

339

this interview please. It will be experience for you. Come with me now and I'll brief you on what will happen."

"Yes Sir."

"Penny and Frank get your report about Colin Tait written up and Fiona will you do me a favour and collect Pippa from school at 3pm for me?"

"Of course I will," Fiona replied.

"I've done the report already Sir," replied Penny.

"Good girl. After the meeting with Philip Gentle, I want to go round and see the Patersons, keep them up to date with what is happening, and also see Mary Gentle for the same reason. They must be wondering and knowing them will not like to contact us. I won't name names but just tell them that we have two suspects in the frame. I also want to see Solomon Fairchild. This might make me late for Pippa and she knows you well enough to come with you. I'll give you a key for the house. Is that OK? Are you going out tonight?"

"No I'm not and it's fine."

Charles decided to see the assistant chief constable first. He climbed the stairs to the next floor and was lucky to catch him about to leave for home. As usual, Fairchild was affable and pleased to hear that the suspects in the two cases had been narrowed to two. Asking Charles to "keep him up to speed", he accompanied him downstairs.

Things were at last speeding up.

CHAPTER 51

Philip Gentle was sitting reading The Herald in the study. No one liked to sit in the lounge now. The bloodstain was still there. It seemed pointless to remove it or get a new carpet when they would be moving out shortly though Mary knew that she could not leave the evidence of the murder for the new minister whoever he or she might be. She had been told by the kirk session that it would probably take a long time for the church to get another minister and that she was welcome to stay for as long as it took for her to find her new house but she wanted to leave as quickly as possible as this house held no fond memories for her or her children.

Unable to concentrate on the newspaper, Philip recalled his mother's words last night. She had told him and Ruth that she had been into an estate agent's that day and knew what she was looking for. She wanted to remain in the south side of Glasgow and she wanted a ground floor flat with a small garden. She asked them to help her by going through to Leven, to the estate agent's there, to get the house put on the market. He and Ruth had said that of course they would go with her and they had agreed to go through next Monday when hopefully the roads would be quieter. Ruth would drive her father's car which they had had insured for both her and Philip. Philip was a bit nervous about driving through Glasgow but would maybe drive on the quieter roads. Ruth having finished her exams, was free till she got a summer job and Philip was free till he returned to Melbourne. He had an open ticket.

He was pondering on what date he should return home which was how he thought of Australia now when the phone rang in the hall. He sat where he was as the chances of it being for him were slim.

He was mistaken. His mother called him out to the hall.

"Philip, it's Detective Inspector Davenport for you dear." His mother looked a bit anxious as she held out the receiver to her son.

"Philip Gentle speaking."

"Mr Gentle I would like you to come into the station this afternoon please. There are some questions I need to put to you."

"What time Inspector?"

"2 pm please. Do you need picked up?"

"No it's not that far. I'll walk."

The Pulpit is Vacant

At 2pm promptly, Philip presented himself at the police station. The constable on the desk was expecting him and showed him along the corridor to an interview room. As he sat at the bare table and looked at the recording machine on the wall beside it, Philip remembered all the crime films he had seen on TV and felt afraid.

This was to be no cosy chat.

Davenport did not keep him waiting long. He and Salma entered the room together and, sitting down, Davenport switched on the machine, saying as he did so:

"DCI Davenport and Sergeant Salma Din, interview with Philip Gentle. May 16th, 2.13pm."

Putting his hands on the table, he motioned to Salma to sit beside him.

"Mr Gentle I have to tell you that you are still in the frame for your father's murder. You were foolish to lie to us about when you arrived in Glasgow and you have no one to back up your story about sleeping in a friend's flat."

"I gave you my friend's address Sir and the names of the people who were there that night."

"Yes but every time we've been across there's been no one in. Phone calls have met with the same lack of success."

"Eric Wilson who owns the flat is a rep and often away."

"Well we'll try Eric again tonight and maybe you would give us his mobile number."

Frances Macarthur

Philip provided the necessary information and Salma wrote it down.

"Perhaps you would now tell us what happened when you did go to the manse on the day of the murder."

"I went across late in the afternoon when I knew that Ruth would be in. I had phoned her on her mobile from Eric's flat.

"Why did Ruth need to be at home Sir?" asked Salma.

Davenport sent her an approving look.

"I needed support and she was the stronger of the two of us. Mum was too in awe of my father to be of any help."

"What happened when you got there?" Davenport asked this question.

"Mum came to the door. We hugged each other, and then Ruth joined us. Then my father came out of what turned out to be his study. If I had hoped for a welcome I was unlucky," Philip said bitterly.

"What did he say?"

"He said, 'So the prodigal returns. Am I to kill the fatted calf?' His tone was really sarcastic. Mum managed to get us all to go into the lounge where we sat, all except my father who stood. He seemed to tower over me. I felt nervous and slightly sick."

"Why should you feel nervous Mr Gentle?"

"Please would you call me Philip chief inspector? Mr Gentle was always my father."

"Why did you feel nervous, Philip?"

The Pulpit is Vacant

"I knew what I was going to say wouldn't please him. Far from it."

"Go on."

"He said had I come to my senses and decided to come home and go to university and I said that I had only come for some of my clothes and personal belongings as I had decided to stay in Melbourne."

"What happened then?"

"Mum gave a cry and said, 'Oh Philip!' Ruth said something like, 'Good for you!' Dad asked me if I was scared of academic work and I said I preferred manual work. He said I could expect no financial help from him and I told him I was going into a surfing business with a friend."

He asked what I knew about surfing and I said that I was going to do the business side of things. I had done well in business studies at school in third year and had taken a course in Melbourne last year."

"What did he say to that?"

"He said I was a big girl's blouse. That was one of his favourite expressions Sir."

"Then what?"

"He just got up and walked to the door. He turned at the door and said, 'You are no longer my son. I disown you.'"

"How did that make you feel?"

"Well I almost laughed. It sounded like a line from a Victorian novel then I felt relieved that there had been no shouting, and then sorry for Mum I suppose."

"Then what did you do?"

"I put my arms round Mum who was crying now. Ruth put her arms round both of us then I said that I had better get my things before he came back and told me to leave so they helped me carry my stuff outside - it was still packed up from their removal. I rang for a taxi which came quite quickly and I left to go back across town."

"How were your Mum and Ruth when you left?" Salma wanted to know.

"Mum was upset and Ruth seemed angry but resigned too. They both knew that I would keep in touch with them as I had before."

"So you felt no hatred for him?" Salma asked.

"I didn't like him, that's for sure. I knew he would blame Mum for how I'd turned out but I knew that I could rely on Ruth to stand up for her as she always does...sorry...did. No I didn't hate him, well not enough to kill him."

"Thank you Philip." said Davenport.

He turned towards the recording machine.

"Interview ended at 2.55pm"

Philip rubbed his sweating hands on his trousers and stood up.

"What now?" he asked.

"Give us the addresses of your friends and we'll pay them a visit. You are free to leave the station. Where are you staying just now?"

The Pulpit is Vacant

"With my Mum and my sister."

"Although you are not in custody till we get your friends' statements, you are not free to leave the country. OK?"

"Of course, Sir. My Mum needs me right now anyway so even if I was not a suspect I wouldn't be leaving yet. I have an open ticket."

Davenport walked him to the door and watched as he walked along the corridor and out of the station.

"Well done Salma. Your questions were good ones. What do you think?"

"I know we need to speak to his friends Sir but I don't think he needed to kill his father. He might have had to endure more unpleasantness if they had met up again but other than that he was escaping back to Australia and need never see him again, so why kill him?"

"Out of anger at how he knew his father would treat his mother, perhaps?"

"But he knew how his father treated his mother and she had survived years of it so why would Philip suddenly become murderous?"

"I don't know Salma. Would you like to be the one to question his friend Eric? Phone first on that umber Philip gave you and arrange a meeting as soon as possible. Take either Penny or Frank with you."

"I'll take Penny Sir."

"How are you getting on with young Frank?"

Frances Macarthur

"Ok Sir but I get on really well with Penny."

Davenport walked with her till they reached his room when he left her to go and ring Eric Wilson. He would have been horrified if he had known what Mary Gentle had had to suffer the night Philip had declared his intention of returning to Australia permanently. Apart from the usual sexual abuse he usually doled out to her when one of their children angered him, in the morning he had made her stand in the corner of the room, naked, for an hour while he sat up in bed and read his Bible.

CHAPTER 52

"Penny. Would you mind coming with me to see Philip Gentle's friend later on? The DCI asked me to go and take someone with me."

"Of course not, Sarge. When will you be leaving?"

"I rang the man, Eric Wilson, and he'll be at home after 6pm."

"Is it Ok if I go home and have my meal first?"

"Of course. That's what I'll do after I've written up what happened at the interview with Philip."

She told Penny what had happened, arranged where they should meet and shortly afterwards Penny left.

Salma walked to her desk, passing Frank's desk on the way.

"Did you hear what I said to Penny about Philip, Frank?"

Frank continued with what he was doing without even looking up. As she stood there feeling a bit foolish, he shouted something across the room to one of the older constables who looked embarrassed at his blanking of the sergeant but answered Frank.

"Think the Paki men have the right idea. They keep their women chained to the sink. Sorry Salma, did you say something?"

"It doesn't matter constable. I wouldn't want to keep you from your work." Salma, her head held high, walked out of the room.

His enjoyment at embarrassing the sergeant in front of the other men was lessened when he remembered that it had been Salma's idea to get Penny to phone him that morning to get him in in time.

Charles had gone to his room after visiting Philip Gentle and eaten some sandwiches he had prepared that morning. He was trying to watch his weight and found the canteen food stodgy. Also he knew that his presence in the canteen tended to stop the natural flow of conversation. The sandwiches were to have been for lunch but he had skipped that. He had a coffee from his coffee maker then put on his jacket and, picking up his car keys, left the room.

He looked into the incident room and saw Salma sitting at a desk. She smiled at him and told him that she had reached Eric Wilson on his mobile and he would be at home that evening.

"I've spoken to Penny Sir and she's happy to come with me. She's gone home now to have her tea. I'm meeting her later."

The Pulpit is Vacant

"Why are you sitting in here Salma?"

"It was quieter to phone from here. The other room is busy."

Davenport glanced into the other room on his way out. Frank and the other two PCs were sharing a joke and a burst of laughter came out to him.

"Her mother's a cornflake. Everyone has her for breakfast. I wouldn't touch her with..."

"Got that report written up Frank?"

"Yes Sir."

As he walked down the corridor he heard someone singing and recognised the words as being "Speed Bonny Boat" - not what he would have thought Selby would have known. The Skye Boat Song! He'd thought that he would have been a modern pop man. He would have been even more mystified if he had heard the laughter that followed.

He would have been angry to know that Salma had moved out of the room because of Selby's refusal to answer her and his racist remark about Asian men. Frank was a popular man and the other two were not brave enough to risk Frank's displeasure by standing up for her. They all chatted with Penny so she figured it was mainly racism that stopped them from talking to her, though in Frank's case it was obvious that her promotion still rankled with him too.

Never mind, she had a friend in Penny she thought as she collected her hat and jacket and left the building. She had heard the song being sung and recognising the tune from school music periods, she knew that the boys were poking fun at the DCI and the DS. It was, she thought, quite clever but she hoped for everyone's sake that neither Davenport nor DS Macdonald found out. They would be embarrassed to be the talk of the station and it might nip in the bud any friendship which was building up there.

Davenport went to the manse first. He had nothing to tell the family but felt it would be polite to let them know that nothing had as yet been discovered. He had had two men searching once again in the manse grounds but no knife had been found.

Mary Gentle led him into the kitchen.

"It's the cheeriest room in the house Inspector."

"Mrs Gentle. You know we've questioned Philip and we still have to check his alibi for the first murder. We're checking the alibi of another young man too. I'll keep you informed."

Mary Gentle smiled.

"I know my son and I'm not afraid for him any more as I was stupidly at first."

Philip came into the kitchen and Davenport stayed just long enough to tell him that Eric was being seen that night and to reassure Mary Gentle that they were still doing their best to find her husband's murderer.

The Pulpit is Vacant

The next visit, to the Patersons, was even less pleasant. Once again he was merely there to reassure them that the police were doing everything they could to find William's murderer. He promised to keep them up to date and left, heading for home.

CHAPTER 53

Fiona Macdonald was outside the primary school at about 3.15. She didn't want to be late for meeting Pippa. She sat in her car and watched as mums and a few dads congregated at the school gate. Some had younger children with them, some had babies in prams. There were a few older folk, no doubt grandparents. One young woman had a beautiful Shetland sheepdog on a lead. It was standing with its long aristocratic nose through the railings, desperate to catch sight of its young owner. Fiona had never hankered after children of her own but somehow the woman with the dog made her feel envious all of a sudden and she wished that she could be here waiting for her own child.

"Don't be an idiot!" she was sharp with herself.

The bell rang and it seemed almost immediately that the first children came bursting out of the building. Fiona got out of the car and walked over to the school gate. When she saw Pippa she was with a boy, slightly older who was carrying her school bag. They were talking animatedly or rather Pippa was talking and the boy was listening. When she saw Fiona, Pippa came running over, the boy following.

"Hi Fiona, Are you here to pick me up? This is Ronald. I'll take my bag now thanks."

The boy, blushing, handed over the Barbie bag and ran off.

"Who's he Pippa, your boyfriend?"

"Don't be silly Fiona. I'm too young for that sort of nonsense. No, he's the school bully."

"What?"

"He bullies everyone, even some of the older boys."

"So why was he carrying your bag?"

"Well he tried to bully me when I arrived and I just gave him a look, like this" - she put on such a disgusted look that Fiona nearly laughed. It was the kind of look you put on when a nasty smell reached your nose - "and told not to be silly and go away and give me peace."

"And?"

"Well ever since that he's been really nice to me and offers to carry my bag. I think he just wants a friend and I haven't made any close ones yet so he can be mine."

There was no answer to that so Fiona led Pippa across to her car telling her as she did so that her Dad was busy and that she had been given the

The Pulpit is Vacant

key and would stay with Pippa till her Dad got home.

Once she was safely in the car and had put her seatbelt on, Pippa announced, "It's cool to be sitting in the front like an adult again. I think those children's seats are for babies, not for someone my age."

Fiona was horrified. Not having anything to do with children, she had forgotten the car seat rule and obviously with other things on his mind, Charles had forgotten to transfer it from his car to hers.

Now what?

"Pippa, we're breaking the law not having you in one of those children's seats. Your Dad must have forgotten. Nip into the back seat and I'll just drive you home and hope that no one notices."

Instead of being annoyed, Pippa found it funny. As she once again did up her seat-belt in the back seat, she giggled, "Wouldn't it be funny if a policeman stopped us and Daddy got fined?"

Funny was not the word Fiona would have used!

Luckily they reached the Davenport house without incident and when they were safely inside, Fiona began to see the funny side of it and the pair of them had a good laugh.

Pippa helped herself to a glass of milk and made herself a sandwich with butter and jam. Fiona put on the kettle for a cup of tea for herself and when Pippa had finished her sandwich she brought out a biscuit barrel and they both had a chocolate biscuit. Fiona was wondering what they were going to do now but she had reckoned without her young charge.

"Now I do my homework Fiona. You can watch me if you like but Daddy usually makes the meal while I do this."

"What homework do you have? Can I help at all?"

"Well I've got some spelling words to learn. You can ask me them once I've learned them."

Thank goodness for an old-fashioned teacher, thought Fiona, though maybe it was a new scheme now. She picked up The Guardian which must have been delivered before they left that morning. She wondered if Charles was a Labour supporter as they were Guardian readers usually. She wasn't really much interested in politics and wondered if he was. She turned to the back and found the crossword on the inside back page. She liked crosswords but she took The Herald and she wondered if Charles did this one. It was blank but then he would hardly have had time to start it this morning before work and taking Pippa to school.

She would hate someone to start on *her* crossword but she tried doing it mentally and had worked out a couple before Pippa announced that she had learned her words. She handed Fiona her jotter. It was a motley selection of words.

"Friend."

The Pulpit is Vacant

"F-R-I-E-N-D."

"Collect."

"C-O-L-L-E-C-T."

"Wednesday."

"Capital W-E-D-E-N-S-D-A-Y."

"No. That's wrong."

"I always get that one wrong. Is it capital W-E-D-N-E-S-D-A-Y?"

"Yes. That's correct."

Something clicked in Fiona's brain. She went through the rest of the words without really thinking about them. Pippa went on to do some maths' work and Fiona sat in deep thought. She had seen that spelling of Wednesday recently. Where was it? Oh yes, on that torn scrap of paper found in the manse garden. That was what she had been trying to remember when she read Pippa's hobby diary and talk notes a few days ago. Pippa must have written 'Wedensday' then too and that was the way it was spelt on the torn paper. Could it have been part of William's school hobby diary?

It was with difficulty that she concentrated on the rest of Pippa's homework, being able to help with everything except maths which was so different from when she was at school.

It was about six o'clock when Charles arrived home. Fiona stayed for a meal again. It was a Marks and Spencer's prepared meal and very tasty though Charles apologised for it saying that he did try to

359

make meals himself but with his busy schedule it was often difficult to fit in the time.

It wasn't until Pippa went to bed that Fiona had the chance to tell Charles what she thought about the scrap of paper.

"Could it have come from William's school hobby jotter? And why was it torn out? Probably nothing important but worth another look at that jotter, don't you think?"

"I certainly do. If Colin and Philip are in the clear - not that they are completely as Colin's partner could be lying to protect him and Philip's friends probably wouldn't have known if he left the flat that night - then we're looking for another suspect and we're running out of folk."

Fiona left about ten o'clock. He had been going to tell her what had transpired when he went to the manse and to the Paterson's house but decided against it as it wasn't fair to talk shop in the evening. They had spent the last hour talking about crosswords and about their shared liking of golf and bridge. Charles had suggested inviting two friends round one evening for a game of bridge, suggesting that Fiona and he could partner one another.

"Only if we don't fall out." she had laughed.

"No. Only married couples do that," he had quipped back.

CHAPTER 54

Penny was ready and waiting for Salma. It was out of Salma's way to come back across for her but she phoned and offered and Penny had accepted. The time in the car would give them a chance for a chat. She and her mother had had their meal together and her mother was waiting for Jack to come for her. They were going to The Citizen's Theatre to see "Waiting For Godot." Penny had heard one of the older PCs talking about it the other day. His wife had persuaded him to go and he had hated it. "Two guys sitting on stage talking about Godot and at the end I still didn't know who Godot was," he had said disgustedly. Penny had not told her mother about this, not wanting her to be prejudiced against the play before she saw it. She liked Jack. Her father had died many years ago. She hardly remembered him and anyway Jack was not trying to become a new father to her; she was too old for that.

The bell rang. Penny opened it. It was Jack.

Frances Macarthur

"Hi Penny, Is your Mum ready?"

"Yes. Come in Jack."

He came in as her Mum came out of the lounge. She looked very attractive in her beige slacks and white blouse. Her hair like Penny's was chestnut brown with just a peppering of grey at the side

"Hi Jack. I'll just get a jacket and I'm ready."

They went out chatting away and Penny went into the lounge and switched off the TV.

The bell rang again. It was Salma this time.

Salma drove them across the city, to a flat in Broomhill Drive. There was no controlled entry here and they walked up to the top floor.

"At least we know Philip didn't climb out of the window," said Penny, laughing.

She rang the bell of the door with 'Wilson' on it.

They heard a cheery whistling and the door was opened by a young man. He was almost bald and had quite a rounded figure.

"Eric Wilson?" queried Salma.

"That's me. You must be the police. Sergeant Din is it? You were the one who rang me."

"That's right Mr Wilson."

"Call me Eric please. Come in."

He took them into a lounge. There was a used mug on the arm of the settee.

"Well Eric. We need you to confirm that Philip Gentle was staying here on the night of May the 6th - that was a Tuesday."

The Pulpit is Vacant

"Yes he was here. We had a bit of a boozy night I'm afraid with two of my college friends. Philip had my spare room."

"How do you know Philip?"

"We were at school together in Killearn. He arrived and went straight into fourth year. He was interested in chess and I was in the chess club. We met there and have been friends ever since."

"Why did he come to you that night?" asked Penny.

"He came straight here from the airport. I knew that he didn't get on with his father who wanted a sports-loving son. Philip was a disappointment to him on that front and then he also refused to go to university. When he emailed that he was coming to Scotland to face his father with the fact that he was staying in Australia, I suggested that he come here first and prepare himself."

"Can you prove that he never left the house that night?"

"Not really. After a spate of break-ins in the area, I always keep both the inner and outer doors double locked and I take the keys into my room so it wouldn't have been easy for him to get out but as I said I was drunk. Mind you so was he. How would he have got across town? He didn't have a car."

"Thank you Eric, you've been most helpful" said Salma and she and Penny moved towards the door.

363

It did not take them so long to get back across to Shawlands as the roads were much quieter. When Salma stopped outside Penny's house, a terraced house not far from the manse, Penny asked her if she had time to come in for a while.

"Mum's out. We could have a drink."

Salma said she would come in and soon she was seated in the lounge. It was a comfortable looking room with big squashy chairs in brown velour and matching brown velvet curtains. A cat lay curled up on one of the chairs.

"Hope you don't mind cats Salma. She's a pet. She won't hurt you."

"No I'm fine with cats. What's her name?"

"Pickle. Mum chose the name and I don't know her reason for it."

"I'm bit afraid of dogs since one went for me when I was wee."

"That's a pity. I would love a dog but it would be unfair as there would be no one in all day. Pickle's a house cat but unlike a dog she doesn't need to be walked."

Salma walked over and stroked Pickle who purred appreciatively.

"Now, what about a drink? Are you allowed to drink or would you prefer tea or coffee?"

"I do have the occasional drink. Not that Mum knows but not tonight, Constable Price. I'm driving remember!"

The Pulpit is Vacant

Salma looked mockingly severe as she said that and Penny grinned.

"Sorry. I forgot. Don't imagine the DCI would be pleased if you were arrested for drunk-driving. Tea? Coffee? Soft drink?"

"I'll have coffee please, black with one sugar."

While Penny made the coffee, Salma got up and looked at the CD collection on one side of the fireplace. She imagined that the collection was Mrs Price's as Penny would have hers in her own bedroom and she was right as most of the CDs were not modern, featuring such artists as George Michael and Lionel Ritchie.

Penny came in with the coffees and Salma sat back down.

"What do you like listening to Penny?"

"I'm not much of a one for music actually. I prefer watching films and reading."

"I prefer a good book to either music or films," confided Salma. "But that's probably because I don't get out much socially."

"I know you don't wear it to work but do you wear the hijab at home or the burka?"

"Mum does. She wears the whole lot but I don't. I was born here and Dad was ahead of his time and told us we could do what we wanted. I think Mum would like us girls to wear the hijab at least but she doesn't make a fuss."

"What school did you go to? Sorry Salma, hope you don't mind all these questions."

"Of course not. I'm going to start on you when you've finished with me." She laughed.

"I went to Holyrood. Dad thought that the ethos of a Catholic school would be better than a non-denominational one. What about you?"

"I went to Shawlands. There were lots of Asian pupils there."

"Yes my cousins go there but they're younger than you of course."

"Personal questions over. Now what do you think about Philip Gentle?"

"I don't think he could have got out and across the city easily. We should really check the taxis, see if he hired one late at night."

"And check the buses too."

"The DCI will probably tell us to do that tomorrow but I think that Philip is innocent."

Salma told Penny of the interview with Philip.

"I still think that Colin Tait is innocent too," Penny said.

"Yet either of them could still be guilty."

"Suppose so."

Salma finished her coffee and stood up.

"Better be getting back. Think I'll get in early to write up the report of tonight's interview with Eric Wilson.

"Do you want me to do it?"

"Let's both do it in case one of us misses something."

"Good idea."

The Pulpit is Vacant

Salma thanked her for the coffee and left. Penny wrote a rough copy of what had happened that night then switched on the TV and was still engrossed in it when her Mum and Jack came home. Neither had enjoyed the play. "We still don't know who this Godot is," her Mum grumbled. "Do you want a drink Jack?"

Jack declined saying that he had had a heavy day at work. He was a painter and decorator and he had many jobs on his books.

Penny and her Mum compared notes of their day. Margaret Price worked in Dobbies' garden centre in Dykebar and had a few tales of whacky customers while Penny told her of the visit to Eric Wilson's. She often talked her work through with her Mum who always listened carefully.

They went to bed shortly afterwards, Penny to dream of Colin Tait chasing Philip Gentle through the local library.

CHAPTER 55

Friday morning and the incident room was buzzing with chat when Charles Davenport and Fiona Macdonald walked in. There was instant silence. Frank would have loved to have whistled the Skye Boat Song just to entertain his mates. He lacked the courage or the temerity which was just as well as the mood became serious with the DCI's first words.

"It's over a fortnight since Robert Gentle was murdered and exactly two weeks since the killing of William Paterson and we seem to be no nearer finding out the identity of the murderer. Let's go over what we know about our two chief suspects. Fiona, would you talk us through the interview with Colin Tait please."

"Colin Tait claims that he was with his partner Hilary Mason both nights. Mr Mason confirms that they were at the pictures on the Friday night and at home on the Tuesday. On the Friday Colin took a phone message from a friend. I've confirmed that there was indeed a call to that address from his friend's address at 10.35 and his neighbour, Carol Livingstone, says Colin was in when she went to borrow milk on the Tuesday evening. She was baking for a family party on the Friday and ran out of milk. She said that she had the TV on and the 9 o'clock news had just started. The second alibi isn't strong as he could have left after she went back home and the phone call places him across the other side of the city after 10.30 on Friday. Still time to get to the South side if Robert Gentle was killed in the small hours of Wednesday morning and if Hilary was lying."

"Surely if Hilary was going to lie for him he wouldn't have kept him from us Sir? "said Penny.

"Exactly Penny." said Davenport. "Now Salma, tell us what happened when you and Penny visited Philip Gentle's friend Eric Wilson."

Salma told of the double locked doors and the fact that Eric kept the keys in his bedroom. His flat was on the top floor so getting out of the window would have been difficult. They were all a bit drunk that night which meant that Philip *could* have got out without Eric knowing but if he too had slept deeply then it seemed that he couldn't have gone. Salma told them that she and Penny were going to check with taxi drivers and the buses from Broomhill to the South side.

One of the PCs said that the bus from Broomhill did not go near Shawlands on its way to Eaglesham

The Pulpit is Vacant

so Philip would have either had a long walk twice or would have had to change buses in town.

"OK. Thanks Salma. I'll give you and Penny time to do the buses. Check at the depot for who was driving from the West End on that night. Don't forget that Philip was living in the manse by the Friday night but as with Colin, if he couldn't have committed the first murder it is very unlikely that he committed the second. Frank, take another two PCs and get on to the taxi side of things. Make a start with the ranks nearest to Broomhill Drive and the ones nearest to the manse."

"Sir, there are two possible ones in the South Side. One near Queen's Park just off Kilmarnock Road and one at the Victoria Infirmary but both would be quite a walk from the manse," one of the older PCs chipped in.

"Thanks. Got that Frank?"

"Yes Sir."

"Sir, if we rule out Philip Gentle and Colin Tait who are we left with?" asked Salma.

"Well we're back with Ruth and Mary Gentle and I suppose Elizabeth French and the Bell twins though it stretches the imagination to see one of those kids as a double murderer."

"Sir," said Fiona Macdonald. "I'll go to the Paterson's house and look at the hobby jotter again, see if any pages have been torn out."

Seeing the puzzled looks on the other faces, she explained that the scrap of paper they had

Frances Macarthur

found after William's death could have been from his hobby jotter as it was in the form of a diary. She had no idea if it was important but they wanted to leave no stone unturned.

"Right. Back here at 2pm. I'm going back to the manse with a question for the Gentle family."

CHAPTER 56

My nightmares were if anything getting worse. On Tuesday night after the sergeant came to ask me if I had known Robert Gentle before and to ask if I knew of anyone who had been to William's hide-out, I had a dreadful night.

The first time I woke sweating. I couldn't remember my dream and Jim was still sleeping peacefully beside me but the second time I woke with him shaking me and saying, "Elizabeth, wake up. It's a nightmare love. Calm down."

I recalled that dream only too vividly.

I was amongst trees, running but getting nowhere and behind me came Robert Gentle. Every time I looked back he was getting nearer. He was wearing our school uniform and shouting, "Mrs French please wait for me!" but in the dream I somehow knew it was a trap and that he would kill me if he caught me.

Jim got up and made us both a cup of tea and when he came back upstairs he sat on my side of the bed.

"You were saying, "No Robert. No William. Who are all these men? Should I be jealous?" He was smiling as he said it. Thankfully he hadn't been annoyed when the sergeant asked if I'd known Robert Gentle before. I had worried that with my past secret coming out, about Peter, that Jim might be wondering if I *had* known him before. I was so terribly afraid of anything coming between us again even something that wasn't true because I had lied to him by omission before and he might not believe me on another occasion.

"I can't remember now what they looked like but it must have been Robert Gentle and William Paterson I was dreaming about Jim."

Was I becoming paranoid?

I drank my tea. Jim got back into bed and I lay in his arms feeling safe and secure until I must have fallen asleep and slept peacefully till morning.

Now it was Friday and we had the weekend to look forward to. Today at school we had had a short funeral service for William's character in our war project. The boys were not going to let it rest until something was done and I was finding it hard to motivate them to other parts of the project. We had eventually agreed that the character could have taken ill and died, undernourished by scarcity of food. They had all made ration cards and were

The Pulpit is Vacant

convinced that nobody could exist without all the food they themselves ate.

Thus it was that at about 2pm we had a short service, helped along by Jacqueline who had been at William's funeral so now felt that she was an expert. I think being the knowledgeable one helped her as she liked telling everyone where to stand and what to do and she had helped Scott Wilson who was taking the part of the minister to write out what he would say. Without this leading role she would possibly have felt upset but children are stronger than we often give them credit for and it all went well. I think I was the only one who remembered the real William as the afternoon progressed.

Once the little funeral scene had taken place, I got them all to sit at their desks and write a letter to the character's mother and father, saying how sorry they were about their son dying. I wrote the word 'condolence 'on the blackboard. Maybe this would come in useful for them in later life. I thought about getting one of them to write a letter to the real William's parents but thought this was a bit maudlin especially since a few weeks had passed and it would probably just upset them when they were trying to piece their lives back together.

Jacqueline stayed behind when the others left.

"Mrs French. Did you ever see William's yellow notebook?"

"What yellow notebook?"

"The one he kept his war notes in at the back. He showed it to me. It was really good and very real though I know he made it all up. He said he was going to show it to you."

"He never did, Jacqueline."

"Never mind, Miss."

She ran off.

Yellow notebook. George had mentioned it too. I wondered if he had told the police.

Mrs Hobson buttonholed me as I was leaving to ask if I had heard anything from Colin since he had left with DCI Davenport last Wednesday lunchtime.

Colin had not returned to school and Mrs Hobson told me now that he had phoned in on Thursday morning to say that he was unwell and would not be back till Monday at the earliest. I told her that I had not heard from him but that I would phone him tonight. We all knew that Colin had gone with the DCI because the janitor had seen them go and had told the auxiliary who had told the school secretary who in turn had told one of the staff with whom she was friendly. Mrs Hobson must have known I imagine but I did not want to mention that I knew as it would have prolonged the chat we were having and I wanted to get home. We were going out to Bill and Alison's that evening. It was one of our first social visits for some time and I was looking forward to it and wanted to get home and have a leisurely bath and wash

The Pulpit is Vacant

my hair before getting Jill and Helen's meal ready. They were eating at our house then we were going to run them to Helen's, where Jill would stay the night, on the way to our night out.

"I hope that Colin is back on Monday or I'll have to call the education offices and arrange for a supply teacher for Tuesday otherwise the rest of the staff will be getting upset at losing what little free time they have."

"Yes Mrs Hobson but I'm sure that Colin will be back. Now if you'll excuse me I must dash."

So saying, I left her and was soon on my way home. I didn't always take the car to school but I had today as I knew that I would have quite a heavy bag to carry home.

I would have to do all my marking and preparation for next week on Sunday as we were thinking of going to the cinema tomorrow night and we really must get some gardening done during the day on Saturday. Maybe if I had a few drinks tonight and got physically tired on Saturday, I might sleep well both nights. I hoped so.

CHAPTER 57

Fiona Macdonald went over to the Paterson house. It was Friday midday so only Mrs Paterson and the youngest children, Robin and baby Sam were with her. When she came to the door, Fiona noticed that her thin face was even more gaunt than before and there were dark smudges under her eyes. She apologised for bothering her again but asked if it was possible to see William's hobby jotter.

Mrs Paterson said that she had read it then given it to George. He had wanted a yellow notebook but it appeared that only George had seen this one and it was nowhere to be found in the house or at school. Mrs French had been puzzled when George had mentioned it. This was obviously a secret record which William had kept.

Mrs Paterson went into the room which William had shared with George and Robin and came back out with the hobby jotter. Fiona flicked through it. There were no pages obviously missing, no Wednesdays missing.

"Do you have any other school jotters in the house?" she asked.

"I think I saw another one in their room," answered Mrs Paterson and disappeared inside once again, returning with a less tidy-looking jotter belonging to George.

Fiona counted the first half of the jotter's pages and did the same with William's jotter. They each had twenty four, forty eight pages in each. No pages missing then.

Thanking Mrs Paterson, she went back to the station.

Charles Davenport made his way by car from the station to the manse as he wanted to back in plenty of time for the 2pm meeting.

It was another lovely day and the sunshine on the brickwork of the old building made it glow. Many manses were modern houses now but this was an old house, lovely in his opinion. He lived in a modern semidetached house in Newton Mearns which was easy to keep clean and was ideal for him and Pippa but he would have loved to have brought his daughter up in a house like this with large grounds and many rooms with high ceilings.

He left the car outside the convenience store, knowing that this would give Nan Brodie something to think about, and talk about no doubt if she was as talkative as his officers said.

The Pulpit is Vacant

He opened the large gates, thinking as he did so that this was where Bill McFarlane and Elizabeth French had met Colin Tait on the night of the first murder. Had Colin told the truth this time? Was he contemplating going home, scared to meet the man who held his secret or was he planning murder?

Charles tended to believe the young man. There was something open about him, just as there was about Ruth Gentle. That was the trouble about this case. There really was no one he would like it to be!

He took his time walking up the path to the front door. The family tended to live in the back rooms of the house so it was unlikely that anyone would see him coming. He walked round the west side of the house, noticing as Frank had the rabbit hutch and the shed which was falling to pieces. Pippa wanted a rabbit. Well she really wanted a dog but that was impossible with his uncertain hours. The pond was untended. The Gentle family had not been here long enough to leave their mark on the garden. Knowing Robert Gentle, he probably would have expected Mary to do most of the gardening.

It was time to get back to work.

He moved round to the front door and pressed the bell. He could hear it ringing in the back quarters.

It was Philip who answered the door. Unlike his father he obviously did not expect his mother or sister to do all the door-answering.

Frances Macarthur

"Hello Sir. What can we do for you?"

"Can I come in?"

"Of course. Sorry. That was a bit rude keeping you outside."

Davenport went in and was escorted to the back of the house.

"Mum and Ruth are in the kitchen."

He ushered Davenport in.

"It's Detective Inspector Davenport Mum."

Charles, walking into the kitchen, thought again how much more relaxed both women looked.

"Sorry Mr Davenport. We're in the kitchen again. We'd only got the back lounge ready. That was why the youth workers' meeting was held in there. Robert spent the first week here getting his study in working order and his dark room. Philip helped us remove the carpet in the lounge yesterday. I hope that's alright."

Davenport reassured her.

"Sorry to bother you again but I have one more question to ask you ladies. Of the people who came to the youth workers' meeting had either of you ever seen the Bell twins, Andrew and Mary before?"

"No Inspector."

"No. I didn't really get a good look at them that night. Mum let them in. I only handed round tea and I was too busy making sure I didn't upset the tray." This came from Ruth.

"What about Elizabeth French, Mrs Gentle.

"No. I saw her three times and...."

The Pulpit is Vacant

"Three times?"

"Yes. She came to the first meeting then she came up to see my husband on her own and then she came to the second youth meeting."

"Have you any idea why she came on her own, Mrs Gentle?"

"Yes. Robert told me afterwards. She came to ask if that wee boy William could keep his den in our gardens. I was surprised that he agreed. He wasn't very fond of children, Inspector."

"Not even his own," said Philip bitterly.

Mary Gentle patted him on the shoulder and he smiled at her.

"You more than made up for him Mum."

"So you hadn't met Mrs French before you came here either?"

"No Inspector."

"Did your husband give you any impression that he had met her before?"

"No."

"Thank you all for your help. I'll leave you in peace now."

Mary Gentle walked him to the door.

"I'm planning on living round here, Inspector. It might seem funny to you but I don't really want to go back to where I was well known and in spite of everything I've felt happy here."

Davenport said he was pleased. Thanking her again, he made his way down the driveway and was soon on his way back to the station.

Frances Macarthur

Another dead end.

The meeting reconvened at 2 pm. Fiona told about the jotter being intact and mentioned the mysterious yellow jotter seen by no one except George. Was it important? It was hard to see why it would be.

Salma and Penny had been to the bus depot and found out who had driven the buses from Broomhill Drive after 8pm and before 2am, the murder having been committed between 9pm and 2am. There were six buses in all and two of the drivers were in the depot. They had been on the early morning shift then and were now on the afternoon one, starting at 12.30pm. Neither had seen anyone on their buses till they reached the city centre as far as they could remember that night and the only reason they were so sure was that it was a rare event to get any passengers at that time of night till the city was reached. The girls had been given the phone numbers of three of the other drivers and had contacted them. They had asked about a man who had been drinking but that hadn't helped as many folk getting on the bus in the evening had had some drinks. The last man was actually at work so Penny had waited till he came off his shift and would be along as soon as she had spoken to him.

Frank reported that few people had hailed taxis from the Broomhill end, and only one from the ranks the PC had mentioned on the Southside.

The Pulpit is Vacant

The switchboards kept records these days and there was no record of a Philip Gentle anywhere. Perhaps he had used a false name, very astute for a man who had been drinking heavily!

At that point a breathless Penny arrived. No luck from the last man. It had been the busy shift for him that night and he would have noticed only someone who had caused trouble and nobody had.

DCI Davenport then told of his manse visit.

"I went to ask if anyone of them had ever heard of Andrew Bell, Mary Bell or Elizabeth French, on the off chance that Robert might have known one of them from one of his past parishes."

Philip had not seen any of them and the names did not ring any bells for him. Ruth and Mary Gentle had seen them all on the night of the meeting and Elizabeth French three times but they said that they had never seen her before or heard her name mentioned.

The information about the knives had come through and none had any trace of blood on them.

It was a despondent group which left the incident room. They started on their reports with reluctance wishing that they could be involved in some action that would lead to solving this case.

There was no point in anyone staying on late that night so it was only Charles Davenport who was there to make a couple of phone calls which gave him the glimmer of an idea.

CHAPTER 58

It was Nan Brodie who told Mary Gentle about the new retirement flats being built in Kingspark and Mary had taken Philip with her to visit the show house. She had been absolutely delighted when the woman in the office there told her that there were two houses still not sold and even more thrilled to find out that one was a ground floor flat with a patio. As they were private flats there was no rule about pets. The woman said that most of the houses had been bought by couples who did not want a garden to take care of and the person who had bought the house across the hallway from the vacant one, was a single woman like herself.

Mary still did not know how much she would get for the house in Leven but Philip was sure that she would get more than was being asked for these modern flats as it was a detached house with quite a large garden in Fife. Mary's father had died some years ago and they had bought the house with the money he had left her, her mother having died eight years previously. She had put the house on the market only last week

Feeling adventurous again, Mary signed for the flat. It had a smallish master bedroom with ensuite, a similar sized guest bedroom, lounge, bathroom and small kitchen with washing machine and dishwasher plumbed in, deep freeze, fridge and oven. French windows opened from the lounge on to the patio. Although this was paved she could either have tubs of flowers or get the paving removed from at least part of the area. The flat would be so easy to keep clean after years of coping with large manses. She hoped that after the sale of the house in Fife she would have enough left over to buy new furniture as she would so like this house to be completely her choice, especially her bedroom.

Her entry date had been fixed at the first week in July so when she got home, she phoned the Leven estate agent. She had got his name from her estate agent in Shawlands as Philip thought he had better not leave Glasgow right now, not even to make the trip to Leven again so Mary had put the house up for sale over the phone. The man told her that there had been, only that day, two people interested in the house and he was hopeful that there would soon be an offer.

On the drive back to the manse, she asked Philip when he would be leaving for Melbourne and he told her that the police had told him to stay in the country meanwhile. Sad, because this meant

The Pulpit is Vacant

that they had not ruled Philip out as a suspect but pleased to have their son with her for a while longer, Mary had told him not to worry as she had every confidence that the police would find out the real culprit.

Over in the station, Davenport rereading reports, noted that Bill McFarlane had said that he had persuaded Elizabeth French to go to the first manse meeting. On a hunch he phoned the McFarlane house and asked Bill, just home from the bank, why Elizabeth had had to be persuaded. "She was busy with school work that night," said Bill, "but when I told her that Robert Gentle had once lived in Sussex, in Aldershot quite near where she had once lived, she had said she would go."

Thanking him, Charles read again the interview with Elizabeth French in which she had said that she had never met Robert Gentle before. She had not mentioned living in Sussex but then it was a big county and there was no reason why she should have mentioned it. Was he clutching at straws?

He rang Colin Tait.

"Mr Tait did you know that Mrs French once lived in Sussex?"

"Yes. We often talked about our childhood there and she lived near Aldershot where I nearly went to train as a soldier. I chose Catterick instead, to be further from my father. Think she knew someone who had also gone there or been a soldier there. She never elaborated on the person I'm afraid."

Was this a new lead? Could Elizabeth French have known Robert Gentle when he was chaplain down South? And even if she had, why would she have killed him? On the other hand, if she had known him then why hadn't she admitted this? A jealous husband? Salma had written that Mrs French had seemed a bit nervous as she told Jim about Salma asking if she had met the minister before and Salma had also noted that Jim French had sounded a bit forced when he had laughed about being a jealous husband.

On an impulse he rang the French house but there was no reply. He would wait and see them tomorrow when, it being Saturday, they would both hopefully be at home.

He put the reports back in his filing cabinet and prepared to leave the station, saying goodnight to the PC at the desk.

CHAPTER 59

Penny had invited Salma to come to her house on Friday night. She promised her that they would not talk shop. She told her to come about 7.30 if she wanted to meet her Mum as Jack was coming for her around 8 pm and they were going out for a meal.

Salma arrived just after 7.15 pm. She was introduced to Mrs Price who she thought looked remarkably like her daughter. Margaret Price asked about her family and Salma told her the names of her sisters and older brother.

"He's a flight attendant with BA. He has a flat just outside London. We tease him about being a trolley dolly".

They all laughed.

"Mum expected him to come home when Dad died as that's the way Muslims do things but Shahid refused. He has his own life and Mum has us girls to look after her. There's Shazia, she's a teacher, just qualified and Farah. She works in the Alliance and Leicester. My baby brother, Rafiq is ten, and spoiled rotten."

"Get Salma something to drink Penny," said Mrs Price.

"What would you like?" asked Penny.

"Just a coke would be great."

"Muslims don't drink alcohol Mum," said Penny as she went off to the kitchen.

"Penny, how rude!" Mrs Price was shocked at Penny's forthright comment but Salma just laughed.

"We're not supposed to drink alcohol. I do have the occasional glass of wine with a meal if I go out. Mum has never touched a drop but I'm sure Shahid drinks with his friends."

Penny returned with drinks for herself and Salma.

"Salma knows it wasn't a racist comment. How are we ever going to get together until we know more about each other? I read at school, "To Kill a Mockingbird". It's a brilliant book and the main character teaches his two kids not to be racist but to get inside the other person's shoes and walk around in them to understand them. That's what I'm doing when I comment on Salma's culture or ask her questions, Mum."

"It's fine, Mrs Price. I'm going to ask Penny lots of questions too."

They sat for some minutes laughing and talking then the bell rang and Margaret Price excused

The Pulpit is Vacant

herself saying that it would be Jack and she would get her coat and they'd be off.

"If you're still here when we get back I'll introduce you to Jack," she promised Salma.

"Do you really not mind me asking questions?" Penny asked.

"I'm used to it. There are two questions I hate being asked. One is, "Where do you come from?' I answer, 'Glasgow' and then they say, 'but where did you come from before that?'

I was born here. I'm Glaswegian. I know what they are really asking but it annoys me every time. I've never even been to Pakistan."

"What's the other question that gets you angry?"

"Do you speak English?"

Salma put her face up close to Penny's and said very slowly and deliberately,

"Do-you-speak-English?"

They both laughed.

"You probably speak better English than most white Glaswegians," Penny commented.

She asked Salma if there was anything she wanted to see on TV but Salma said she could do enough of that at home and would rather just chat.

"Penny. Why is Frank so racist?"

"I think it's his parents. He told me once that his Dad would like to be in the National Front but doesn't join because it might look bad on his CV. His Mum told him never to come home with anyone black or Protestant. He doesn't seem to object to the Protestant bit so much. I mean he knows I am and yet we are friends - most of the time- but he seems to have soaked up his Dad's hatred of black people."

"He's against gay people too."

"Yes and I bet he's never really talked to a gay man. It's just fear, I think, of anything that's unknown."

"Very wise young Penny," said Salma in a schoolteacherish voice and they both laughed.

"Is there anything you want to ask me?" said Penny.

"What *is* the difference between Catholic and Protestant?"

"Well Catholics believe they really are eating the flesh of Jesus when they take communion but Protestants think the bread is a just a symbol of his body. It's the same with the wine. We don't think the wine changes into blood. I'm sure there's more to it than that. I know in the chapel the crosses have Jesus on them but in our churches they don't. I think we worship Jesus alive and risen but they worship him crucified. I could be wrong but that's what I mean about ignorance. When we don't know about something we can get scared of it or mock it. If Frank would only take the time to talk to you and get to know you as a person as I'm doing, maybe he would change in time."

"Have we got that long?" said Salma with a grin and the serious mood was broken.

The Pulpit is Vacant

Of course, in spite of their promises to each other, the talk turned to the murders.

"Let's take everyone one at a time and do the 'for' and 'against'," said Penny.

"Right. The manse people first. Mrs Gentle."

"Against. She's too nice but - for - she could have snapped at being bullied."

"I agree. Philip Gentle?"

"I don't think he could have come across the city. We've checked with buses and taxis but then again he could have got a lift."

"And also he was going back to Australia so didn't need to get rid of his Dad."

"True. Ruth Gentle?"

"Too honest but it could be a double bluff admitting that she hated her father."

"Colin Tait?"

"Your turn. What do you think?"

"Too gentle and he now has an alibi."

"Elizabeth French?"

"No motive that we know about."

"Kevin and Bill are too tall unless that woman saw one person and another came along."

"And Claire is too short."

"The Bell twins?"

"Why on earth would they want Robert Gentle dead?"

Realising that they were getting nowhere, they decided to put on the news and by the time that was finished, Salma was getting up to go home.

Frances Macarthur

"I've really enjoyed my visit Penny. It's your turn to come to me next."

"I'd like that. You can tell me the difference between Sunni and Shi'ite Muslims."

Salma laughed.

"Getting your own back eh?"

They had reached the door by this time.

"See you on Monday unless anything happens before then."

Just at this point, Mrs Price and Jack arrived home.

"Just made it in time," laughed Margaret. "Salma, this is Jack: Jack, Salma."

The two shook hands.

Not wanting her Mum to worry about her, Salma left.

CHAPTER 60

We were to be at Bill and Alison's for 7 pm but had to run Jill to Helen's house on the way. We were about to leave when Colin phoned.

"Elizabeth. Colin for you," called Jim from the hall.

Shrugging into my jacket, I took the receiver from him.

"Colin, how are you? Did everything go alright with the police?"

Colin told me what had transpired and told me about his partner Hilary. I wasn't surprised. I had always felt an affinity towards Colin and we had often shared confidences as I would normally have done with a girlfriend and they say that homosexuals make good friends for woman. I had read that somewhere.

"Do they suspect you because you hid Hilary from them?"

He said that he thought they had at first but that Hilary could now give him an alibi for both nights so he wasn't sure where he stood. He had been warned not to leave the country.

"I am glad you phoned me, Colin as I wanted to phone you but didn't like to."

Colin went on to say that he had had a call from the DCI a short time ago asking if he knew that I had once lived in Sussex. Apparently Bill had mentioned it to him recently. Colin wanted to warn me that I would probably get another visit from the police and he had wanted me to be prepared for it. I thanked him very much and told him that I had no dark secrets to hide. I was glad that Jim had gone back into the lounge and couldn't hear me say this.

Colin said that he would be back at school on Monday.

I hung up the phone, called Jill and Helen from the kitchen and we left shortly afterwards.

We dropped the girls off at Helen's, Jill with her overnight bag, and drove on to the street where Bill and Alison lived. We had not been before and I hoped that I would like Alison and that Jim would like them both.

I had bought wine and flowers and once in their hallway, I gave the flowers to Alison and Jim handed over the wine to Bill.

Alison laughed. "I leave the flower-arranging to Bill I'm afraid. He's so much better at it than I am."

"And she's the wino!" Bill laughed.

Jim and I had admired their front garden as we had walked up the path and I asked who did the gardening.

"Bill mostly," said Alison, "Though I have a vegetable patch at the back which I tend."

General chit chat about gardens and flowers followed as we took off our jackets and walked into the lounge. I admired their décor, saying I liked the strong red of their suite. Jim and I sat on the settee, Bill taking one of the easy chairs and Alison remaining standing.

We were asked what drinks we would like. Jim opted for a whisky and soda and I took a soft drink. I was driving that night and would have one glass of wine with the meal.

"So it's the same in your house is it?" Alison said laughingly. "Bill drives us there and I drive back."

"We take it in turns," I said, not wanting to admit that this was our first social visit for some years.

Alison left, presumably to see to the meal.

"While Alison is out, I'd better take the chance to tell you Elizabeth, that DCI Davenport rang me earlier this evening to ask if you been reluctant to go to that first manse meeting and how I had manage d to persuade you to go."

"What did you say?" I asked.

"I told him that when I mentioned that Mr Gentle came from Sussex, you were interested because that was your home county."

Frances Macarthur

"Yes that was right. That did make me go. It's funny how you have an affinity for the place where you were born, no matter how long you've lived somewhere else."

I felt weak with relief that Bill had not mentioned Aldershot. Jim might have linked Aldershot with the fact that Peter was a soldier and I didn't want all that raked up again.

At that point Alison came in to say that dinner was ready and we made our way through to their dining room. I commented on their most unusual very high backed chairs and glass table and Alison said that they had been her parents' and they had given them to her and Bill when they moved to a smaller house.

I enjoyed the starter which was very light, egg mayonnaise with prawns but when the main course arrived I suddenly lost my appetite. I had not been eating very well since the death of William and now this heavy meal of steak pie was too much for me.

"Alison. I'm so sorry. I hope you don't mind me leaving so much. It's delicious but my appetite has gone these days."

"No problem Elizabeth. Is it the death of the wee boy? Or do you not want to talk about it?"

"It would only spoil a nice evening."

"She won't even talk about it with me," said Jim. "I want her to have counselling but she won't hear of it. She did at least go to the doctor and get sleeping pills."

The Pulpit is Vacant

"Well, how can I make a fuss when poor Mrs Paterson is having to cope? It would be like those folk who cry at funerals when the immediate family are holding up."

Bill, realising I think that this was getting a bit heavy, for me in particular, changed the subject to their new baby. Alison was only too delighted to talk about little Graeme.

"We were going to have him christened but there's no minister."

"I'm not sorry," said Bill. "I know that's a terrible thing to say but I didn't like the man."

"He was a bit prosy when I heard him," said Jim, "but you actually met him didn't you?"

Bill said he had and recounted the way the man had treated his wife and daughter.

"Mind you," said Jim. "I had to agree with some of his views. If we kept to the Ten Commandments as he said in the sermon I heard him preach, the world would be a better place. No murders; no adultery."

Alison added, "I wonder what God thinks of abortions. That's murder too."

Jim agreed.

The conversation was in danger of leading back to murder so I turned it to the proposed closure of Jim's school, Bradford High. My school, Southview Primary, was one of its feeder schools but as I was not on the school board I wasn't really involved. I obviously felt sympathy for Jim who loved his school. Also I did not want Jill to have to change schools. She was happy there after a shaky start when she'd had to leave Southview. I was glad when Jim started to talk about their plans to fight for the school. It would do him good to talk about it to two people who were not involved although the school would be wee Graeme's when he got to eleven unless they planned to send him to a private school.

When we had exhausted the topic of school closures, I asked Bill about the bank. He had told me at BB recently that he was applying for promotion. He was happy to talk about his chances. He wanted to move up the ladder but on the other hand he did not want to move house which he might have to depending on where the bank was.

Luckily Alison had made no dessert, bringing in biscuits and cheese which it was easy for me to say no to without embarrassment. I saw Jim look at me but no one else seemed to notice. I enjoyed my coffee though I knew that it would not help me to sleep that night.

We left about 11pm knowing that the new parents would probably be up half the night.

As we drove home, Jim commented on my lack of appetite. I explained that it would come back but that William's death was hard for me, seeing him every weekday as I had. I told him about the mock funeral and being a teacher he understood

The Pulpit is Vacant

probably better than anyone else would have, the effect that an empty desk had on a teacher.

I didn't tell him that I had only taken the sleeping pills once. I didn't want to sleep because of the dreams. To misquote Hamlet, "For in that sleep what dreams would come."

CHAPTER 61

On impulse, Charles phoned Fiona on the Saturday morning. It was only a trivial thing he was going to ask Elizabeth French about but it would be nice to have company, especially hers.

She answered, sounding a bit breathless.

"Did I get you up Fiona?"

"Almost," she laughed. "I was in the shower."

"I'm sorry. I'm going to see Elizabeth French at some time today and wondered if you'd like to come along. Please be honest and tell me if you had anything planned."

"I did," she replied.

He was surprised at how disappointed he felt.

"No problem."

"Yes. I had housework planned and you've no idea how glad I would be to have an excuse to forget it."

They both laughed.

"Great. When would suit you best?"

"I think we should go as soon as possible in case they decide to go out."

"They were out last night. I did phone. If they're out it doesn't matter. It can wait."

"I can be ready in about half an hour. Why don't you pick me up about 9.30?"

"Make it 10 o'clock. I have something to do first. Give me your address."

He had no problem with Pippa as she was up and ready to go. She had made a new friend called Hazel and had been invited to her house in Newlands this morning. They were going to go swimming with Hazel's Dad first then have lunch.

True to his word, it was just after 10 o'clock when Davenport drew up outside Fiona's house. She lived in a tenement in Shawlands and was standing outside waiting for him.

On the way he told her about the phone calls he had had with Colin Tait and Bill McFarlane and the fact that the reports showed that Mrs French was a bit nervous when asked if she had known Robert Gentle before.

It was about 10.10 when they pulled up outside the French house. Jim answered the door.

"Hello Mr French. Could we please have another word with your wife?"

Jim looked annoyed.

"She's upset enough, Inspector, without questions. She can't get William's death out of

The Pulpit is Vacant

her head. She's not sleeping well and having nightmares."

"I'm sorry Sir. This won't take a minute I promise you."

Jim, not looking the least bit mollified, left the hall. When he returned from the kitchen Elizabeth was with him. Her eyes were dark-rimmed.

"Inspector, what can I do for you?"

"I just wanted to ask once again if you had ever met with Robert Gentle before?"

"I told your officer that I hadn't."

"I know. I just wondered if you'd had any new thoughts. Maybe you were at a church where he preached. He was an army chaplain at Aldershot. Does that ring any bells?"

Elizabeth French looked exhausted but she was quite calm when she replied that she definitely had not seen Robert Gentle before or if she had, she had no recollection of it.

Charles thanked her and they left.

"Poor woman. William's death has hit her hard I think." said Fiona.

"Yes, she saw him Monday to Friday and I think took a lot more interest in him than his poor mother did."

They were driving back to Fiona's and had to pass the manse. Mary Gentle was getting out of a driving school car. They stopped. Charles wound down the window and she came over to them.

"Driving lessons, Mrs Gentle?" said Charles.

Frances Macarthur

"Yes Inspector. Robert would never let me learn to drive. He thought I'd be no good at it but I'm surprising even myself."

"Good for you."

"Oh by the way, I'm moving out shortly. I've had an offer for our house in Leven and I've bought a new retirement flat in Kingspark."

"Quick work," said Fiona.

Mary Gentle looked distressed.

"Do you think I've been too quick? I just didn't want to stay in the manse. I couldn't face the lounge and I knew that I would have to get out as soon as the church got another minister so it seemed right to get it all over with."

"I *am* sorry Mrs Gentle," said Fiona. "I didn't mean to sound critical. I think you are so right both with the driving and the new house."

Looking relieved, Mary left them. As they watched her walk up the path, Charles commented on the spring in her step.

"There goes one person who's benefited from Gentle's death."

They had hardly driven any distance when they spotted George Paterson standing outside his house. Davenport wound down the window and waved to him. George waved back.

"That reminds me," said Fiona. "I was wondering last night. What if there *was* a yellow notebook and the murderer wrenched it out of William's hand

408

and tore a bit of a page out of it and that was what we found."

"Could be, Fiona. Look let's stop for a drink somewhere and think that one through.

We're due a break. Could this be it?"

CHAPTER 62

Over coffee, Charles and Fiona discussed the yellow notebook. George had been adamant that it existed. He had seen William writing in it and said that he wrote about his war findings at the back of it. It was possible therefore that the boy had had it with him on the night of the murder in which case the murderer must have taken it when he or she killed William.

"We'll need to question the kids in William's class, Fiona."

"How about seeing his only friend in the class, Jacqueline something?"

"Jacqueline Beaton."

"Let's not wait till Monday. Let's go to the Paterson house and see if anyone there knows where the girl stays."

They finished their coffees and were soon at the Paterson house. It was Arlene who answered the door, baby Sam in her arms.

"Mum and Dad are out," she said.

Frances Macarthur

This was not the time to tell her that they should not have left a girl Arlene's age alone with the younger children. He would remind Mr and Mrs Paterson if he saw them again but they had had enough trouble to be getting on with.

"Is George in?"

"Yes he's in his room playing with Robin. Come in."

The two policemen entered and were shown to George's room. When they went in George was playing with leggo and wee Robin was watching him, fascinated.

George stood up.

The DCI asked him if he knew where Jacqueline Beaton lived and was told that she lived two doors down. "I play football with her brother Tom."

They thanked him and left.

They were again lucky as when they rang the doorbell, Mrs Beaton said that Jacqueline was in.

"She's not one for going out to play. She prefers to read in her room. I'll get her for you."

Mrs Beaton went into another room and Jacqueline followed her out.

"Hello Jacqueline," said Fiona. "We're two of the police officers on the case of William Paterson and we want to ask you about a notebook belonging to William."

"Oh, his yellow notebook. He took it everywhere with him. He wrote down notes about his birds and

412

The Pulpit is Vacant

at the back he wrote down pretend things about the war."

"Did you ever read it? What sort of pretend things?" asked Davenport.

"Oh he sat in his den and watched what went on at the manse and made up stories about the people who came and went there. He wrote that bit at the back. He showed me it once or twice."

"Do you know if he showed it to anybody else?"

"I think he'd either shown it to Mrs French our teacher or he was going to because he said he had asked her if she would like to see it and she had said yes."

Thanking Jacqueline and her mother, Davenport and Fiona went back to the car.

"Well that's interesting Fiona. According to Jacqueline, Mrs French knew about the notebook and may even have read it."

"Why would she lie about it?"

"There's only one way to find out. We'll have to pay her another visit."

"Her husband is going to be really annoyed at us for worrying her again."

"I can't help that. This *is* a murder investigation."

This time it was Jill who answered the door. She said that her mother was out, having a walk to clear her head and that her father was out in the back garden doing some weeding.

Not wanting to bother Jim French and not being able to see Elizabeth, Charles decided that

413

they would telephone later and come round when she was at home.

"Tell your Mum we called and we'll come back when it's suitable," said Davenport.

Jill said that she would pass on the message and shut the door.

Fiona asked where Pippa was just now and got the answer that she was at the house of her new best friend and would be there till he collected her at around 3pm. The friend's mother had invited her to stay for lunch and there was a DVD which both girls wanted to see and which had been bought the day before.

Fiona asked if Charles would like to come to her house for some lunch and he readily agreed.

She lived on the top flat and told him that it had been her home, with her Mum, for many years.

"It's all a bit old fashioned but it's home," she told him as they walked up the stairs.

"Mum only died two years ago and I haven't changed anything yet."

She took him into a kitchen which was also obviously where she sat in the evenings as there was a TV there and two easy chairs. She ate there too as there was also a dining room table and four chairs.

He felt rather than knew that he was the only man to have been invited in here and that was confirmed by her words.

The Pulpit is Vacant

"I've always taken guests into the 'good' room as we call it. You're honoured."

He sat in one of the easy chairs while she busied herself with lunch, noticing that she read The Herald and did the crossword as the paper was open at that page. It was yesterday's paper. He knew that if he read the paper through he would not see anything about their two murders as there had been no developments for some time. Hopefully this was going to change. He had a feeling about this yellow jotter.

As if reading his mind, Fiona said, "Charles, if Elizabeth French is hiding something about this yellow notebook, it might hold something important."

"Maybe she's protecting someone. Maybe Colin Tait is mentioned in it. Maybe William noticed him on the night of the first murder and wrote his name down."

"That's possible. Colin would be known by William. Colin might have come back up the path that night and William might have noted his second appearance. Hilary might not have seen him till a bit later than he said."

They ate their lunch of cold meat and salad, washed down by coffee and then Charles, using his mobile, phoned the station for Elizabeth French's phone number.

Getting what he wanted, he rang the French house.

415

Jill answered.

"Hello Inspector. Mum has just come in. I haven't had time to tell her you wanted to see her. Hang on and I'll get her for you."

He heard Jill calling for her mother.

"Hello Mr Davenport. Elizabeth French here. What can I do for you?"

"Would it be suitable if we called round in about half an hour? I want to ask you again about William's jotters."

"Fine. See you then."

As it was only a minute's walk from Fiona's house to where Elizabeth French lived they decided to walk after downing a quick coffee.

CHAPTER 63

Once again they walked up the driveway to the French's front door. This time Jim French answered. He looked surprised and annoyed when he saw who was standing there.

"Not again. Have you not bothered my wife enough, Inspector?"

"She knows we're coming Sir. We 'phoned about half an hour ago."

Jim looked nonplussed.

"But she never told me and she's gone out again. She said she had something to give Bill McFarlane for the BB."

Something was not right here.

"How was she when she left? Did she say anything else?"

"No just gave me a hug and left."

At this point Jill came into the hall. Seeing the police officers she looked anxious.

Frances Macarthur

"Dad is Mum OK? She gave me a great big hug and told me she loved me. Then I heard the door banging shut. She hasn't had an accident has she?"

Jim went over to her and put his arms round her.

"Don't worry pet. The police are here to talk to Mum, not to give us bad news."

Jill, looking relieved, shrugged out of her Dad's arms and went back into the other room she had come from.

"I want to speak to your wife immediately she comes home Sir," Davenport told Jim. "And I mean immediately."

"She shouldn't be long if she's just handing over something to Bill."

Once again Charles Davenport and Fiona Macdonald left the French house, deciding that the station was the best place they could go to right now. They went there, telling the constable at the desk to alert them as soon as Jim French called. They went into Fiona's room.

"I'm worried about Mrs French. If she knows anything and our murderer finds out, she could be in danger," said Charles.

"We'll just have to wait till her husband rings."

There was a silence. Both were busy with their own thoughts. Davenport broke the silence.

"How do you think Salma Din's getting on now, Fiona?"

The Pulpit is Vacant

"Fine, Charles. I'm glad to see the friendship between her and Penny."

"Penny's a lovely girl. What about Salma's relationship with the others?"

Fiona reminded him about Franks' racist comment about the smell of curry and he remembered another comment Frank had made about Western cultures being different from Asian ones.

"Ask her how she's getting on Fiona or even better ask Penny. She's so transparently honest. She'll tell you the truth whereas Salma might not like to be seen to be telling tales about a fellow policeman."

"OK."

"How do Penny and Frank get on?" he asked.

"Quite well I think. His reports have improved recently and I suspect that she's been helping him."

They had put on Charles's coffee machine so they helped themselves to another drink.

The phone rang. It was Jim French.

"I'm getting worried. I phoned Bill's house and Alison said they haven't seen my wife today. Where could she have got to?"

Davenport reassured Jim as much as he could, then hanging up the phone, he asked Fiona to get Penny and Frank to the station if possible.

"I'll try to get Salma. Leave the others just now. Five of us should be enough."

Frank was available. No one answered at Penny's. Davenport got Salma.

Soon the four of them were in the Incident Room.

Davenport brought them up to date and told them that he was worried about Elizabeth French.

"Frank. She may have gone across to Colin Tait's. You go there. If she is there, try not to alarm Colin Tait and bring her back here. I don't want to phone and warn him."

"Salma, check the streets between the French house and Bill McFarlane's."

"What about Penny Sir? She'll want to be in on this. Will I try her mobile?"

"Good idea."

Salma raised Penny who was at her grandmother's with her Mother. She told her to get to the station as quickly as she could.

When Penny arrived, DS Macdonald brought her up to date. Elizabeth French might know more about the murder than she had let on. Now she appeared to have gone missing. She told Penny where Salma and Frank had gone.

Where else could she be?

Penny had a thought.

"What about the manse? The other suspect is Philip Gentle. She might have gone up there."

Penny was dispatched to the manse with the same instructions. If Elizabeth French was there, she had not to alarm Philip Gentle.

The Pulpit is Vacant

About half an hour later Frank called in. Colin Tait and Hilary had not seen Elizabeth French that day. Colin did not seem anxious,in fact he looked more relaxed than Frank had seen him.

Salma had arrived back quickly having seen no sign of Elizabeth either. She had called in to see Bill and Alison and they had commented on the fact that she had seemed unwell the night before, not finishing her meal.

About ten minutes late Penny returned from the manse. She too had drawn a blank. Philip Gentle was out and his mother and sister had not seen Elizabeth French that day.

It was stalemate.

CHAPTER 64

Davenport rang Jim French and told him where they had looked. Jim had had no word from his wife. He sounded frantic.

"I've sent Jill to her friend Helen's and phoned Paula, Helen's Mum to ask if she would keep Jill for a while. I don't want her worried about her Mum."

"Have you any idea where your wife might go if she was upset or worried?"

"I would have said Colin's. She was fond of him and he knew William and knew about the murders but her car's still here and it would be unlike her to take a taxi across. There's no one else I can think of except Paula and that was the first place I tried."

Each promising the other to get in touch if there was any news, they rang off.

"I know it's clutching at straws but might Mrs French go to William's hide-out if she was upset about him?" This came from Penny. She looked a bit sheepish about her idea but Davenport, having

Frances Macarthur

no other ideas, suggested that she take Salma or Frank and look there.

Salma, who would like to have gone, saw how keen Frank was looking and, knowing that he and Penny had been good mates before she came, said quickly, "Take Frank, Penny. He was with you when you found William. He knows the area."

"OK. Come on Frank." Penny knew that she had been ignoring Frank recently and was grateful to Salma for her consideration.

They went by police car in case they found Mrs French and knowing that the Gentle family would be curious as to why they were in the grounds again, they went to the manse door.

It was Ruth who answered.

"Hello Miss Gentle," said Penny. "We're just going to have a look in the grounds. Someone involved in the case has gone missing."

Ruth thanked them for letting her know and shut the door.

Penny and Frank hurried to the undergrowth where they had found the body of William Paterson. Pushing aside the bushes which skirted the path, Penny went to move further in and found her way blocked by a large mound on the ground.

She stopped so suddenly that Frank bumped into her.

"Penny what the..."

They stood together looking down. In the gloom they could make out that it was a body.

The Pulpit is Vacant

Frank bent down and shook it but there was no reaction. Dreading a repeat of the bashed in head of William Paterson, he felt around the head. There was no wetness. He took one hand and felt for the pulse. Nothing.

They backed out onto the path. Penny took her mobile from her pocket and rang the station asking to speak to DCI Davenport.

"Sir I think we've found Elizabeth French. She's dead but there are no obvious injuries to her head."

She listened then rang off.

"They're coming. We've to warn the family here."

Back to the manse front door they went. Again it was Ruth who answered their ring.

"Sorry to come with bad news Miss Gentle. We've found a body in your bushes, in William's hide-out to be precise. I can't tell you more right now but we'll keep you informed."

"Oh no! Who now?"

"Ruth what is it?"

"Mum, they've found another body in our bushes."

Mary Gentle's face was ashen.

"Another murder? When will this stop?"

"Sorry we have to go. Here's the boss coming now."

Frank and Penny went back to the bushes and Davenport and Fiona Macdonald joined them, leaving their car at the front door behind the police car.

Davenport had brought a torch and it didn't take him long to identify Elizabeth French and find no obvious reason for her death.

He looked around. There was nothing suspicious lying about this time.

He rang the station and asked Salma to get in touch with the police surgeon.

In the half hour it took for Martin Jamieson and the SOC team to arrive, Penny, Frank and Fiona Macdonald had returned to the station so it was only Davenport who was there to receive the news that Elizabeth French had taken an overdose of pills, the bottle which contained them having been found in her pocket by one of the team.

"Sleeping pills, Sir. The bottle is empty. It could be murder but it is more likely to be suicide." Martin Jamieson handed Davenport two envelopes.

"These were in her other pocket."

The body was taken away to be examined further and Davenport returned to the station, having paid a visit to the manse to reassure the family that this time murder was not suspected.

Davenport rang Jim French, telling him that he should come to the station. He said nothing more. It was not the kind of news that could be broken over the telephone.

When Jim arrived, he was shown to the DCI's room. Davenport shut the door.

"There's no easy way to say this Sir. Your wife's body has been found in the manse gardens. We have no reason to suspect foul play. This letter to you, and one to me, were found in her jacket pocket. I've read mine. I'll leave you alone to read yours."

Back in the Incident Room, Fiona Macdonald was reading out loud to the other three the letter addressed to DCI Davenport as he had asked her to do. He stood by the door and listened.

"Dear Mr Davenport

I killed both Robert Gentle and William Paterson. I went home after the meeting, did some school work and when Jim was asleep I went back to the manse. I got in through the bathroom window. I had been to the toilet during the meeting and opened the window a little. It was a warm night and I was sure that nobody would close it, thinking that someone else in the house had opened it. There was a light on in the lounge. I crossed the hallway and went in. Robert Gentle was sitting with his back to me but turned round as I came in. When he saw who it was he stood up and came towards me, smiling. He probably thought I had come to plead with him. He knew about a previous relationship I had had and about a pregnancy I had had terminated. I stuck the knife in his ribs and pulled it back out. I was lucky. He fell backwards. There was very little blood and what there was oozed out rather than spurted.

Frances Macarthur

I went back out the way I had come in. He could have been in bed. I was lucky I suppose.

I washed the knife and gave the knife set to the church nearly new sale which takes place every Wednesday. Jill was the only one who noticed the new set and it was easy to tell her that the knives had become blunt.

The next day in school, William asked again if I would read his notebook - yes the yellow one Inspector. I said I would read it on Thursday when another teacher took the class for PE. I did that. He had been in his hide-out two evenings before, taking notes for his war diary. He wrote that he had seen us all coming and going from the meeting and then later he had heard someone return. That person had stood very near him and he had smelled the perfume - the one I wore. He had watched me go into the manse and come out again and had noted the times and my name. He had written that I was a spy. What could I do?

When I took him up on his offer to show me his hide in the manse garden, he whispered to me that he had been so thrilled when I had gone into the manse through the window. "You're a spy Miss. It's so exciting. I won't tell anyone."

He meant it, bless him, but if the police had questioned him which they would have when they found out that he hid in the gardens at night, he would have told them. I found myself holding a large stone and the next thing I knew I was hitting his head with it. He was clutching his notebook and I had to pull it from his fingers.

I got home somehow. The fire was still burning in the grate and I burned the notebook. I don't know why you were so interested in the book but tonight I started thinking - Jacqueline had seen it too. What if you questioned the class? What if Jill told you about the new knife set? What if Colin was arrested for murder, that lovely young man who had done no one any harm? I couldn't kill Jacqueline and I certainly could not kill Jill. Could I stand by and see Colin imprisoned?

I knew you were getting close when you rang tonight to say you wanted to ask me more about William's jotters. You knew now about the Aldershot connection.

I can't put Jim and Jill through the pain of seeing me arrested and tried for murder. I couldn't bear to see the look on their faces. I killed a monster but I also killed a loveable, innocent little boy. My dreams haunted me. They were getting worse.

I got sleeping pills from my doctor to please Jim but I didn't want to sleep in case I gave something away in my sleep. I have enough to end my life.

I am going to die in William's den, a fitting place to die. I am so sorry.

Elizabeth French

There was silence.

"Thank God she killed no one else," said Penny.

"Except herself," added Frank.

Frances Macarthur

At that moment they heard footsteps. Davenport, still outside the room, turned round. Jim French was coming down the corridor. As the door to the Incident Room was open, the team heard him speaking.

"You'd better read this letter, Inspector. You'll need to know everything."

"May I read it to the team, Sir?"

"I don't see why not. It will no doubt come out soon enough."

"Can someone take you home, Sir?"

"No thanks. It's not far. I'll need to go for Jill. What on earth am I going to tell her?"

"I would tell her the truth Sir. As you say it's bound to come out and it will be better if she hears it from you. Children, I've found, are more resilient than we give them credit for."

Jim French, ashen-faced, stumbled to the swing doors. As he went out, silence came in to the room again. Davenport entered.

"Mr French has given me permission to read his wife's letter to him."

He cleared his throat

"Dear Jim

By the time you get this letter I will be dead. There is no easy way to tell you this. I killed Robert Gentle and William Paterson.

I did know Robert Gentle before, down in Aldershot. Not only did I sleep with Peter, I

The Pulpit is Vacant

became pregnant by him. I was only sixteen. He paid for me to have an abortion. After a while he began to feel guilty about what we had done so he asked to see the chaplain at Aldershot - Robert Gentle. Gentle asked to see me too. I suppose he counselled us by his way of it. He made it clear that he did not approve of what we had done.

Peter went to Ireland soon after that. I never saw him again. I came to Glasgow to stay with my aunt and uncle and go to Jordanhill College. Mum and Dad knew about Peter but not about the abortion. They were glad when we stopped seeing each other and delighted when I asked to go to a Scottish training college as it took me out of Peter's range.

I was told that I would never have children.

You were so horrified when you found out that I had had an affair with another man that there was no way I could have told you the rest, especially the reason why we could not have children.

We had just started to get our old lives back when Bill McFarlane came on the 'phone to ask if I would represent the BB at the manse meeting. He told me that the new minister had been a chaplain at Aldershot barracks. Bill was on the vacancy committee and knew all the details of Robert Gentle's past life. This was the first time I had heard the man's name. I went in the vain hope that this was not the same man, although the name was uncommon.

Frances Macarthur

That first night Robert Gentle made a comment about never forgetting a face. I went back to see him on the pretext of asking if William could keep his hide-out in the manse gardens and he told me he remembered me. I was so scared, Jim, that you would speak to him at some time. He was so straight-laced - remember his first sermon here. I just feared that he would think it was his duty to tell you about me. Maybe I was wrong but I just couldn't take the chance.

I murdered him Jim and I can't say I am sorry. Mary Gentle has been freed from his domineering ways, Ruth can happily marry her Kevin but - I killed William and I can never forgive myself for that. He was so trusting, so innocent but he was a threat to my life with you my darling.

It was when I started thinking about others who might be a threat that I realised that it was myself I had to kill this time.

Maybe Jill will eventually be comforted by the fact that I am not her real mother. Encourage her to find her mother please, Jim.

All I can hope for is that in time you will find it in your heart to forgive me.

All my love,
Elizabeth

No one spoke.

Charles Davenport felt drained. There was a nasty taste about the ending of this case. He felt

The Pulpit is Vacant

no satisfaction but he was the leader. He must rally his troops.

"We need to go to the manse. Frank you do that. Tell them what has happened. Philip is free to go back to Australia now. Tell him that.

Penny, get on the 'phone to Colin Tait. Tell him he's in the clear."

Penny and Frank left and Charles turned to Fiona and Salma.

"Salma, you're lucky. There's no one else to tell though on Monday you can go to the school and tell the head teacher. Fiona, would you come with me, please? We have the unpleasant task of informing Mr and Mrs Paterson."

Fiona left to get her jacket from her room.

All that was left now was to inform the chief constable that the case was closed. Usually this gave Charles pleasure but the ending of this case did not give him any pleasure at all. Elizabeth French had murdered to keep her husband's love. Now she had killed herself and left him and their young daughter.

Threads bind us all together. The web that was Robert Gentle's had disintegrated and the flies were all free but Elizabeth French had spun a web which now trapped the ones she loved.

Charles Davenport gave himself a mental shake. He knew that his team must be feeling as he did. He would suggest a staff night out very soon.